Lairds of the Isles

Should duty come before love?

The windswept islands of the Outer Hebrides
are a close-knit community, where the local laird
lives to serve his people, and outsiders aren't
always welcome. But as the MacDonald family
moves between London and the isles,
all that could be about to change...

A Laird for the Governess
The Laird of Ardmore has sworn never to remarry...
until he meets his feisty new governess!

A Laird in London
When the Laird of Broch travels to London, he
doesn't expect to find himself a wife!

A Laird for the Highland Lady
Max is leading an empty life in London,
until he moves to the Hebrides and finds
himself falling for a Highland lady!

All available now!

Author Note

I hope you have been enjoying my Lairds of
the Isles. While each book can be read stand-alone,
if you have read *A Laird for the Governess* and
A Laird in London, you will already be familiar with
the MacDonalds of Benbecula and their trials. This
time, we are accompanying Eilidh and Max as
they journey with their siblings from London to the
Hebrides. Max, a gentleman of the *ton*, has some
decisions to make that will change not only his
own destiny but that of Eilidh Ruadh MacDonald.

I have loved writing my Scottish series, and I hope
you've enjoyed reading it. Next, I'm returning to the
heart of the *ton*, as the Lennox sisters are about to
take London society by storm!

CATHERINE TINLEY

—

A Laird for the Highland Lady

HARLEQUIN®
HISTORICAL™

Recycling programs
for this product may
not exist in your area.

ISBN-13: 978-1-335-72390-1

A Laird for the Highland Lady

Copyright © 2023 by Catherine Tinley

For questions and comments about the quality of this book,
please contact us at CustomerService@Harlequin.com.

Harlequin Enterprises ULC
22 Adelaide St. West, 41st Floor
Toronto, Ontario M5H 4E3, Canada
www.Harlequin.com

Printed in U.S.A.

Catherine Tinley has loved reading and writing since childhood, and has a particular fondness for love, romance and happy endings. She lives in Ireland with her husband, children, dog and kitten, and can be reached at catherinetinley.com, as well as through Facebook and on Twitter, @catherinetinley.

Books by Catherine Tinley

Harlequin Historical

Christmas Cinderellas
"A Midnight Mistletoe Kiss"
A Waltz with the Outspoken Governess

Lairds of the Isles

A Laird for the Governess
A Laird in London
A Laird for the Highland Lady

The Ladies of Ledbury House

The Earl's Runaway Governess
Rags-to-Riches Wife
Captivating the Cynical Earl

The Chadcombe Marriages

Waltzing with the Earl
The Captain's Disgraced Lady
The Makings of a Lady

Visit the Author Profile page
at Harlequin.com.

Chapter One

St James's Park, London, Monday 11th March 1811

Max ran full tilt, enjoying the feeling of the wind on his face and the air in his lungs. Ahead of him in their impromptu race was his younger sister, her head start agreed due to her smaller stature and hampering skirts. Their destination was a pale statue at the end of the walkway, but Isabella was—for now—still ahead.

Summoning all the spirit of competitiveness they had enjoyed throughout their childhood, and which occasionally resurfaced in moments of madness such as this, Max pushed himself harder. Stride by stride, moment by moment, he got ever closer to her, his long legs eating up the distance between them.

I may well best her this time!

Focusing only on Isabella, and entirely failing to notice the two people emerging from a side path to his left, the first Max knew of their presence was when someone stuck out a foot and tripped him.

Deliberately!

Sailing through the air, Max was conscious of shock, disbelief and a strong sense of outrage. Then he hit the ground with an almighty thump, his right hip and shoulder making painful contact with the unforgiving gravel. Out of the corner of his eye, he saw that Isabella too had been floored, having collided with the second person with full force. *How dare they?* He barely felt the pain of impact, rage making him scramble to his feet to face his own attacker.

His jaw sagged. *A woman!* A shockingly beautiful woman, in fact. His gaze quickly roved over her, noting unruly red curls barely contained in the semblance of an elegant style, bright blue eyes, a delightful form and an expression bordering on smugness.

'Nicely done, Eilidh.' Max's gaze swung round to the second assailant—a tall, chestnut-haired man in full Highland dress.

Scottish—naturally! Papa always said these people are only half-civilised. He was instantly furious with himself; that was his father's thinking, not his own.

Normally Max did not endorse such sweeping generalisations, but his current provocation was severe.

The Scot advanced on Max, knife held threateningly in his right hand. 'Now then, *a bhalaich*,' he murmured threateningly, 'what do you mean by chasing a lady through a park?'

Max, with all the agility gained from spending most of his summers at sea, crouched to face him, fists ready to fly. With fire in his eyes and his face twisted in anger, he growled, 'What I *mean* by it? What I *mean* by engaging in a harmless race with my *own sister*?.' Briefly, he glanced towards her. 'Isabella, how do you?'

The woman who had tripped him was now helping his sister to rise.

'I am well.' Isabella straightened, a glint of humour

in her eye. 'Max, may I introduce to you Mr MacDonald. My brother, Maximilian Wood.'

Max gaped. *Isabella knows them?*

The Scot's face cleared. Slipping the knife back to its hiding place, he bowed. 'A pleasure to meet you, Mr Wood. This is my sister, Miss MacDonald.'

A pleasure? I think not.

Still, the forms had to be observed. Stiffly, for he had no intention of forgiving them, Max made his bow to the Scottish pair.

The woman—Miss MacDonald—was openly grinning at him, no sign of maidenly mortification on her pretty face. Eilidh, her brother had called her.

Ay-lee. An unusual name.

'Come now, Mr Wood. Surely you can see that our intention was to aid your sister?'

Despite her lyrical, sweet accent and her heart-stopping smile, Max remained unmoved, his chagrin at being intentionally tripped up by a lady probably all too apparent to the entire party.

Miss MacDonald was undeterred. 'Indeed, you should be thanking us for coming to your sister's aid again!' Clearly, she cared little for the humiliation she had just doled out.

She turned to Isabella, and as they conversed Max was conscious of a feeling of dislocation, as though something earth-shattering had occurred, rather than a simple fall from a deliberate trip.

What on earth—?

Mr MacDonald was speaking. 'May we walk with you a little way?'

'Of course!' Isabella spoke quickly, and Max understood she feared he would make some excuse on behalf of them both. Which, naturally, was absolutely the case. The last thing he wanted was to extend the painful encounter.

Isabella indicated the path to their left. 'Shall we?'

She walked off with Mr MacDonald, leaving Max to accompany Miss MacDonald whether he wished to or not. His expression shuttered, he indicated with a gesture that they should follow Isabella and Mr MacDonald. Determined to give Isabella a severe trimming just as soon as he was able, he reluctantly stepped out beside Miss MacDonald. The sooner this unwanted assembly could be brought to an end, the better!

Eilidh suppressed a smile. The man walking alongside her—Mr Maximilian Wood—was bristling with indignation, and not even attempting to hide it. When Isabella had introduced them just now his bow had been stiff and shallow, clearly demonstrating he was suffering from the effects of wounded pride. Eilidh stole a look at him, noting how tall he was, and how handsome. His eyes were the same dark brown as his sister's—strange how much more compelling they were in a man's visage.

At present his good looks were marred by a slight frown. Indeed, she observed, he was a picture of boyish frustration, though he must be five-and-twenty or so—just a few years older than she. Having handled her brother Angus all these years, Mr Wood's severity did not disconcert her in any way. She had, to be fair, robbed him of all poise by her actions just now.

Allowing the silence to build for quite some minutes before deciding enough was enough, Eilidh offered in a deceptively mild tone, 'We really ought to be conversing, you know. For the sake of politeness.'

He flashed her a glance, and the frustration in it sent a giddy delight running through her.

Lord, men can be so haughty when their dignity is threatened!

Peeking up from under her lashes, her gaze roved over him. He was undoubtedly a fine-looking specimen—for an Englishman. Tall, broad and strong, with a handsome face, a shock of dark hair and dark, dark eyes currently flashing fire in her general direction. He looked very like his sister, Isabella, whom Eilidh and Angus had met by chance in the same park a few days before.

Quite why she wished to incite him further, she could not say. Perhaps it was a desire to sting him into retaliation, or simply because she wanted to know if he was as lively as his sister underneath all of his lofty coolness. Whatever it was, it made her long to throw caution to the four winds and allow her tongue to run away with her.

A small voice of caution within reminded her that she and Angus had an important task to accomplish in London, and irritating members of the *ton*, London's high society, might jeopardise their chances of success. She ignored it.

'We might speak of the weather perhaps,' she declared silkily, 'or comment on how delightful St James's Park is today.'

He cleared his throat. 'London is blessed to have such beautiful parks, I daresay.'

My! A full sentence!

He remained in high dudgeon, and she had to suppress a bubble of laughter.

I should not laugh at him.

To add such an insult after tripping him up could only make matters worse, and yet she often used humour to cajole Angus out of his occasional sulks. Was

Mr Maximilian Wood even capable of humour or play-fulness?

She raised an eyebrow. 'From what I have seen—and I have been here only a few days—London needs such parks, for never have I seen so many people in one place!'

'Is this your first time in the capital, Miss MacDon-ald?' His tone was purely polite, giving no indication he was in any way interested in her response.

'It is, and I must declare it is very different from my home.'

'Which is?' His expression remained disengaged, almost languid.

'Benbecula.' Her reply was deliberately brief, forc-ing him to ask for clarification. 'It is an island off the west coast of Scotland, part of the Western Isles.' He shrugged. 'The Hebrides?' she persisted. 'Perhaps you have heard of them?'

'Ah, yes. I believe Mr Johnson and Mr Boswell wrote an account of their journeys there, some thirty or forty years ago. My father had a copy in his library.' His tone now was neutral—an improvement on the previous stiff hostility, yet still she had no sense of who he truly was.

'Are you and your brother here as visitors, Miss Mac-Donald,' he continued coolly, 'or are you planning to make your home in London?'

'We are here for a visit only. A *short* visit,' she em-phasised. 'As soon as our business here is done, we shall return home to Scotland.' Shuddering, she added frankly, 'I could not imagine what it must be like to live in a place such as this.'

'You do not like London?' A sharpness in his tone warned her to be careful.

'I have no doubt it has many good qualities,' she offered in what she hoped was a conciliatory tone, 'and that there are many who may love to live here, but it would never do for me.'

Rather than respond to this, his expression simply hardened and they walked on, ambling down a tree-lined path that in other circumstances might have been delightful. An idyllic setting, a handsome man, yet the silence between them was growing once again, stretching with tension on his part, suppressed laughter on hers.

Eilidh was determined to seem unperturbed. 'The weather at present is unseasonably warm, do you not think, Mr Wood?'

'I do not,' he returned shortly. 'Today is rather cool. Early March is normally much warmer than this.'

Pressing her lips together to prevent them curving into a grin, she realised she was enjoying the encounter much more than she ought. He sought to irritate her, but she was having none of it. Tilting her head to one side, she gave him the full benefit of her dazzling smile. 'How interesting! In Scotland the weather stays cool until at least June!'

'Hmph!' His noncommittal response was further evidence that he remained cross about her tripping him. Being from the Hebrides and having been reared amid fiery Scots, she was well used to male pride and took no insult from his bad temper. Instead she decided to speak openly.

'I am sorry for…what happened before,' she offered demurely. The word 'trip' was not mentioned.

No point in emphasising it.

Thinking back, she reviewed the incident in her head. As she and Angus had stepped out on to the main path, Eilidh had been astounded to see a young lady running at top speed towards them, a man in hot pursuit. It had all happened in an instant. Eilidh, her protective instincts surging, had stuck out a foot just as the man—Mr Wood—had been about to catch up with the young lady. It was only afterwards she had realised it was Isabella, the lady they had met a few days before in this very park. And of course she could not have known Isabella was engaged in a light-hearted race with her own brother.

My timing was impeccable, she thought now, with a decided sense of satisfaction.

Mr Wood—who had to be over six feet tall and naturally much heavier than her, had been caught off-balance and had sailed through the air, landing on the gravel with a sickening crunch.

It must have hurt his body as much as his pride.

'Are you, though? Are you truly sorry?' He glared at her, clearly seeing her masquerade for what it was.

Interesting. Not many men are so perceptive.

'Well, yes—and no.' She sighed. 'I believed your sister to be in trouble, and I can have no regrets about coming to her aid.' Sending him a glance filled with devilment, she added, 'But I do regret that you turned out to be undeserving of my…er…intervention.'

'Ha!' His bark of laughter seemed to surprise even himself, his face settling quickly back into disapproving lines, but that brief glimpse was all Eilidh needed.

He has humour after all, and a sense of the ridiculous.

Quite why this realisation gave her such satisfaction was unclear.

'Take care!' He placed a hand briefly on her arm, for she had been about to step heedlessly into the road.

Caught up in conversation, Eilidh had quite failed

to notice the park was behind them, and the bustle of London was suddenly swarming her senses. Since the greatest road congestion known to the Islands was when two carts tried to pass one another in a narrow lane, the sight of The Mall, with its myriad conveyances and terrible noise, was still bewildering to her. After only six days in London, she was no closer to being able to manage the terrible assault on her senses.

She caught her breath, her heart pounding. Was it the carriages, riders and pedestrians all around that had disconcerted her so, or was it the simple touch of a man's hand on her arm? *This* man's hand.

Briefly, a flash of memory came to her. Another man, a handsome face, a dazzling smile.

False colours.

It sounded a warning. Not since Edinburgh, and Mr Ross, had Eilidh found herself attracted to a gentleman. But there was no more time to think, for Isabella and Angus were crossing in front of them, and Eilidh and Mr Wood followed carefully behind.

Chapter Two

Max fell into step beside Mr MacDonald, maintaining idle conversation as the ladies forged ahead. They seemed to be greatly enjoying one another's company. Thrusting the beautiful Miss MacDonald from his mind, his thoughts drifted back to his conversation with Isabella in the park, just before their daring decision to re-enact their childhood races.

All is not well with Bella.

Following a visit to their ailing great-aunt this morning, Isabella had suggested they walk in the park, and Max had been quick to agree. Somehow he had to find ways of getting through each day, filling his time with adequate activity in the hope of being tired enough to sleep at night. Caught up with his own darkness, he could not have failed to notice his sister was also in low spirits.

'Why such a sigh, Bella?' he had asked her gently.

'Prudence. Freddy. Marriage. All of it. Even visiting Great-Aunt Morton has depressed my spirits.'

'I know what you mean,' he had replied. 'She is remarkably cheerful, given her circumstances and the fact she has such a cough. That house!' He shuddered now, recalling how rundown the old lady's home was becoming. 'She is clearly in strained circumstances. A pity, because her husband had a reasonable fortune when he was alive.' His tone had been deliberately mild, belying the frustration he felt on their elderly relative's behalf. They would continue to visit her regularly, and when the end came it would sadden them both, for Great-Aunt Morton was Mama's only other living relation.

Responding absentmindedly to a comment from Mr MacDonald, and watching the two ladies exclaim over a bonnet in a shop window, he recalled Isabella's wonder that their older brother Freddy—Frederick, the Viscount Burtenshaw—had not made financial provision for Great-Aunt Morton. He had no such expectation of their parsimonious brother. Freddy had no interest in impoverished distant relatives, and no notion of looking after their great-aunt.

And yet he could, if he chose to.

Listening to Freddy opine at the family breakfast table, one might think the Burtenshaw fortune was tiny, and the family close to being paupers. Yet when Max had been included in matters of business before their papa's death, it had been clear to him that the family wealth was comfortable, and Freddy's fortune secure.

And I worked hard to learn the responsibilities of leadership, only to be condemned to a life of meaningless pleasure and empty ease as the unneeded second son.

Isabella had been charged with choosing a husband this Season, and had expressed some frustration with the notion. Earlier he had asked her if she did not wish to marry someday, and she had indicated that she would, but not because her hand was forced.

This he understood, although his own circumstances

were different. Rather than being forced to marry, he had been deprived of the opportunity. Freddy kept Max on a tight financial leash, his allowance enabling him to live the life of a fashionable buck, yet his brother steadfastly refused to buy Max a pair of colours, or allow him to take up a profession.

Max's yacht—currently moored near the family home in Sussex—was his only luxury.

Not a luxury. It is my sanity.

Being out at sea, working hard alongside his friend Cooper and the crew, he felt alive, purposeful. *Useful.*

There was no chance Freddy would allow him to marry. None. Max had always understood his role as 'spare', should anything happen to Freddy. But now that Freddy and his wife Prudence had two sons of their own, Max was of no practical use to the family. The useless second son. Bitterness rose like bile in his throat.

I am condemned to a cycle of ton *parties, card games, drinking and purposelessness.*

His allowance was enough to maintain the yacht and pay his tailor and his club, but not enough to freely pursue his own course.

He had tried to explain it to Isabella earlier, and she had asked if he enjoyed the parties and card games.

'At the time,' had been his reply. 'Sometimes.' He suppressed a sigh as the same weariness washed over him once more. 'It may sound good, but it is…empty.'

Empty.

The word resonated with him now, even as he devoured the sight of the beautiful Miss MacDonald smiling at something Isabella was saying. Any distraction, no matter how temporary, might distract briefly from this eternal gnawing hollowness.

Earlier, Isabella had caught her breath at the word.

'Empty…yes, exactly! I feel the same way. Oh, why do they not *see*? But Max, at least you can escape. After the Season, you are free to sail and hunt and fish all year if you wish. For me, though—' she had swallowed, a frown creasing her forehead '—if Freddy carries through on his threat, then I shall be forced to choose a suitor by early summer, and will no doubt be married shortly after.'

He grimaced inwardly now, recalling his response. 'I have no answers for you, Bella, save a hope that something may turn up. It is, after all, how I live my own pointless life.'

On they went. The ladies emerged from yet another shop, and Max was struck anew by Miss MacDonald's beauty. It was not just her features, though he could find no flaw in those pale blue eyes, reddish curls or perfect complexion. There was something about her liveliness that drew him. She had a…a *vigour* that he had lost somehow, somewhere.

He looked away as a wave of pain arced through him. Not a distraction, not any more. Now she had reminded him of his own emptiness, and it was too much to bear.

Unnerved by the flash of memory that had taken her back to Mr Ross's betrayal, Eilidh had moved to walk with Miss Wood, leaving the gentlemen to follow behind. The young ladies exchanged shy smiles. 'I am glad to see you again, Miss Wood,' Eilidh began, discovering that she sincerely meant it.

'And I you. I have been thinking of you both these past days, wondering how you are. Thank you again for your kindness the other day.'

Eilidh waved this away. When they had met before, Angus had rescued Miss Wood from a stampeding herd of cattle—not an event Eilidh had anticipated as she and Angus had made the long, difficult journey by boat to Glasgow, then by road all the way down to London. .

Cattle in a city park? How peculiar!

'Think nothing of it,' Eilidh declared now. 'Why, anyone might have done the same!'

'And again today. How were you to know that I was racing with my brother in a dreadfully hoydenish way, rather than being attacked by an assailant? You and your brother seem to have a talent for being there when I needed you. Twice now.'

'Somehow I think it is less of a coincidence than it might seem,' Eilidh replied dryly, given that she had specifically been hoping they would bump into Miss Wood again—though perhaps not literally.

Miss Wood was the one person from London society they had managed to converse with so far, and that had occurred only because she had needed assistance. Eilidh knew that Angus could do no business with any-one in the *ton* unless they were known and accepted within those hallowed social ranks. As Laird at home, Eilidh's brother commanded respect. Here in London, no one had even heard of him, or of Broch Clachan, their ancient home in the Islands.

She stifled a sigh. All of it made their aim of per-suading an English Lord to sell back ancient lands to the Islanders more difficult.

We do not even know how to approach this Lord Burtenshaw, never mind approach him in such a way as to make him likely to sell the precious lands back.

Yet they had to believe it was possible.

Fools look to tomorrow, she reminded herself. *Wise folk make the most of today.*

Small steps might help them achieve their aim. And

besides, she quite liked Miss Wood for her own sake, regardless of whether or not she might advise them on gaining access to the drawing rooms of Mayfair.

Time to change the topic of conversation.

Eilidh paused outside a milliner's shop, commenting on a pretty bonnet displayed in the window. Miss Wood stepped inside with her and together they viewed some bonnets, Eilidh deciding she would return another day to make some purchases. Afterwards they wandered up to Piccadilly, stopping frequently to peruse shops and stalls and forcing the gentlemen to follow in their wake.

Hopefully Angus is making more headway with Mr Wood than I did.

Eilidh had decidedly the easier task, for Miss Wood was as open and friendly as she had seemed the first time they had met.

'I am surprised to say it, but I find that shopping in your company, Miss MacDonald, is actually enjoyable!'

Eilidh gave her a puzzled look. 'But you are so fortunate to have all of these merchants and wares right on your doorstep. I must order unseen from Glasgow or Edinburgh, then wait for weeks or months for my purchases to arrive.'

'I suppose I take such things for granted, Miss MacDonald. Thank you for opening my eyes.' She gave a small laugh. 'I take no interest in matters of fashion and am not womanly enough for my sister-in-law.'

Eilidh was astounded. 'But your gown! Your hair! You look delightful!'

Miss Wood shrugged. 'My maid, Sally, sees to such matters.' She smoothed her gown. 'Although I must admit to a little vanity at times. I do like this gown.'

'Our fashions in the Islands are a little different, I

must admit.' Eilidh indicated her own gown. 'I shall be glad to see my new dresses on the morrow.'

She glanced sideways at Miss Wood. *I might as well ask.*

'Would you like to come with me to the dressmaker's in the morning?'

She held her breath, but Miss Wood agreed without, it seemed, any hesitation. Eilidh felt a twinge of guilt. Was she being deceitful with Miss Wood? Should she tell her of their purpose in London? Reassuring herself with the thought that she *liked* Miss Wood and would always have wished to prolong the acquaintance, she determined to speak with Angus before making any such revelation.

All too soon it was time to part ways, Miss Wood regretfully informing the MacDonalds that she had social engagements to return to. 'But I shall call on you tomorrow, Miss MacDonald, if you can give me your direction?'

At this, Angus produced his card, and Miss Wood bent her head to glance at the details. 'Chesterfield Street. I know where that is.'

Angus had turned his attention to Mr Wood. 'Might I have a word with you?'

'Of course.'

They stepped to one side, and Miss Wood's gaze met Eilidh's, a clear question in her expression. Eilidh, her eyes twinkling, bent closer to report in a confiding tone, 'I think he wishes to apologise for my tripping him up.'

Isabella rolled her eyes. 'Gentlemen suffer indignity very badly, do they not?'

Eilidh grinned. 'There is little difference, it seems, between gentlemen here and gentlemen back home in that regard.'

The gentlemen had, it seemed, finished their conversation. Eilidh made her farewells, bestowing a warm smile on Miss Wood, and favouring her brother with something altogether cooler, yet still allowing him to see a hint of her continued amusement at his stiffness.

I should not, she thought, *for we need to make friends here.*

But his unyielding attitude had been as provoking as it was amusing, and just now she cared not if he knew it.

Max stomped along Piccadilly in silence, still irked by the look Miss MacDonald had sent him as she made her farewell, and the fact that Isabella—and common politeness—had forced him into prolonging the acquaintance, when every instinct within was screaming at him to keep as far away from Miss MacDonald's lively beauty as he possibly could.

'Well?' Isabella's tone was challenging.

'Well, what?'

'What is your opinion of Mr MacDonald and his sister?'

'I have no opinion,' he lied. 'They seem pleasant enough.'

'Pleasant? Is that all you have to say? When they are both so charming, and attractive, and…*Scottish*?'

He remained unmoved, allowing himself to recall his earlier humiliation.

Tripped by a woman! Thank the Lord none of my acquaintances were there to see it.

'Do you not think that Miss MacDonald is beautiful?' A sly glance was sent his way. 'I know you normally are very interested in noticing beautiful ladies.'

'I suppose she was fairly handsome.' His voice remained flat, yet inwardly he had to acknowledge yet again the impact of Miss MacDonald's wild beauty. Not just that glorious face and form, but something about her attitude. The spark of *knowingness*, and humour, and intelligence in her eyes. She had more liveliness than a dozen dreary debutantes, forcing him to acknowledge the deadness, the lethargy within him.

Stop thinking of her!

'What did you and Mr MacDonald speak about just now?'

He ran a hand through his hair at this. 'He apologised and…he wishes to invite me for dinner later. At The Clarendon.'

'And will you go?'

His jaw hardened. 'I could not refuse. I wish I had.'

'Why?'

Abruptly, his terseness vanished, replaced by an outburst delivered in a tone of great frustration. 'Isabella, we know nothing about them. Who are they? Why are they in London? Do they have any proper connections? One must always be wary of soldiers of fortune and their allies. She may not even be his sister!' In his mind, unwanted, was an image of his papa, frowning. Papa had always been protective of the regard due to the Burtenshaw family.

I am a viscount, he would say. *Never forget it.*

Max never had, not for a moment. Well, how could he? Pride and consequence had been, it had always seemed to him, Papa's primary focus in life. Any childhood transgression on Max's part had earned him beatings and sneering humiliation, until he had learned to comply as best he could.

Isabella snorted. 'Anyone can see from a mile away that they are brother and sister. They are very alike—just as we are.' She laid a hand on his arm and he stopped to face her. 'Max, I know you think me too trusting, but is it not possible that you are too *untrusting*?'

'Look…' he spread his hands wide '…I have agreed to meet him for a short dinner. I shall stay long enough for politeness, but I think it prudent to be cautious until we know more of them.' He had no intention of prolonging the connection. Not only because of the unfortunate circumstances of their initial meeting, and his unlooked-for attraction to the Highland lady, but also because what he had told Bella was true. They might be anyone.

His sister had withdrawn Mr MacDonald's card from her reticule and was studying it more carefully than she had earlier. She stopped. 'Max!'

'What is it?'

'He is not a *nobody*. He is a laird!'

'Let me see.' He perused the card. 'The Much-Honoured Angus MacDonald, Laird of Broch Clachan… Hmm… These Scottish titles may be very dubious, you know.' Still, he felt a little more reassured. If the man was titled it meant he and Isabella could acknowledge the acquaintance, and Max might be able to discover more about him and his lineage. 'I shall consult Mr Debrett's book and ask around for what may be known of him and his title.'

Once again he felt a flicker of unease. Surely he should be judging the MacDonalds on *character*, not connections? And yet family pride had been ingrained in him for so long that he could not help but respond reflexively, as if Papa were standing just behind him, belt in hand.

He shuddered, focusing briefly on the knowledge that Miss MacDonald was sister to the Laird.

She will doubtless marry her own kind, he told himself.

Perhaps, indeed, she was already promised to some neighbouring laird in the Islands. The thought gave him

Chapter Three

Tuesday 12th March

Max awoke in his chamber in his brother's townhouse with a cloudy head but a surprising sense of satisfaction. Despite his worst fears beforehand, his evening with Angus MacDonald had gone very well. After dinner they had enjoyed a few hands of cards in a gaming hell followed by a couple of brandies in Max's club. He had signed his new friend in without any qualms, having by this stage formed a fair notion of the man.

When they had parted not long before dawn Max had clasped Angus's hand with genuine amity, feeling as though he had found a friend. While still needing to overcome the twin barriers of inertia and scepticism, last night he had found himself willing to build a friendship with the Scot. It had helped that the man's beautiful sister was nowhere in sight, clouding Max's judgement and making him feel things he would rather not feel.

This morning his customary cynicism was reasserting itself, and yet he resolved to pursue the acquaintance.

It cannot hurt to do so, surely?

Either Angus would turn out to be as solid, quick-witted and entertaining as he had seemed, or he would fail the scrutiny of sobriety and be dropped as unsuitable.

Yes, for now he would make a friend of Angus.

Because of himself or because of his beautiful, lively, maddening sister?

Max shook away the thought, rising to wash and dress. Angus had earned his approval last night, irrespective of his sister.

To Max's disappointment, Isabella was not at home, and so he forced himself to endure the company of his sister-in-law: Freddy's wife, Prudence. Thankfully Freddy had yet to join them in London, being due to arrive on the morrow.

Late in the afternoon, Isabella finally returned, and he was swift to signal to her that he had something to say. Leaving Prudence to her embroidery in the drawing room, he accompanied Bella to the elegant morning room on the ground floor.

'Well, and how do you today, Bella?'

'I am well, and have so much to tell you. But you first. How was your evening with Mr MacDonald?'

He shrugged, suddenly unwilling to admit how much he had enjoyed it. 'It was tolerable.'

Her face fell a little, and she gave a weak smile. 'Oh.' She lifted her chin. 'Well, I am forced to tell you that I like Miss MacDonald very much, and I mean to make a friend of her.' She eyed him anxiously. 'But I do not wish for you to disapprove.'

He touched her arm reassuringly. 'You may do so with my blessing, such as it is—although a little caution may still be required as we assess whether our first impressions have been correct. I have checked their credentials, and they are who they say. Angus seems to have a well-formed mind.'

'He does, does he not? His sister too.' Her eyes widened as she realised what Max had said. 'Angus? You are using first names?'

He grinned. 'After a lot of wine and a few brandies it seemed churlish to maintain formalities.'

'Did he…did he tell you why they are in London?'
Strange question.

'No. But why should he? He is a laird, and has every right to visit London if he wishes.' Her gaze dropped, and suddenly he was all alertness. 'So why is he in London?'

'He wishes to buy an estate near his home from its current owner.'

He thought about this, but could see no reason why she should suddenly seem uneasy. 'A perfectly ordinary reason, then. Or is there more to it?'

'The current owner is Freddy.'

His jaw dropped. '*Freddy?* But—' His mind swiftly ran through all of the Burtenshaw holdings. 'The Scottish estate. Of course!' He frowned. 'Has he spoken to Freddy?'

'Not yet, for they know few people in London.'

His jaw hardened as he put the pieces of the riddle together. 'I see.' So Angus's friendly invitation, his attempts to court Max with amity… 'They mean to reach Freddy through us.'

'But no! They did not even know we are related to him!'

He gave a cynical laugh. 'And I am a two-headed donkey! Naturally they knew, and fooled us both.' He shook his head, hurt piercing his gut. 'I did wonder if they were not what they seemed, but I was quite persuaded by Angus's seeming openness. It looks as though my first instincts were correct, and I should not have succumbed to their charm.'

'But listen, Max! They were astounded when I told them today that Freddy is our brother. Honestly!'

His lip curled. 'I have no doubt that you believe what you were told. But can you not see that there may be another story here? One where they deliberately sought us out to befriend us.' A thought occurred to him. 'Who will make their introduction to the *ton*?'

'I did wonder if we should offer to do so, for they know no one in Town. No, listen, Max, it would be a kindness—particularly since they have been so helpful twice now.'

'They know no one, yet they just *happen* to befriend you and me within days of arriving?' He shook his head. 'Wait—they helped you *twice*?' His brow furrowed. 'I vaguely recall some mention of them helping you *again* when we saw them in the park. Was there some previous occasion? And how do you know them, Isabella?'

All his instincts were screaming that he and his sister had been taken in by deliberate and studied charm.

I knew it! I knew they had to be false.

Disappointment and pain coursed through him, much more intensely than it should for so casual an acquaintance.

I have only known them for a few days. It should not matter.

Yet it did.

'It was last Thursday,' Isabella began. 'I was drinking milk in St James's when some idiots on horseback decided to scatter the cattle there. If not for Mr MacDonald, I would surely have been trampled. He moved in front of me and took the impact, and he was winded for quite some time afterwards. His lips were blue and I thought he would die.' She hid her head in her hands, and he saw that she was trembling.

His jaw sagged in shock. 'Oh, Bella, Bella!' Throwing an arm around her, he spoke to her in a comforting tone. 'If what you say is true, then that was brave indeed, and we are surely indebted to him. But—forgive me, I must ask. Was there really such danger, or are your memories coloured by your liking of him and his sister?'

'No, truly, it was terrifying. Sally was there, and can tell you the whole.' She exhaled slowly, and he saw her bravely push away the troubling memory. 'I was certain I would die then and there, and *oh*… Max, what an ignominious death it would have been! My inscription would have read, "Here lies Miss Wood, who died by cattle". Can you imagine?'

He laughed with her then, but had much to think about. Afterwards, Sally, his sister's maid, corroborated Isabella's tale, confirming that not only would Miss Isabella have likely perished, but that the Highlander had put his own life in danger to protect her.

The tale did not tally at all with the notion that the MacDonalds were bent on deceit and self-interest. They could not possibly have foreseen such an event. Perhaps then, despite his earlier scepticism, Angus and his beautiful sister *were* worthy of his friendship after all. And more, Angus had not so much as mentioned the incident to him. He was discreet then, and not a man to seek accolades.

Max frowned, needing to navigate a cautious middle road—one which allowed for both possibilities, that the MacDonalds were scheming adventurers, or that they were genuine, honest people. If Isabella was to see them again, he would make sure to be present.

I must thank him for his service to my sister, as soon as I may. And I must tell him I shall not interfere in his business dealings with Freddy.

Once it became clear to Angus that Max would not assist him, Max would soon discover whether their burgeoning friendship would vanish like a sea fret burnt by the morning sun.

Friday 15th March

'Max! Are you to accompany us?' In the act of donning her long evening cloak, Isabella glanced at Max's knee breeches, which clearly signalled his intention to go out in company tonight.

'Indeed, yes. I procured an invitation from Craven. I believe he was happy to have more of a balance of guests tonight.' Mr Craven was one of Isabella's suitors, and once Max had heard that the MacDonalds were to be included in the party, he was quick to angle for an invitation.

This will be an opportunity to observe them further and consider what their game may be—if they are duplicitous.

'I had wondered. In terms of gentlemen, there are but three, with five—or possibly six—ladies, as I understand Mrs Bell may also accompany us to the theatre.'

He gave a short laugh. 'Some of my friends would consider me lucky, I suppose, with Miss Bell, Miss MacDonald, *and* Miss Sandison to entertain!' All three young ladies had been invited as part of Mr Craven's theatre excursion, yet Max knew he would have eyes for only one of them. He longed to see her again, yet dreaded it. Tonight he hoped to discover if she was true or false, worthy of the inconvenient fascination that had been plaguing his mind since the day in the park or not. Yet he suspected the fascination would remain even if he discovered her to be an adventuress, using deceit for personal gain. It made no sense.

Isabella was watching him so he added hastily, 'I suppose that Craven will attempt to monopolise your attention.'

She sniffed. 'Well, I should hope I know not to let him! For I am no green debutante, ready to have her head turned by a smile or an empty compliment!'

'True.' He shook his head ruefully. 'Keep both feet on the ground and be ready to see the difference between gold and gilt. Mama raised us well in that regard. As did Cooper.' Cooper was their dearest friend, an older man who had worked for the family in Sussex since before they were born, having travelled from Scotland as a sailor on a ship bound for Newhaven.

They exchanged a warm glance at this mention of the people who were so dear to them both, then he offered her his arm and they followed Prudence outside and into the carriage. Freddy, thankfully, would not accompany them tonight.

They arrived at the Haymarket Theatre at the same time as the MacDonalds, Max feeling decidedly uncomfortable now that he saw them again. Were they friends or deceivers? Their greetings were warm and natural, and he replied with as much enthusiasm as he could muster. Following them upstairs to their box, he was relieved to see that the front row of seats had already been taken by Miss Bell and her mama, along with Miss Sandison. Tonight, he would much prefer to remain in the shadows.

With a flourish, Mr Craven led Prudence to the last remaining front row seat, then indicated that he would seat himself in the centre of the row behind, with Isabella to one side and Miss MacDonald to the other. Since siblings did not normally sit together, this meant that Angus sat next to Isabella, while Max took the empty seat to Miss MacDonald's right. She smoothed her gown and he gave her a formulaic compliment, to which she responded with the raise of an eyebrow that could only be described as ironic. This was rather unfortunate, for she truly looked stunning tonight, her hair deftly styled with side curls framing her beautiful face and a silk gown enhancing her fine form. Swallowing, he forced himself to listen to the wider conversation, turning his head away from her.

Eilidh could only be relieved that his gaze was gone from her. Having convinced herself that she had exaggerated Mr Wood's handsomeness and ability to fascinate, she was rapidly discovering her error.

Oh, dear!

Having suffered the ignominy of Mr Ross's false attentions in Edinburgh a few years before, she had thought herself immune to male charms, and yet... Foolishly, she had assumed Mr Ross to be without major flaw, based only on his handsome appearance, warm smiles and charming compliments. When his true colours had been revealed, she had vowed never again to be taken in by charm before discovering someone's true character.

Mr Wood had been in her thoughts very frequently since they had first met, and she was unsure why. He seemed as closed as his sister was open, as dark as Miss Wood was bright, as cynical as she was trusting. But something about the way her mind kept turning to him reminded her of her earlier fixation with Mr Ross.

A fixation that had ended cruelly with the announcement of Mr Ross's betrothal to Miss Black, who had five thousand pounds and a house in Galashiels.

During the past few days—and nights—her mind had drifted repeatedly to Mr Maximilian Wood. His looks. His irritated demeanour. The moment when she had realised he shared her sense of humour. Seeing him tonight in full evening wear had disordered her senses—so much so that she had said little since their arrival. His compliment towards her just now had been delivered in an offhand way, which came as something of a relief since she could not believe it. Thankfully, it seemed he had no intention to charm her, for which she could only be glad. Somehow she suspected he was capable of being very charming indeed, and she needed to guard against him.

Max settled back in his seat. Tonight's play was *Rule a Wife and Have a Wife*—a title to which Isabella, naturally, objected.

'*Rule* a wife?' she declared. 'I think not!' Max stifled a grin, hearing in his sister's pronouncement; the echoes of his rebellious mama, and of Cooper too. The servant had always behaved as a friend to his employer's two youngest children, and he abhorred class strictures.

Mr Craven—clearly interested in Isabella's opinion on such matters—was suddenly all ears. 'You do not believe a wife should submit to her husband, Miss Wood?'

Oho! This should be interesting.

Isabella had her own mind on such matters, much to Freddy's chagrin. She seemed to answer carefully. 'I certainly believe that the most felicitous marriages are those where neither the man nor the woman can be said to rule.'

Max pressed his lips together. Their own parents' marriage had been deeply unhappy, with their father continually attempting to dominate Mama, and she resisting and rebelling as best she could. Peace had reigned in the house only when Papa went to London, and Mama had always seemed much happier then.

It had been a blessed relief to all of them when Papa had succumbed to apoplexy and died when Max had been fourteen and Isabella nine. Freddy, already a young man of twenty-three, had stepped into Papa's shoes and had married Prudence soon afterwards. Mama had been happy then for a time, until she too was carried off—by a fever—eight years later.

'But it is the proper order of things for a man to be master in his own house,' protested Mr Craven. Glancing briefly at Max, who eyed him levelly, his gaze slid away and he turned to the Scot. 'Mr MacDonald,' he appealed, 'surely you will support me on this?'

Max watched with some interest.

How will Angus handle this?

'He can certainly be Master…' the Highlander began, and Mr Craven smiled in satisfaction '…as long as his lady is Mistress.' The smile faded on Mr Craven's face. 'I come from a long line of strong women, Mr Craven,' Angus continued. 'Indeed, the Islands are full of them, as my sister can confirm. It does not make a man weak when women are strong, for they have a different kind of strength to us.'

'How so, Mr MacDonald? How does a woman's strength differ from a man's?' Isabella asked, and Max was conscious of some discomfort as he saw how intently she focused on Angus's answer.

The Scot thought for a moment. 'A man can withstand physical pain—the pain of hard work, or wounds from battle, but a woman endures childbirth. A man may hide his fear on the eve of battle, but at least he can act. The women must hide their fear from the children and the old ones, while being strong enough to endure the waiting.' His eyes lost focus, as if another thought had occurred to him. 'Men fear ridicule and rejection, while women fear assault and violation.'

Mr Craven's jaw dropped. 'Surely, sir, you do not intend to suggest that all men are capable of such…such abhorrent acts?'

'Not all men, no.' Mr MacDonald had refocused on Mr Craven, and there was a teasing glint in his eye. 'But I'll wager those who feel the need to rule have the greater likelihood.'

Now put that in your pipe, Craven, and smoke it!

Max could not help but be amused at how effectively Angus had scythed through Craven's self-important pomposity. *Nicely done!* He glanced towards Miss MacDonald, who looked decidedly displeased by her brother's audacity.

'I think,' she offered, her soft Scottish accent setting off a ridiculous fluttering throughout Max, 'that where there is a meeting of minds, the notion of one ruling the other is less relevant. It is certainly true that men and ladies have different expectations put upon them. And yet I could not see myself choosing to marry a man who was too soft, for example. A man should be…manly.'

'What then, is your definition of "manliness", Miss MacDonald?' Max could not help himself: he had to ask.

'I can only speak from the perspective of a woman, and a Scottish woman at that.' Her voice was low, and he leaned closer to hear her. 'Manliness is…it is all that is *good* about men. It is strength, yes, but a strength that shows itself in subtle ways. A man is active. He makes things happen, but not through domination. He gets things done, and takes responsibility. And he also knows there is a strength in tenderness, in caring for others, in sharing his pain with those who care about him. That is not softness, it is simply another form of strength.'

'Yet you said you could not marry a man who was too soft.' In his mind's eye, he pictured an unknown laird, the epitome of *manliness* as envisaged by Miss MacDonald.

'Ah, yes. What I meant by that is the softness of idleness, of selfishness, of self-indulgence. In the Islands we do not have such luxury as this.' Her hand fluttered vaguely towards the other boxes, where *tonnish* parties dripping with fine jewels laughed and chatted as they waited for the start of the play. 'In my home, every man must work, and work hard.'

'Even the Laird?'

'Especially the Laird.'

She paused, and they simply looked at one another for a moment—a moment in which Max felt himself to be drowning in her eyes. Then she blinked and gave a little laugh. 'How foolish you must think me! Who am I to say what a man is, after all, when all I know is womanliness?'

The play began then and Max directed his gaze to the stage, but inwardly he felt as though he had been shattered like glass by her words. *Idleness. Selfishness. Self-indulgence.* It felt as though she had gazed into his very soul and found him wanting. How would a lady such as she judge his empty, vacuous life? A life where the choosing of his waistcoat was one of the most significant decisions in his day.

Self-loathing—that familiar demon—rose like bile within him.

I would never meet her requirements in a man. I do not even meet my own. What am I then? A boy in a man's boots? A half-formed thing of no import and no strength? Something useless, and hapless, and worthless.

All around him he could hear the others commenting to one another about the play, but he found himself entirely incapable of speech. It was all he could do to maintain a neutral expression on his face and brace himself for the first interval. It came, and Miss MacDonald disappeared briefly to the ladies' retiring room with Isabella. Max stood with the others, pretending to listen to their empty words, yet inwardly focusing entirely on maintaining his self-control.

I must master this!

If his thoughts continued to circle as they currently were, it would bring the darkness of low spirits on him again. He had managed for months to keep the demons that plagued him at bay. The last thing he needed was for them to swarm over him now, when he would be expected to be in company for the next three months. And he could not even seek the haven of his yacht, for it was moored at home in Sussex and he would not sail again until summertime.

The two ladies had returned. Desperately, Max focused his attention on other matters. The way Isabella was looking at Angus. The way Miss Bell was smiling at Mr Craven. The way Mr Craven was smiling at Miss MacDonald.

Is she on the catch for a husband here, perhaps?

The notion sent a pang through him, which he ruthlessly rejected.

I hardly know the woman, and it is no business of mine whom she marries!

Eilidh knew not what to think. Normally, she believed she was a good judge of character, but Maximilian Wood confused her. Who was he? A hedonistic dilettante, as heedless and useless as the drunken young men who had scattered the cattle last week? Or was there more to him? Was there depth, feeling, self-reflection? She could not tell for sure, but during their conversation earlier she'd had the curious sensation that her words had caused him hurt.

I should not have spoken so forcefully. No, nor allowed myself to be inveigled into such a conversation.

As they took their seats again for the second act she had the grace to feel rather ashamed, and so set out to make conversation with him in an attempt to smooth over any uneasiness. Her first sally—a bland enquiry as to whether he was enjoying the play—was met with a blank expression, before his eyes narrowed and he made some equally bland comment about it being 'delightful'. They maintained a light conversation during the act, commenting now and again on the performances in the brightly lit theatre.

All the while she felt on edge, uncertain, somehow needing him to offer her reassurance. Yet he remained closed to her, distant, unreadable. Quite why his good opinion mattered to her, she could not say. Once she returned to Benbecula, she would never see him again. And if he was, as he appeared, a vacuous and self-indulgent *tonnish* gentleman, as shallow and inconstant as Mr Ross had turned out to be, then so much the better, for never again would she allow any gentleman the opportunity to bruise her heart.

The play ended and they stood to mingle and chat with other members of their party. Max, thankfully, was feeling a little more in control of his unseemly emotions following Miss MacDonald's too-accurate barbs earlier. Gazing abstractedly to where she was making conversation with Miss Sandison, he tried to figure out why, despite the danger she presented to his peace of mind, he still felt so drawn to her.

Perhaps it is because of the danger, not despite it.

Never before had he encountered anyone—woman or man—who had seen into his soul with such devastating accuracy. The notion was terrifying.

'Max!' Isabella signalled for him to join her.

He managed a half-smile. 'Well, Bella. Did you enjoy the play?'

She shrugged. 'It was entertaining, I suppose.' She lowered her voice. 'I am certainly enjoying the company of Mr MacDonald and his sister. Is there nothing we can do for them? You know how Freddy hates the Scots.'

'Hate is too strong a word.' Yet his sister was right. Freddy had always had an antipathy towards Scotland and the Scottish. Papa had been just the same. 'He was certainly fed a diet of anti-Scottish sentiment by our father. I remember Papa ranting at length about Jacobites.'

Why have I never questioned why they felt that way?

Max's own views of the Scottish had been largely coloured by Cooper—a servant in name but in reality Max's confidant, adviser and friend. Cooper lived on the family estate in Sussex, and Max would not see him again until summer. Yet another reason to hate the Season.

She acknowledged this, but added, 'Still, someone should warn Mr MacDonald. Prepare him. Advise him.'

'By "someone" you mean me, I suppose?'

She nodded. 'Will you do it, Max? They are good people, and Freddy can be so…mercurial when making decisions. It is nothing to any of us if Freddy sells this small estate. But it would mean much to the people there.'

At her words, anger rose up within Max as the memory of Miss MacDonald's earlier words hit him again with full force. 'Why should I put myself out for strangers? After all, I am nothing but a good-for-nothing layabout!' The words erupted from him, fuelled by the self-loathing currently swirling within him. Being angry with Miss MacDonald was irrational for she had spoken only the truth, yet he could not help but feel injured that she, of all women, thought so badly of him.

Isabella's jaw dropped but she rallied instantly, adopting a scolding tone. 'For goodness' sake, Max! Quit being so self-critical. You know full well you are better than that. And here is your chance to do something that has meaning. Will you not take it?'

They are good people.

Ironically, Miss MacDonald's scathing criticism of the *ton* was what had finally convinced him that she and her brother were not adventurers. Someone trying to cut a wheedle would not have been so critical.

Isabella is right. As she often is.

'I suppose…' His jaw hardened. 'But any such conversation will remain private to me and Angus only. No one is to know—particularly Mi…particularly our sisters. So you are not to ask me about it after tonight. Agreed?'

'Agreed. Thank you, Max.' She touched his arm. 'So when will you speak to him? Tonight? Tomorrow?'

He grimaced. 'You are too impatient, Isabella. I shall choose the time and place—' she opened her mouth as if to argue '—or I shall not do it at all!'

Isabella nodded in agreement, then made her way across to Miss MacDonald and Miss Sandison, joining in their conversation with easy grace. Max, looking towards them, felt unaccountably uncertain—almost lost.

Pull yourself together, man!

Gathering himself, he walked towards Craven and Angus. Just now he could not face the ladies.

Eilidh was feeling concerned. Concerned and rather ashamed. Really, her words earlier had been uncalled for. Knowing she needed to attempt to make things right with Mr Wood, she took her opportunity as soon as it arose. Mr Craven had bid them wait to leave their box until the crowds from the pit below had gone, and she now saw that their departure was imminent. Moving to where Max was standing, she spoke swiftly, knowing she might otherwise lose her nerve.

'Mr Wood,' she began as he turned towards her, and she was hit with the full force of his handsome face and shuttered gaze. 'There is something I must say to you.'

'Yes, Miss MacDonald? I am all ears.' Was it her imagination, or was there suddenly a new tension in the line of his broad shoulders?

Courage.

Taking a deep breath, she continued. 'Two things, actually. The first is that I wish to apologise for any offence caused by my blunt words earlier. I know nothing about the people of the *ton*, and should not presume to judge them.' She grimaced ruefully. 'I have the terrible habit of speaking my mind—a great failing, I know.'

'Not at all,' he replied smoothly. 'I admire your plain speech.'

She eyed him doubtfully. No, she could not read him. Was he simply giving the expected polite reassurance or did he truly mean it?

'And the second?' His dark eyes held hers, and this time there was a definite frisson of...*something* between them.

'The second?' Her mind was suddenly blank, having been evicted from her body, it seemed, by her racing heart and roaring pulse.

'You said two things.'

'I did. I wish to be honest with you about our reason for travelling to London.'

He blinked. 'Plain speech indeed. I confess I did not expect you to raise the topic so directly.'

'Then you know about it?'

'My sister said that you travelled to London because you wish to discuss a matter of business with my brother, Burtenshaw.'

She nodded. 'We wish to buy back a Benbecula estate. Angus intends to offer a fair price.'

He raised an eyebrow. 'And so you decided to befriend us in the hope of gaining access to my brother?' His tone was questioning, but she heard the accusation in his words regardless.

'Not at all! We discovered only yesterday that he is your brother. It was the purest coincidence when we first met your sister near the milch herd, and of course the second time she literally ran into my brother!'

A gleam of humour lit his eyes. 'And you were coming from quite the opposite direction. No,' he mused, 'I cannot see how you might have deliberately contrived to rescue her twice.' His expression became thoughtful. 'I am in your brother's debt for the incident with the cattle.'

She waved this away. 'Not at all! That is not how things work where we come from. Everyone helps with no expectation of reward, and as the world turns and seasons pass, everyone is helped in turn when they require it.' Daringly, she added with a twinkle, 'Besides, my brother's assistance to your sister was quite undone by my tripping you up!'

At this, he threw back his head and laughed, and once again she was forced to consider how handsome he was. '*Touché*, Miss MacDonald. Very well, we shall count any debts settled.'

'As to our presence here tonight, Mr Craven was there when we called on your sister yesterday, and included us in his invitation. Your sister played no direct part in it, I assure you!' She glanced to where Miss Wood was chatting with some of the others. 'I like her. That is the truth of it. It matters not that she happens to be Lord Burtenshaw's sister. And I like...' About to say 'you', she suddenly thought better of it and diverted her words to something a little less particular. 'I like *both* of you.'

There!

Now, would that make up for any hurt she had caused him earlier? She would hate to think she had caused pain to anyone. And she did like him. Mostly. Despite... everything.

His eyes widened briefly and he seemed momentarily lost for words, so she hurried on. 'Anyway, Mrs Bell has just invited all of us to a soirée she will host in three days, so I hope to see you there.'

'I shall look forward to it.'

He bowed gallantly, and still she could not sense how he was feeling. His social mask was in place, that was certain. Yet beneath it she was vaguely aware of a maelstrom of…of something.

He has more depth than he shows to the world.

Quite why she suddenly believed this, she could not say. But he was a puzzle to her, a riddle she was increasingly determined to solve.

Despite her earlier misgivings, based on her experience with Mr Ross, she knew that apologising for any hurt she might have caused Mr Wood had been the right thing to do. The fact that it had forced her—forced them both—into a meaningful conversation, something beyond the social chit-chat that would be expected at this stage in their acquaintance…well, that could not be helped. But something had changed between them tonight, something that prevented her from seeing him as a stranger to her, and it could not be undone.

As she walked away it did not occur to her to wonder yet again why she was developing such a fixation with him. She simply let it be. Relief was the dominant emotion she was feeling, and hope that his wariness might in time give way to something warmer—something that indicated he had truly forgiven her for her harsh and unfeeling words. And if he was simply a self-indulgent London gentleman with no depth then so much the better, for someone with such a character could never earn her true admiration. No, nor retain it.

And besides, I shall be gone soon.

There would be no time for Mr Wood to wheedle his way into her expectations as Mr Ross had… Vague memories of flowers and poetry, of dancing and compliments in the Edinburgh Assembly Rooms came to her now, and she was gratified to feel not even a mild pang of pain. Even the anger had died, it seemed. All the pain was gone, leaving only the learning she had taken from Mr Ross's duplicity. This time, she was forewarned and forearmed. This time, her heart would be safe.

Standing outside and breathing the crisp night air in the noisy street, Max waited with the others for the carriages to be brought round. Inwardly, he remained unsettled, a tempest of emotion swirling within him.

She likes me! She despises me!

Having no idea which was the truth, he considered this.

I am rightly despised—do I not know better than anyone how useless I am?

'Angus!' He spoke impulsively, knowing he would not be able to sleep for hours yet. 'Shall we go to my club again?'

Angus grinned. 'An excellent notion! You keep much later hours than we do at home. I can tell I shall be quite corrupted into sleeping late in London!'

Corrupted.

Knowing Angus spoke in jest, he ought to take it in the manner intended, yet still the word pierced Max, sharp as the sting of a wasp. Even compared to sleepy Sussex, London had much of corruption in it. How it must seem to Islanders, he had no idea.

A few moments later, they made their way up to Jermyn Street then across to St James's, where the gentlemen's clubs were clustered. Inside, they were both greeted by name, the staff having made it their business to memorise Angus's name and title from his last visit. It was the raucous time of night and the place was busy, filled with young bucks in the full swell

of wine-fuelled bravado and cheer. To Max, who like
Angus had imbibed only a few glasses at the theatre,
the young men seemed universally foolish and commonplace.

Idleness. Selfishness. Self-indulgence.

Eilidh's words returned to him once again and, honestly, he could not argue with them. Not just for himself,
but for many of the young men of the *ton*. The difference was the others accepted it as if it were a *right* to
be idle and useless.

Yet if he had any hope of sleeping later in the night,
particularly after his earlier encounter with Angus's sister, he knew he would need to sup more wine and, later,
brandy. And so he ordered a bottle, and then another.
He and Angus chatted about everything and nothing,
cementing their burgeoning friendship through learning more of each other's history, attitudes and family.

'Is your brother much older than you?' Angus asked.

'Nine years.'

Angus's eyes widened. 'Nine? And then you and
your sister were born much closer in time?'

'Yes. Why?'

'Have you never wondered why there was such a gap
in time between you and your brother?'

Max shrugged. 'My parents did not enjoy a cordial
union. They may well have been estranged for a time.
No one speaks of such things, so I suppose I shall never
know.'

'As your brother was much older, I assume you have
never therefore enjoyed a close friendship.'

'No, not at all. He was…he was something like a distant young uncle to me. Always there, but never really
engaging with me or with Isabella. At times he seemed

little more than a prefect, doing my father's bidding. He was, naturally, Papa's favourite.'

'I see.'

Do you, though?

'Papa disliked the Scots, I am sorry to say.'

'And so your brother may refuse to sell, simply because we are Scottish?'

Max took another sip of brandy, shrugging. 'Freddy is entirely predictable in many ways.' He frowned. 'And occasionally unpredictable.' He narrowed his eyes. 'What I can say is, tread carefully. Once he makes his mind up, it is difficult to change it.'

The quiet part of the night was upon them, finding them seated in a comfortable corner of Max's club. The boisterous young men had lately departed, and the clock had struck three times just now.

'So, your advice?' Angus prompted.

Max shuffled uncomfortably. 'He is my brother. I cannot advise you too strongly. But I see no harm in him accepting a fair price for an estate that he has never even visited.' He thought for a moment. 'He sets much store by the views of the *ton* and I do believe he is more likely to do business with an acquaintance rather than a stranger.'

Angus snorted. 'Then he is no different to anyone else in that regard!' He took a swallow of his own drink. 'Still, I am making some headway in terms of *ton* events. Eilidh and I were invited to the theatre tonight, we have Mrs Bell's soirée next, and after that, who knows?'

'Prudence—my brother's wife—might host a soirée or something this Season, for there is Isabella to be fired off. She may well invite you—' Max grinned briefly '—though not if you turn Isabella's head from her suitors!'

Angus sent him a sharp glance. 'And why should anyone think I would or could do that?'

No need to be coy with me, my friend. I have seen the way you and Bella watch one another when you believe yourselves to be unobserved.

Aloud he said only, 'I know Prudence of old. She can be tigerish in her pursuit of a goal, and any barriers to it are dealt with ruthlessly. She may not yet be aware that you are not in Town to find a wife. Once she is, expect yourself to be struck off her list and ruthlessly ignored. Her one aim this Season is to see poor Isabella leg-shackled!'

'*Poor* Isabella? She will be forced into marriage?'

Max considered this. 'I cannot imagine so. But they will pressure her, yes. Freddy has told her she must marry this year.'

'And if she does not? What then?'

'He will choose her husband himself. You shake your head, but it is not so bad as it sounds. Isabella is more than ready to leave behind the life of a spinster, ready to be mistress of her own household.' He shook his head. 'It is hard for her, living under Freddy and Prudence's eye. I at least have some freedom.' His mouth twisted. 'Such as it is.' He remained silent for a moment, his thoughts turning inexorably to Angus's sister, Miss MacDonald. *Eilidh*. 'What of your own sister? Do you not have a duty to see her settled?'

Angus laughed shortly. 'Nay, she knows her own mind, our Eilidh. She will choose a husband when she wishes to, or remain unmarried if she prefers. It is of no matter to me, for I want only her happiness.'

'Yes. I see.' Max dared not dwell on Eilidh's potential future husband, whoever he might be. 'That is very different to the expectations on Isabella. Freddy seems to take it as a personal slight that she is unmarried. I believe he thinks it reflects badly on our house and lineage.' He heard the hint of bitterness in his own final words.

'It is good to be proud of one's name, surely?' Angus smiled. 'We MacDonalds are known for fighting each other, until a common enemy unites us.'

'A common enemy? Like the English?'

'I was thinking more of the MacNeills or the Campbells. But yes, oft times it has been Scot against English.' He paused. 'I bear no ill will towards individuals who have done no harm to me and mine.'

'I am happy to hear it!' There was a moment of companionable silence. 'I am promised to Gentleman Jack's tomorrow, for some boxing practice. Should you like to join me?'

'I should, and thank you.' Angus grinned. 'If only all our woes could be settled by fisticuffs, the world would be a better place!'

Two hours later Max made his way home by hackney in the pre-dawn light. His assessment of Angus as a 'good fellow' after their meal in The Clarendon had been correct and just. It was a pity the MacDonalds would leave London soon, once the matter of the Scottish estate had been settled, for Max had few true friends. Oh, there were many who would style themselves that way, yet with Angus he had felt an affinity that was unusual.

Perhaps it is because I do not belong here, among the ton. *I have never felt easy with my lot.*

Angus lived a different life as Laird, a life with purpose and meaning, and Max envied him. Envied him, and yet was fiercely glad that he now knew men like

Angus even existed. Men who carried the burden of responsibility without complaint, as though it was their very purpose in life.

He reflected on Freddy's overdeveloped sense of duty. Despite frequently disagreeing with his older brother, Max knew how seriously Freddy took his responsibilities as head of the family. Isabella knew it too, which was why she needed to choose from among her suitors swiftly, for otherwise Max suspected Freddy would soon choose for her, as he had told Angus.

Eilidh had no such threat hanging over her and would be free to marry whoever she chose. Picturing her beautiful face and recalling the intelligence and insight in her eyes, Max was unsure if there was any man in the world worthy of such a jewel. Despite the fact she had unintentionally hurt him with her direct words and had the frightening ability to see directly into his soul, he could only admire her. While he had multiple reasons to keep a distance between them, he already knew in his bones that whoever she chose would be the luckiest man on earth.

Chapter Four

Monday 18th March

The Bell mansion was an elegantly appointed house in the heart of Mayfair, with stone steps, a stuccoed porch and a smiling hostess. By the time Eilidh and Angus arrived it was already packed with guests, their elegance and wealth on conspicuous display, as was the considerable expense Mrs Bell must have laid out on tonight's event.

Scarcely daring to believe that they had achieved their first aim of gaining access to a *ton* event, Eilidh curtseyed gracefully as Mrs Bell introduced her and Angus to innumerable people. Some were barely polite, clearly disapproving of the Scots, but most people were perfectly friendly. Eilidh's new gown—a green silk over a bronze and red underdress—had already gained multiple compliments, and she and Angus were handling the social niceties with ease. Less than two weeks since their arrival in London, and never could she have anticipated being invited to a *ton* soirée so quickly.

All of society was here tonight, it seemed. Would Lord Burtenshaw be among them? She scanned the crowds, looking for Max's tall, broad figure, for surely, in order to find Lord Burtenshaw, she first had to find his brother or sister, and the crowd was simply too dense for her to see Isabella. She had seen Mr Wood briefly yesterday and he had been a little stiff with her. This caused her some sadness and regret, but she hoped to melt his coolness, if given the chance.

'What a pleasant young man!' one elderly lady declared loudly as they moved off. 'And the sister is quite the diamond!' Exchanging a quick glance with Angus, she saw that the amusement in his gaze mirrored her own.

Would they think me so ladylike if they saw me milking cattle, or tying lines on a boat, or waulking the tweed?

Still, she would take encouragement from those members of the *ton* who had welcomed them.

Eventually they spotted Prudence, Lady Burtenshaw, whom they had met the week before, and crossed to make their greetings to her. Responding affably, she introduced them to her friend Mrs Edgecombe, a middle-aged lady. A moment later her husband joined them, along with Max… Mr Wood.

Finally!

Eilidh's heart was beating faster. It was nothing to do with Mr Wood's presence, of course. It must be because at last she was in the company of Lord Burtenshaw.

Burtenshaw.

A name that was infamous in Benbecula. The absentee landlord who cared nothing for his tenants. The current owner of lands that should never have been taken from the Islanders. The man whose agents insisted on rents being paid in full and without fail, uncaring of the troubles the tenants might have endured in that quarter.

Stealing a glance at him, she noted with irrational surprise that Burtenshaw looked no different to the other lords and gentlemen here tonight. Similar clothing, similar hairstyle, the same confident air. He looked older than Max and Isabella too—there could be perhaps ten years between Max and his older brother. Since Isabella and Max looked so alike, Eilidh had expected their older brother to resemble them closely, but he did not. Not at all. The notion pleased her greatly.

'Angus!' Max greeted him in a friendly way before turning to Eilidh. 'Miss MacDonald.' The contrast in the tone of his greeting was marked, and Eilidh felt it.

He is wary of me yet.

She swallowed hard.

Greetings and introductions continued and Eilidh watched as her brother shook Burtenshaw's hand.

I must believe he is as reasonable a man as his siblings. Perhaps he is unaware of his tenants' suffering. If he would only sell the Lidistrome estate to us, we may begin to put things right.

Conversation continued, and the group remained together until supper was called. Max and Isabella invited them to take a tour of the Tower of London on the morrow, and Angus accepted in a relaxed way. Angus was doing well, Eilidh knew, and she made sure to play her part.

Two of Isabella's suitors joined them then—a Lord Welford and a gentleman introduced as the Honourable Mr Barnstable, whose eyes roved over Eilidh's form in a decidedly unsettling manner. Stifling a shudder, she reminded herself they were in the heart of London society, where the mores and standards might be different to those in which she was accustomed.

She must, though, focus on their reason for being

here. Now was their opportunity to build a respectful connection with Lord Burtenshaw before Angus raised the thorny issue of the sale of the Lidistrome estate. Hopefully Burtenshaw's agent did not in fact speak for his employer, and Lord Burtenshaw would see Angus's proposal as a reasonable request from a reasonable man.

After supper the musicale began, and Eilidh and Angus took their turn among the performers, Eilidh singing 'Red, Red Rose' by Burns, with Angus accompanying her on the piano. She had sung it a hundred times at home, for musical evenings were common, particularly in winter. Never had she sung in such a setting before, being rather more used to stone castle walls rather than glittering chandeliers and delicate French furniture. Performing with all the passion within her, as was customary among her people, she was astonished on finishing to hear a brief silence, followed by fervent applause.

The comments were equally gratifying.

'Wonderful!'

'Delightful!'

'That was beautiful, my dear!'

Eilidh smiled and curtseyed, then changed places with Angus. As she played for him while he sang 'Ae Fond Kiss', she could not help but wonder if Max—she had stopped calling him Mr Wood in her head—had enjoyed her performance. He was clapping politely when she glanced his way after Angus finished, and she stifled a sigh. Really, she should not allow Burtenshaw's brother to distract her from their mission.

Should not, but reality was altogether different. There was just something about him that bothered her. Each time she was in his company, she noticed him. Not just with her mind, but with her tingling body and racing heart. And there was more. Somehow, in that moment in the theatre, when she had said those hurtful words and they had looked at one another, there had been an unexpected sense of connection, something she had never hitherto experienced.

His opinion mattered to her. His happiness too. And yet the more she knew of him, the more she understood he was a typical *tonnish* second son. He had no responsibility, no profession or commitment requiring his time and attention. It was impossible for her to conceive of such an existence.

How does he pass the days, weeks and months?

She shuddered at the thought of *years* of such a life.

Looking around her, she realised that many of the men here would have no difficulty in spending a life of idleness. The odious 'Honourable' Mr Barnstable for one. As she watched, Mr Barnstable took a seat at a card table with Lord Burtenshaw and Max, and a moment later she saw Angus join them.

Good! Make the most of this opportunity, Angus, for the sooner we finish our business here and return home, the better!

The card games would likely go on for two hours or more. Eilidh held a few conversations with new acquaintances then searched for Isabella and joined her friend with some relief. Isabella clearly felt the same way.

'I am so happy to have you here, Eilidh!' she declared. 'Without you and your brother, this evening would be so dull!'

Eilidh eyed her curiously. 'Is there no one here whose company you enjoy?'

'Well, there is Max, naturally—although he does not

usually stay very long at these sorts of events. There is a…a restlessness within him, particularly in London.'

Eilidh's heart skipped a beat at the mention of Max. 'Then outside of London he is different?'

'He is more settled, yes.' Isabella thought for a moment. 'Like me, he is happier in the countryside, or out at sea. Does that seem strange?'

'Not to me, for *this* is what is strange. It looks a little like a Gathering such as we have at home, but the air is altogether different.' This was encouraging. Perhaps then Max had another side to him—one that was not apparent in the drawing rooms and ballrooms of the *ton*.

Isabella seemed only to be half-listening. 'Oh! There is someone else here for whom I have a great liking. Mrs Edgecombe, who was my mama's dearest friend. You met her earlier, remember? Shall we go and speak to her, for I see she is alone at present?'

'Oh, yes, your sister-in-law introduced us earlier.' Accompanying Isabella across to where Mrs Edgecombe sat, they joined her for some pleasant conversation.

'So, Isabella,' Mrs Edgecombe said after a while, 'I am glad to see that you managed to find your friends and that they are here tonight.'

Isabella nodded. 'It is wonderful to have them here tonight. We also went to the theatre together on Friday, as part of Mr Craven's party.'

'You did?' Mrs Edgecombe glanced across to where Mr Craven was conversing with Miss Bell. 'Mr Craven seems a very worthy gentleman.'

'Worthy. A good word.' Isabella grimaced.

'He is not to your liking?'

'I like him well enough, I suppose.'

'But you do not *like* him.'

'I…no. No, I do not.' She sighed. 'Which is a pity, for I cannot say what is wrong with him. He is everything that is…worthy.'

'Is there anyone that you *do* like, Isabella?' Placing a hand on Isabella's arm, she added, 'I do not mean to pry, my dear, but I think your mother would have wanted me to watch out for you.'

Isabella flushed, and Eilidh had a sudden notion that there was indeed a man that her friend liked. Unfortunately, Eilidh also suspected she knew exactly who he was.

'None of my suitors are particularly inspiring,' Isabella replied.

Mrs Edgecombe was not done. 'Your taste runs elsewhere?' she asked archly, a teasing twinkle in her eye. 'You are your mother's daughter in that regard.'

'What do you mean?'

Mrs Edgecombe leaned closer, speaking directly to Isabella. 'Your mother, despite doing her best to comply with society's strictures, was something of a rebel— a trait that was not appreciated by her husband. But I must say no more. Your brother Burtenshaw does not like it when I speak so.'

Eilidh grinned, liking the sound of Isabella's mother. Perhaps that was why her friend seemed different to other London ladies. Was Isabella, in her own way, as rebellious as her mother had been?

'No. I see that,' Isabella replied thoughtfully. 'I remember them arguing when Mama refused to travel to London for the Season. Papa went without her after that.' She considered this for a moment. 'Freddy is very like Papa, I think.'

'Like peas in a pod—in looks as well as character.'

She expanded on this, and Eilidh saw understanding dawn in her friend's eyes.

'It is true! Papa's portrait could well be Freddy in old-fashioned clothing—apart from the eyes. We all have Mama's dark eyes. People always used to comment about how alike Papa and Freddy were. They have never said that about Max and me.'

Eilidh, fascinated, was hanging on every word. So Lord Burtenshaw was like his father in character, while Isabella was not. And Max?

'You both favour your mother.' Mrs Edgecombe's reply was not unexpected. She took Isabella's hand. 'She would be proud of the young woman you have become, Isabella.'

'Thank you.' Isabella's voice trembled a little.

Patting her hand, Mrs Edgecombe then turned her attention to Eilidh, addressing her with the same directness. 'I assume since your brother is Laird that your father is gone, but is your mother yet living, Miss Mac-Donald?'

'No. She is also deceased. Miss Wood and I have this in common.'

'And what brings you to London? Are you on the catch for a husband, perhaps?'

Eilidh laughed. 'Oh, no! I do not think of marriage— I have plenty of time for such things in future.'

'Then has the Laird come in search of a suitable lady?' Mrs Edgecombe's eyes twinkled with humour, and Eilidh saw Isabella blush again.

Oh, dear!

'Lord, no!' she replied airily. 'I expect when the time comes that he will marry a girl from the Islands. He definitely has no such intentions here.' Eilidh glanced at Isabella as she spoke.

Best that she knows and does not hold any futile hopes.

She and Angus were here for business reasons only, and needed to return home just as soon as the matter of the Lidistrome estate was resolved. Marrying an English person could not be part of their plans. Surprisingly, a pang of something that felt suspiciously like loss went through her and she was unsure whether it was the thought of losing Isabella or...

Shaking herself, she explained to Mrs Edgecombe that they would be in Town for just a few short weeks, after which they would return to their home in Scotland. No, they would be unlikely to return to London after that.

This I must remember too.

Max sent Angus a knowing look as the Honourable Geoffrey Barnstable once again praised Freddy for playing a good card, even though his brother would have been better playing it in the previous round. Freddy believed himself to be a skilful player, with all evidence to the contrary ruthlessly ignored. Angus, Max noted, was deliberately throwing away good cards on occasion, in order to prevent Freddy from being completely disgraced. Max thought it both mortifying and hilarious—and a good distraction from his unwanted preoccupation with his friend's sister. Eilidh was looking exquisite tonight, and her singing earlier had caused a surge of emotion within him.

Taking another sip of wine and desperately focusing on other matters, Max decided to invite Angus for another few rounds in the boxing ring. Boxing was always a useful way to vent whatever frustrations he was feeling. 'So Angus, shall we return to Gentleman Jack's on the morrow, so you can try your hand at besting me again?'

'Yes, why not? We can go before accompanying the ladies to the Tower.' Angus grinned. 'I am keen to learn more of the "science" of pugilism as practised in London—if only to defeat you, Max!'

'Ah, boxing!' The Honourable Geoffrey sighed. 'I was a reasonable fighter in my day. What of you, Plank? Did you enjoy a round of fisticuffs in your youth?'

'I am not yet in my dotage, Geoffrey! And I do not like to be called Plank,' Freddy retorted. 'But since you ask, such vices have never interested me. I leave such activities to men like my brother.'

'What do you mean by that?' Max knew that tone and abruptly he decided that tonight he would not allow Freddy's insults to pass him by.

Freddy sniffed, a familiar disdain showing on his face. 'Simply that I have more weighty matters with which to fill my time.' He sighed dramatically. 'The life of a second son must be truly blessed. They know not the burdens we carry.'

Max was in no mood to let this pass. 'Angus has time for boxing, and he is head of his family and Laird of— what is the name of your place, Angus?'

'Broch Clachan,' Angus muttered.

Freddy raised an eyebrow. 'A Scottish title? Not at all the same thing, Max. The Scots are half-civilised at best—and that only because of English influence. The Burtenshaw line is long and noble, and its preservation and continuation rests with me.'

Half-civilised. Papa's words.

Max could scarcely believe his brother's effrontery. Used to being on the receiving end of his brother's condescension, nevertheless he was shocked at Freddy's blatant insult towards Angus, and indeed all of Angus's countrymen. Speechless, he dared not continue without giving his brother a bloody nose.

'And now you plan to marry off your sister, eh, Burtenshaw?' The Honourable Geoffrey, showing a severe lack of awareness and good judgement, decided this was a good moment to press his case for Isabella's hand. 'What are you looking for in a suitor for her, eh?'

Freddy lifted his chin, clearly unaware that his behaviour tonight was doing the Burtenshaw name no favours. 'Someone of impeccable breeding. A family who deserve to be aligned with mine.'

Max brought a hand to his head. *Deserve?* Had Freddy any notion just how arrogant he sounded?

'Ah! Well, you may look no further. The Barnstables came with the Conqueror, you know!'

A gleam of interest lit Freddy's eye, and it was all Max could do not to groan aloud. 'They did?'

As Barnstable began listing his noble connections—throwing into his litany the fact that Henry VIII was reputed to have spent a night at their country estate, Max and Angus exchanged a look of disgust. Freddy could not seriously be considering Barnstable as a possible husband for Isabella, surely?

'One last hand, gentlemen?' Max, barely holding on to his self-control, drew an end to their playing. The last round, thankfully, was brief, and Max rose from the table with more anger than he had felt in an age. It was, he dimly realised, not just his brother's appalling insults tonight. Having lived with years of similar frustration he should have been equal to it.

Tonight, though, had been worse. Much, much worse. Freddy had exposed all of his venal self-importance before Angus, who was a man of sense and good taste, and who was brother to Eilidh, who already thought ill of Max. The only saving grace was that Eilidh had not heard the exchange directly.

'Such a pity we cannot play on!' The Honourable Geoffrey was pouting like a disgruntled child. After a moment his face cleared. 'Ah, gentlemen, I have it! I shall host an evening of cards at my house this Season. Next month, perhaps. Will you all come?'

Max and the others agreed, and Geoffrey undertook to write to them with the details. Max cared not when he would invite them. His focus was simply on getting away from the table without offering violence to the Honourable Geoffrey or his own dishonourable brother.

Tuesday 19th March

'I hope you did not say anything to Lord Burtenshaw last night about the land.' Angus and Eilidh were enjoying a late breakfast following their first soirée. Eilidh had not slept well, her initial impressions of Lord Burtenshaw being less positive than she had hoped. Add to that Max's coolness with her, and Isabella's *tendre* for Angus… Yes, the entire situation was becoming a tangled mess.

Angus snorted. 'I am not so foolish as I look!'

'And a good thing too!' she countered, smiling at their familiar raillery.

'We played cards, talked of nothing, and I was able to form something of an impression of him.'

'And?' Her breath caught. 'What manner of man is he, Lord Burtenshaw?'

'Well,' her brother began cautiously, 'we know already how agreeable and pleasant Max is. His sister too.'

She sniffed. 'I am not so sure. They are certainly *real*

with us—a refreshing contrast to the false smiles and simpering we have encountered in some of the others—but in this case it may be as much a curse as a blessing. Isabella is a darling of course. Which reminds me—you really ought not flirt with her, you know. She is being forced to choose a husband over the next few weeks and if she thinks you are eligible, it may prevent her from… from seeing other men clearly.'

He grinned. 'What? Are you giving me an indirect compliment, sister? You think me more eligible than the dour Mr Craven? Or the delightful Honourable Geoffrey Barnstable?'

'Ha! The ladies have apparently dubbed him the 'Dishonourable Geoffrey' because of his habit of wandering eyes and wandering hands.'

Angus's jaw slackened in shock. 'Indeed? Do let me know if he attempts any such thing with you, Eilidh. He shall have my fist to answer to!'

'I shall make it my business to avoid him—as do most of the young ladies, I am told. Isabella, Miss Bell and Miss Sandison warned me about him on separate occasions.'

'I see. Such a man would soon be banished at home, if he could not learn to behave himself.' He frowned. 'Would Lord Burtenshaw know of this? Or Max?'

She shrugged. 'I know not. Possibly not, for they seem to have unwritten rules about matters that can be discussed with gentlemen and matters that are for women's ears only.'

'Well, that is no different to home, for there's many a conversation that we get shooed out of, for it concerns "women's business".'

'Aye but here, there's much less plain speaking generally. Everything is done with a nod of the head or a tilt of an eyebrow. Have you not remarked upon it?'

'True, but something like a dishonourable man should be spoken of plainly to the menfolk.'

'We shall be here for only a matter of weeks, Angus. We cannot change them.' Wise words, if she could but heed them herself.

Do not be tempted into too much involvement with Burtenshaw's family. Remember why you are here.

'Now, you were about to tell me your impression of Lord Burtenshaw.'

He took a sip of tea. 'I was, and I had just stated that Max and his sister are both likeable. You agreed in respect of Isabella, but am I to understand that you dislike Max?'

Her jaw fell open at his directness, for she had hoped to avoid the topic of Max. 'Dislike him?' she replied carefully. 'No, at least I think not. But he…vexes me.'

And I cannot stop thinking of him.

Angus frowned. 'But why? He is perfectly amiable. Has a quick mind and a ready wit. Boxes well too,' he added ruminatively. 'He will probably best me again today.'

'He is…he is like a pretty boat adrift on the ocean. He looks good, but is unmoored and lost, and you just know he will sink beneath the waves eventually.' Her gaze became unfocused. 'This *ton* life is cruel to second sons.'

'Aye, but he cannot help his birth. None of us can.'

'But I am not speaking of his birth. I am speaking of his *life*! He does nothing, besides…besides *being* a second son all day long. He does not even *try* to find some purpose. Isabella too seems sometimes possessed

of a certain *ennui*…' She shuddered. 'I could not stand
to live in that way.'

*He cannot help his situation, but he could at least
try to find some purpose beyond wine and cards and
boxing.*

'I see and hear your frustration, but you have already
pointed out that we will only be here a matter of weeks.
We cannot fix the ills of London society. My point is,
Lord Burtenshaw is nothing like Max and Isabella. He
is as unlikeable as they are likeable, as lacking in humour as they are witty, as mutton-headed as they are
bright and rational. In short, they are nothing alike—
a fact which makes our task much more challenging.'

She sighed. 'I knew it. While I spent much less time
than you in Lord Burtenshaw's company, that was my
impression too.' Grimacing, she added, 'It also explains
why Isabella and Max are so close to one another, and
why they seem to avoid his company as much as they
can. Their nature seems similar to ours, and to people
we know at home, rather than many of the *ton*.'

'Their older brother also detests Scotland.' Briefly,
he told her of a scathing comment Burtenshaw had
made at the card table.

'What an *amadan*!' She shook her head. 'This is wor-
risome indeed. Still,' she added more brightly, 'we are
not yet defeated.' She held up the pile of society invitations that had arrived so far that morning. 'These invitations will help, for even if Burtenshaw does not attend
the events himself, our acceptance in society—which
is by no means assured—must be something to strive
for. He is a man much given to conformity, I think.'

He nodded. 'Aye. Maintaining and enhancing his
family reputation seems to be his main spur, his duty
as he sees it.'

And if we are accepted by society it will make Angus's task easier.

'Very well.' She picked up her pen. 'I shall accept all of these, and hope for more.'

Chapter Five

'So how did you enjoy your first *ton* soirée?'

The two young ladies had met in Gunter's and were idly watching the other parties present while enjoying delicious ices. The gentlemen were boxing and would come for them in an hour, for they intended to visit the Tower together.

Eilidh smiled. 'Well, I did enjoy it, Isabella. Meeting new people is always diverting. The music was excellent, as was the company.'

Isabella gave an answering smile. 'I do not know how I shall manage when you return to Scotland. You think as I do on so many topics, and I have never met anyone like that before. At least, apart from Max. But you are the first true friend I have had. Most of the other young ladies think only of gowns and compliments and dancing. I care little for such things.'

Eilidh's eyes gleamed with humour. 'And yet you and I also spend time together looking at fashion plates and even visiting dressmakers.'

'That is true! And I am learning to appreciate a pretty gown. But those are not the *only* things we speak of. Why, today we have already discussed the creation of the Regency, the need for both rationality and sensibility, and Napoleon's antics in the Peninsula! And I have loved hearing more about your home.'

'And I am going to risk having you judge me for an excess of frivolity—'

'Oh, no! Never!'

'I am glad to hear it. I wish to ask you about dancing.'

'What of dancing?'

'We have our own jigs and reels in the Islands, and I learned some dances at school in Edinburgh, but I think that Angus and myself probably need to familiarise ourselves with dances popular in London at present.' She shrugged, adding ruefully, 'Not that we can be sure of being invited to any balls. But if we are, I do not wish for us to disgrace ourselves. Can you suggest perhaps a school or a dance teacher who might—'

'I know the very man! Monsieur Dupont is quite simply the best dance teacher in London. I did some classes with him a few weeks ago to catch up on the latest steps, so that Prudence could satisfy herself I was able to hold my own on the dancing floor without disgracing the family name.'

'Thank you! I knew you would advise me. Could you possibly get me his direction?'

'I shall do better than that. He is in such demand, you see, that he is unlikely to take on anyone new this Season. But, given the fact he has already completed some lessons for Prudence and me, I shall simply book a few more and you and Angus can join me.'

Eilidh regarded her dubiously. 'Naturally I am grateful for your kind offer, but would Lord Burtenshaw or his wife not object to finding a couple of Scottish cuckoos in their elegant nest?'

'Oh, stuff! Why would they object? Indeed, Freddy

does not trouble himself with such things and would not care in the slightest!' When Eilidh did not reply she continued, 'Monsieur Dupont may not even be available, but I shall ask.'

'And can you check that your sister-in-law agrees?'

Isabella nodded, adding, 'Monsieur Dupont has an assistant who plays the piano during lessons. He must be fifty if he is a day, and has the most diverting eyebrows—as though two caterpillars crawled up his face and decided to rest on his brow.' This provoked a smile. 'Oh, I do hope you get invited to a ball!'

'Well, I do too—even if it has little to do with our purpose in coming here, I admit to a certain curiosity about a *ton* ball. It is an experience I shall never have again, so I do not think it an unreasonable wish.'

'No, indeed! And in the meantime there are soirées, and the theatre and tomorrow's jaunt to Greenwich.'

'Yes, tell me, what shall we do there?'

'The Sandisons will have invited thirty people or more. We shall drive out in carriages to the place with a view over London, and the servants will bring food in wicker baskets for us to enjoy outdoors. It is a way of enjoying the natural landscape.'

'I see,' Eilidh replied, though she did not, not at all. At home, one did not need to consciously enjoy the landscape. It was simply there—beautiful and powerful and dangerous all at once. 'Well, I do not fully understand, but no doubt it will be an interesting experience. Tell me, will your suitors be there?'

Isabella sighed. 'I expect so. The thing is…' She bit her lip. 'May I speak plainly?'

'I should welcome it.' Even as she said the words, Eilidh was conscious of a little anxiety.

Please do not speak of your tendre *for my brother,
for soon we shall be gone, and I would not see you hurt.*

Isabella took a breath. 'My difficulty is that I have
this foolish notion of wishing to *like* my husband. And
there are no gentlemen I like half so well as Max and
Angus, and I cannot marry either of them!' Her voice
trembled a little, and Eilidh felt a rush of sympathy
for her.

'I understand you. Angus is by no means perfect,
but he is a good man. Max is…he is definitely far from
being perfect, but I like him too.'

It was true. She did like him, which was probably
why she felt so bad about the continued coolness between them. Still, coolness was probably preferable to
the clear warmth between Isabella and Angus, which
was creating a different problem entirely.

'And frankly,' Eilidh continued, 'if I try to imagine
myself married to the worthy Mr Craven…' She shuddered. 'And as for the Dishonourable Geoffrey…!' They
eyed one another in mutual understanding. 'What will
you do, Isabella?'

Isabella's shoulders dropped and her wry smile
faded. 'I do not know. Would living with Mr Craven
be worse than living with Freddy? Perhaps not, but why
should I have to choose between impossible options?'

'When must you choose?' Eilidh could hardly bear
the thought of the unthinkable choices that lay before
her friend. Mr Craven was the least offensive of this
year's known bachelors, and that was probably the best
she could say about him as a suitor. Eilidh, frankly,
would not have wished to marry any of them.

Isabella shrugged. 'It is by no means guaranteed that
any of them will even offer for me. Manly pride being
what it is, it is expected that a lady shows a gentleman

some encouragement, and the truth is that I do not wish to encourage any of them.' There was a brief silence. 'But enough of my troubles. The sun is shining, we are eating ices in Gunter's, and today all is well!'

Wednesday 20th March

The trip to the Tower was both interesting and delightful and, although nothing was said aloud, Eilidh felt she had made some progress with Max. Since Isabella and Angus had insisted on walking together as usual, Eilidh had found herself in Max's company for more than an hour as they wandered around the White Tower and its environs. Their conversation had been light, friendly almost, the only moment of tension when the Jacobite rising had been discussed.

Eilidh need not have worried, for both Max and Isabella had shown themselves to be both rational and compassionate and had seemed to understand the Scottish perspective. When Angus and Eilidh had spoken of clearances and killings and the Gaelic language being frowned upon, Max and Isabella had listened with intent and with sympathy.

'There has been bad blood between our nations,' Max had said, and Eilidh recalled how serious he had looked in that moment. Even remembering, her heart turned over in her chest and warmth gathered behind her breastbone.

Her own answer had also been conciliatory. 'Aye,' she had said, 'but it need not echo between us.' They had looked at each other momentarily then—one of those looks that made her heart temporarily still and breathlessness travel through her body, leaving her tingling with…something.

I am glad we do not have our national conflicts between us, she thought now, as they travelled in Prudence's coach to Greenwich for Mrs Sandison's visit to Nature. *And he has definitely thawed towards me. I am forgiven for any hurt, I hope.*

It meant she could look forward to a day in his company without any qualms.

They were part of a cavalcade of over a dozen carriages, with the Sandisons leading the way. Eilidh was unsure what would happen when they arrived at their destination, and a little disappointed that Lord Burtenshaw had not accompanied them, but was determined to make the most of the opportunity to make further inroads into being accepted by London society.

The carriage was sizeable, which was a blessing as it currently contained three ladies and two gentlemen. Max was opposite her, and it was all she could do not to keep looking at him. Instead she looked out of the window, in her mind's eye seeing every detail—his long legs and athletic frame, his deep brown eyes and dark, thick lashes, the way his dark hair curled over his collar, how his handsome face looked when he was relaxed, or laughing, or cross. Or hurt.

Her reverie was broken by a shout from the carriages ahead. Max leaned out, confirming a moment later that their destination was in sight. Instantly everyone sat up straighter, the ladies checking for their reticules. Despite enjoying the company on the journey, they were all keen to stretch their legs and explore their destination.

A few minutes later, the carriage drew to a halt and Max and Angus jumped down to lower the step and hand the ladies out. It was a task normally carried out by the footman after descending from his perch at the rear, and it was a courtesy for the two gentlemen to perform this small service for the ladies. Lady Burtenshaw seemed particularly gratified by their gallantry. 'Thank you, Max. Thank you, Mr MacDonald,' she murmured as they each took a hand and assisted her out of the carriage. Eilidh stifled a grin.

Nicely done, Angus.

Eilidh was next, and Angus gave way as Max offered both hands to her. His dark eyes met hers as he took her hands, and she felt herself flush. There was again no sign of the coolness that had characterised their previous interactions. Now that it was gone, Eilidh realised the warmth which seemed to have replaced it created a new difficulty, for her heart was suddenly pounding and her hands tingling at the warmth of his firm grip through her thin gloves. Oh, she still knew herself to be in some danger from him so far as her heart was concerned, but could only hope to be gone before he had the chance to truly insinuate his way into her affections.

I have warned Isabella—now I must warn myself.

All around them ladies and gentlemen were pouring out of carriages, gentlemen donning beaver hats and some of the ladies opening parasols as they greeted one another, all the while exclaiming at the surroundings. A few people commented on Angus's Highland dress, but in a complimentary way, thankfully. Eilidh took part in the general exchange of greetings before returning to Isabella and Max.

Angus too did his duty by all his acquaintances, including Miss Sandison and Miss Bell, before returning to them. Lady Burtenshaw had been immediately claimed by one of her friends and had wandered off contentedly, leaving just the four of them.

Eilidh looked about her with interest. The place was beautiful indeed, and very different from the raw glory of the Islands. A wooded area was nearby and Eilidh immediately felt a longing to walk under a canopy of spring-green trees—a treat denied her at home.

Almost immediately Mr Sandison announced they could wander at their leisure for an hour, during which time his servants would prepare the food. 'Feel free,' he said, 'to explore the woods and fields. For those keen for exertion there is a pretty stream about half a mile in that direction, and for those who wish to sit and rest, we shall have cloths laid out immediately. The views, as you see, are spectacular.' He indicated the edge of the hilltop and the four of them went directly across to drink in the vista. From up here the sky looked huge and Eilidh took a deep breath, glad to be away from the oppressiveness of the city.

'It reminds me of home,' she murmured, and Angus sent her an understanding glance.

'I was just thinking the same.'

'How so?' Max seemed genuinely interested. 'Is the landscape similar?'

'Not at all,' Angus responded. 'We have very few trees, and at this time of year the heather and bracken give the landscape as much bronze as green. But yes—' he nodded to his sister '—it reminds me of home too. It is the bigness, I think.' He laughed lightly. 'That is not a real word, I know, and yet…'

'If your Islands are anything like as picturesque as this, I wonder why you would ever leave it,' Isabella murmured.

'Needs must.' Eilidh shrugged. 'But I confess I shall be glad to be home again.'

'I too,' Angus replied. Turning to Isabella and Max, he bowed formally and Eilidh realised with dawning horror what her brother was about to say. 'I should like to invite you both to visit Benbecula as my guests, should you ever wish to travel there. It is very far away, and I do not expect you to come, but I make the offer nevertheless.'

No! I need to be free of Max and his effect on me!

The last thing she needed was to imagine Max in Benbecula. Sitting by the peat fire in the Broch, enjoying whisky and raillery. Climbing Rueval with her and exclaiming at the views. Sitting together amid the wildflowers of the machair…

Stop thinking such things!

'But I should love to come!' Isabella exclaimed instantly—a response which did not surprise Eilidh in the least. 'To see Broch Clachan, which I have heard so much about, and to visit your cousin's castle at Ardmore! To see the hill and the heather and the beaches… it would be a dream come true!'

Unlike his sister, Max was frowning. 'I thank you for your offer, Angus, although, as you say, it is far away and it is unlikely we shall be able to take you up on it.'

Quite against all rationality, Eilidh felt a pang of disappointment at Max's words. Naturally, he would not wish to go all the way to Benbecula.

Well, why would he?

Isabella looked as crestfallen as Eilidh felt. 'Yes, of course, Max. One must be sensible.' She looked directly at Angus, adding softly, 'But it was a lovely notion.'

There was a pause until Eilidh decided to take charge.

Enough of all this nonsense!

'Now!' She adopted a brisk tone. 'I have a fancy for—what did Mr Sandison call it—exertion? So I should like to suggest we find the pretty stream he mentioned.'

'A capital notion!' Max concurred. He offered Eilidh his arm. 'Shall we?'

Isabella and Angus fell in behind, and they made their way towards the woods down the narrow path that Mr Sandison had pointed out. Max's arm was warm through the sleeve of his superfine jacket, and Eilidh was once again conscious of his nearness.

I shall enjoy his friendship, she told herself, *and resist any silly thoughts or wishes. Our purpose here is simply to buy back Lidistrome, and today is simply a pleasant interlude in our visit to London.*

And so they meandered down the woodland path, Eilidh enjoying the way the sunlight danced through the trees and spotting pretty celandines and daffodils under the trees and in the clearings. They talked of everything and nothing—of politics and philanthropy, music and books. She found him to be well-read and well-informed and, while they did not agree on everything, their debates were fairly fought and skilfully argued.

Surrounded by beauty, in the company of a handsome man, it was little wonder that Eilidh had a sense of dreaminess about the whole walk. Never could she recall feeling so in harmony with another person. Naturally, it would have no lasting bearing on her life, for it could not, but somehow she knew she would never forget this day.

About fifteen minutes later, they came to the stream, which was delightfully pretty, the sunlight dancing on its shallow pools and spring flowers adorning its banks. They had clearly been walking at a faster pace than their siblings, for Angus and Isabella did not appear for quite five minutes. By that time Max and Eilidh had seated themselves on the mossy bank overlooking the stream and were laughing quietly together at some pleasant raillery between them. Eilidh was conscious of a slight feeling of disappointment at the arrival of the others, as though she and Max had built a kind of wall around themselves—a wall against reality. It was a strange feeling, and one that she should not welcome, and yet…

Returning to the main party, the ladies walked together and Eilidh was conscious of being a little quiet. In truth, she was feeling rather glum.

I shall master this, for it is only a pleasant interlude, of no great significance in my life.

Isabella too was unusually quiet and both young ladies walked silently together through the woods, Eilidh absorbing the healing balm of the pleasant surroundings.

The rest of the excursion passed without further incident, but Eilidh was conscious of a feeling that once again something had changed between herself and Max. *A deepening.* This was both a blessing and a source of worry.

He is, she reminded herself, *a second son with no profession, no responsibility and no notion of acquiring any.*

The fact that she sometimes sensed he was unhappy with his lot made little difference, for he had done nothing to change his path.

Such a man—a man of leisure, lethargy and idleness—would never do for her. And yet her foolish heart insisted on fluttering, turning over and glowing each time he looked at her just so, or when their hands accidentally brushed, or when they discovered yet another point of agreement between them. Really, she needed to be more careful, or she would be in serious trouble from him when the time came to leave.

Chapter Six

Thursday 21st March

Max strode through Mayfair, his long legs eating up the well-worn path between Great-Aunt Morton's house and the Burtenshaw residence. The old lady had welcomed his visit, but each time he called, she seemed to have faded a little more. Today, Mama's aunt had looked paper-thin, her frailty more and more pronounced each time he visited. He had frowned again at her frugal surroundings, and had passed what money he could to her only servant for the purchase of food and fuel.

Despite her failing body, her mind was just as sharp as ever, and she had even managed to question him about his low spirits. Having initially resisted being open with her, her constant probing and sharp instincts had undone him, and he had told her of his *ennui* with his lot as the second son. The arrival of a certain lady into his life had ensured that such thoughts were constantly near the surface.

'But what would you do differently if you had the means, Max?' Great-Aunt Morton had demanded to know.

'Something. Anything!' he had replied with passion.

'I would become a lawyer or a doctor, or buy a pair of colours and help in the Peninsular campaign. Anything would be better than this empty life of parties and gaming!' He had apologised then for the manner of his speech, but she had waved this away, advising him to speak to Freddy again about his frustrations.

So now he was on his way home, his mind awhirl.

Is there even any point in raising the matter again?

The last conversation with his brother on the matter had not ended well. Yet things were different now. *He* was different, and he knew exactly why. Miss Eilidh MacDonald had erupted into his life and held up a mirror to him, forcing him to once again face who he had become.

What was more, she was becoming something of an obsession with him—an unwelcome circumstance, for they were from different worlds and there could be no hope of a future for them. Spending so much time in her company yesterday at Greenwich had brought him as much pain as joy, for he could not even kiss her—a notion that had crossed his mind more than once during their private walk together. His heart was tortured with unattainable dreams, and he was unsure of his best path.

'Max!' The call brought him back to the present, and his face lit up as he saw who was approaching the house from the opposite direction.

'Cooper!' They embraced briefly, Max caring little if word got back to Freddy that he had been seen embracing a servant in the street. He cared not, for Cooper had never seemed like a servant to him. 'So it is true that Freddy has called you to London!'

'It is. I took the stage and am not long arrived.' The older man's Scottish burr hit Max's ear with a new freshness.

Of course—Cooper is Scottish! Is that why I was predisposed to like Eilidh and Angus?

Cooper's Scottishness was embedded in Max's mind as much as his greying hair, wiry frame and dark eyes that were usually brimming with humour. Usually, but not today.

'Have you any idea what Lord Burtenshaw needs me here for?'

'I have no clue,' declared Max frankly. 'The grooms and footman do the physical work here, and Freddy has never had any interest in buying a boat... Honestly, your time would be better spent at home, caulking and generally preparing the boats for the summer ahead.'

Cooper shrugged. 'Mine is not to question my lord.' He glanced sharply at Max. 'How do you, Max?'

Max grimaced. 'The same. I had a notion to speak to Freddy again about buying me a pair of colours.'

Cooper placed a hand lightly on his shoulder. 'I know how frustrated you are but, believe me, joining the Army may not be the answer.'

'The law, then. Or the church! I care not.'

Cooper shook his head. 'That is the problem, right there, Max. You do not like your current life, but you have no clear calling to another. Until you know for certain, best to keep your powder dry.'

He was right, Max knew, but Cooper's wisdom was entirely unwelcome just now.

'I shall think on it.'

'See that you do, now,' Cooper adjured, his lined face creased with concern. He sighed. 'I suppose I shall go inside and hear what your brother wants of me. May I find you later?'

'Of course!'

They separated then, Max to enter by the front door

and Cooper via the servants' entrance, down the steps to the right. The divisions between them were always there, yet Max knew Cooper was one of the few people in his life who genuinely cared for him. He had been with the family forever, it seemed, and his boathouse workshop had been a haven for Max and for Isabella when Papa's and then Freddy's criticisms and expectations became too hard to bear.

Making his way into the house, he made for the drawing room, where he found Prudence and Isabella. Prudence was commenting on how delightful the trip to Greenwich had been, and how proud she was of Isabella for taking seriously her duty to choose a suitor this Season. Isabella grimaced a little at this, and Max saw her twisting her handkerchief in her lap.

Lord! he thought, taking a seat. Hard as it was for him not to have any hope of a life with Eilidh, how hard must it be for his sister, who clearly preferred Angus over the other gentlemen. He stopped short, abruptly realising the direction of his thoughts.

When had he begun thinking of Eilidh as a woman he would like to marry? He could not say, and yet his heart thundered at the very notion. It mattered not, though. He could not afford to marry, and Eilidh would likely not accept him anyway.

What a fix!

When asked, he spoke about Great-Aunt Morton, hoping that some of his concerns about her perilous finances might reach Freddy via Prudence. Each time he had broached the subject directly with Freddy, he had met the same sort of obdurate resistance he had when asking his brother to finance a profession for himself. Freddy was highly skilled at obduracy.

Finally, it was time to dress for dinner. Although he

did not need the same time to prepare as the ladies, still the escape to his own room for a while was a welcome relief. A knock on the door made him sigh briefly, before he realised who was likely to be there.

Sure enough, Cooper entered on his call, and something in the man's demeanour set his senses on edge. 'What? What is it, Cooper?'

'I am to be let go.' As if saying the words aloud brought fresh realisation, the older man's face crumpled. 'I am dismissed, Max.'

Max leapt to his feet. 'What? *Dismissed?* Impossible! Who has said so?'

'Lord Burtenshaw, and I know he has every right to dismiss any worker he wishes. It is just… I never expected…'

'I shall speak to him right this instant! How dare he dismiss you, when you have worked hard and faithfully for…for…how many years, exactly?'

'Twenty-eight.'

'Twenty-eight years—since before I was born! How dare he? How *dare* he?'

Cooper laid a hand on his arm. 'Now then, do not be hasty, Max.'

'Hasty? It is not *hasty* to respond to an injustice such as this. Wait here.'

Despite Cooper's protestations, he stormed out, making his way directly to his brother's library. The butler was present but after taking one look at Max's turbulent demeanour he bowed himself out, closing the door tightly behind him.

'What do you mean by it, Freddy? How could you do such a thing?'

Freddy sighed. 'If you are referring to my decisions about which staff to keep and which to let go—'

'I am not talking of staff. I am talking of *Cooper*! How dare you dismiss him, after so many years of faithful service?'

'Max, really. Certain economies must be made, and you know nothing of the decisions I must make, the burdens I bear.'

'I know when you have done something wrongheaded!'

Freddy adopted a sullen look. 'You know nothing, Max. Nothing! Now, return to your boxing and your drinking and leave the difficult decisions to those of us who understand what it means to hold responsibility!'

Max leaned across the table menacingly. 'If I did not know what a weakling you are, I would be strongly tempted to plant you a facer!'

Freddy flinched, but managed in a tight tone, 'I am doing my best to protect this family, including you and your sister.'

'Then explain! Help me understand your reasoning!'

Freddy opened his mouth, then closed it again. 'I cannot. You will have to trust me on this.'

Max's lip curled. 'Trust you? I believe I shall never trust you in the same way again!'

Turning on his heel, he departed, leaving the door ajar. As he climbed the stairs back to his chamber, each step felt like a hundred, and his legs like lead.

How am I to face Cooper when I have failed to assist him?

Failed.

Failed.

Failure.

Cooper eyed him neutrally as he entered. 'You were unable to persuade him to change his mind.'

'He would not listen.' His shoulders sagged. 'I am so sorry, Cooper.'

'Did he give a reason? What did he say?'

'Oh, a lot of nonsense about his responsibilities. Nothing I have not heard a hundred times.'

Cooper let out a breath. 'He does his best, you know.'

'Does he?' Max sent him a bleak look. 'What will you do now?'

Cooper shrugged. 'Look for work. What else can I do?'

'But—forgive me—at your age?'

'Ach, never worry about me, lad. I shall be right as rain. I have a little money set aside. But I shall miss you and your sister.'

'And we shall miss you.' His mind was reeling. Impossible to imagine life without Cooper. 'I must apologise again, Cooper. You deserve better than this.'

'Aye, well, as to what I *deserve*, I'll leave that to the good Lord to decide on Judgement Day. I am no saint— no, not by any means.'

An idea occurred to Max. 'Cooper, there is something I should like you to do for me.'

'Which is?'

'I would like to hire you for the next month, your task being to prepare my yacht, hire a crew and bring it to London.'

At least this way he can say his goodbyes and gather his belongings in Sussex and will have another month's pay.

Max could barely afford it, but knew instinctively it was the right course of action.

'To *London*? But why?'

Max thought quickly. 'Because if I know I can escape on the yacht at times I am much more likely to survive the rest of the Season without breaking my brother's nose!' Cooper sent him a sceptical look. 'No, really! You cannot know how difficult…and there is Isabella.'

Cooper's gaze sharpened. 'What of Isabella?'

'Freddy is determined to marry her off—whether she wishes it or not.'

'And is there a gentleman she favours?'

'Well, there is,' Max replied frankly, 'but he is not seeking a wife. He is Scottish, actually.'

Cooper grinned. 'I always knew Isabella had impeccable taste.' His brow creased. 'So what will Burtenshaw do?'

'Choose for her, if I am not mistaken. And his taste is questionable, to say the least.'

'Max—' Cooper's look was intent '—I cannot speak out of turn, but I know that your mother would have wanted you to protect your sister.'

'Indeed. And Mama always valued your judgement, Cooper. But I do not imagine she expected Isabella would need protection from *Freddy*!'

Cooper left soon afterwards. He would stay in the servants' quarters tonight, before departing on the morrow for his last ever trip to what had been his home for twenty-eight years. And Max could do nothing about it. Never had he felt more useless, more trapped, more frustrated.

Torment—the same torment that had been his closest friend for years—screamed within him. He had no money of his own, no freedom to take up a profession, no liberty to choose a bride.

And, besides, she would never have me anyway.

With an exclamation of disgust he left his chamber, intending to go directly to his club, there to drink wine until such time as his senses were dulled and the torment, temporarily at least, silenced.

Saturday 6th April

'Dancing lessons? Please tell me you are jesting!'

Max, attending his sister in the empty ballroom on the ground floor, stood aghast at the news that Angus and Eilidh were expected any minute, along with Isabella's dancing master.

Isabella's face fell. 'Please do not deny me this, Max! I am trying to help them prepare for when they are invited to a ball!'

'Yes, but why must I be here?' Since his realisation that there was no one but Eilidh he wished to marry, he had ensured that his evenings had been spent at different events to his sister and her Scottish friends.

'Is it not plain? I can partner Angus, but I need someone to partner Eilidh. They will learn much faster if they have us, rather than be forced to partner each other.'

He sighed, knowing he was trapped. Having spent the last two weeks and more carefully avoiding Eilidh, all was undone by his sister's well-meaning meddling. 'So they still have not been invited to any balls?'

Isabella bit her lip. 'No. It seems as though everyone is waiting until someone else invites them first.'

'So they are accepted in society, but not by all?' The prejudice against Scots—a legacy of the Jacobites—lingered still, sixty-five years after the rising.

'Freddy will note such things and use them to fuel his dislike of Angus—of both of them. It cannot help Angus's case.' She eyed him worriedly. 'It is so unfair! When does Angus mean to broach the matter of the estate with him, do you know?'

Max ran a hand along the back of his neck. 'I am unsure. I imagine it must be soon.' The truth was he had not spoken to Angus much recently, having pretended to be 'busy' on a couple of occasions when his friend had suggested meeting.

I am a poor friend. And a poor brother. And a poor friend to Cooper.

The door opened then, admitting Monsieur Dupont, a diminutive Parisian with a delicate step and an impressive paunch. His assistant, a middle-aged chap with dramatic beetling eyebrows and a folio of sheet music under his arm, followed.

'Bonjour...bonjour!'

Monsieur Dupont was all effusiveness, greeting them with a deep bow and a broad smile. Max, biting down on his frustration, managed a reasonable level of politeness but his self-control was tested to its limits when, ten minutes later, Eilidh and Angus arrived.

Lord, how beautiful she is!

The sight of Eilidh in a day gown of rose-coloured muslin, which seemed to enhance her colouring rather than clash with it, almost literally stole his breath and he was glad that Angus, Eilidh and Isabella exchanged greetings first, leaving him a moment to recover. He managed his part, and less than five minutes later, her hand was in his as Monsieur Dupont began taking them through the dances currently popular with the *ton*.

It was exquisite torture, having her this close yet knowing he would never kiss her, never lie with her, never tell her...what? What could he say to this woman, a gem of sharp wit and warm insight? Nothing. His only hope was to hide his true face from her as best he could, in the hope that she would leave for Scotland with a reasonably positive opinion of him. Hell, he did not even need it to be positive. Even neutral would suffice.

'What is making you frown so, Max?' she asked him as they twirled their way about the room following

Monsieur Dupont's shouted instructions. Naturally, she was an adept dancer and was picking up the new figures quickly, that sharp mind of hers remembering the sequences after only a couple of repetitions.

'Was I frowning? I was not aware of doing so.'

She bit her lip. 'Is something troubling you?'

Yes. I cannot tell you how you have enchanted me. And I cannot show you my true worthless self.

'Nothing of importance. But what of you? I hear your days and nights are filled with engagements.'

'Yes, we have plenty of callers now, and many invitations to soirées and routs. No balls though.'

'Not *yet*. I am sure an invitation will not be long in coming.'

'I do hope so.' She smiled. 'You dance well, Mr Wood.'

'Why, thank you.' He acknowledged her compliment with a nod, turning her smoothly before adding, 'This surprises you?'

'Not at all! I imagine dancing to be an activity you practice frequently.'

He frowned. 'You mean to suggest, I suppose, that I have the time for such frivolous activities because I have no profession?'

Her jaw dropped. 'No! Not at all! I was not even thinking—'

'And yet it is what you believe of me, is it not?'

'I—'

She had no answer, he saw. His jaw hardened as he felt, like a punch to the gut, just how superficial she believed his life was.

And she is right, damn it!

All the joy leeched from him after that, and they completed the lesson in near silence.

After almost two hours, the caper-merchant declared himself almost satisfied.

'Mademoiselle Wood,' he announced, 'I thank you for bringing me two such apt students. One more lesson, I think, is all that I shall require! The same time tomorrow, perhaps? I regret I have not many gaps in my appointment book, for this year's debutantes...' He rolled his eyes. *'Oh là là!'*

The following day, the lesson proceeded much as the first one, except this time Max knew about it in advance. It was unclear to him whether this made it easier or more difficult. The almost sleepless night had left his head foggy, but there was a perverse joy in the anticipation of seeing her again.

Today's gown was in a delightful shade of pale green, and as they danced, one recalcitrant auburn curl managed to free itself from its pins. Despite the almost unbearable urge to touch it, he managed not to by the simple expedient of reminding himself that she would not want him to, and as a gentleman, he could not violate her dignity. She thought little of him, yet all he could think of was her.

And yet...was she trembling now as a turn brought their faces close together and his breath briefly caressed her cheek?

Thank heaven we are not alone, for this is madness!

'Sir.' A footman had entered the ballroom, and the music stopped. 'A messenger from Mrs Morton's house.'

The man's grave expression was telling. With a swift glance towards Isabella, Max bowed and made his farewells.

I may never dance with her again, was his fleeting

thought as he turned his attention to his great-aunt's messenger, bracing himself for the man's news.

Thursday 11th April

Great-Aunt Morton's funeral had been a quiet affair as only Isabella and Max, along with her servant, seemed to grieve for her loss.

She was the last of my mother's family, Max thought, refusing to judge Freddy for his lack of emotion. *And Freddy hardly knew her.*

Freddy had made it clear that she was a distant relation and as such they did not need to go into formal mourning, but still Max was a little shocked that the Honourable Geoffrey's card party would proceed just one day after the funeral.

Being decidedly light in the pocket after paying Cooper, Max had brought only a small amount of cash and managed to retain most of it during the early stage of the evening. Angus, he noted, was being similarly parsimonious, which met with his approval. Freddy, on the other hand... He frowned as his brother lost yet another hand, and two guineas along with it. The Honourable Geoffrey and his friends were now suggesting increasing the stakes, and Max knew this was his moment to depart.

Following an exchange of nods with Angus, he announced, yawning theatrically, 'Freddy, we should go. This has been a delightful evening, but I fear we must leave you. I have an appointment at a ridiculously early hour tomorrow. Freddy, shall we call for the carriage? Angus, may we offer you a ride home?'

'But I am not ready for home yet!' his brother declared sullenly. 'And why should you have any sort of appointment, when you are only a second son? What business could you possibly have?'

With considerable effort, Max did not rise to this, instead replying calmly, 'I am promised to my great-aunt's solicitor on the morrow.' He smiled ruefully. 'Lord knows what the old girl has left me, if anything, for she had hardly two farthings to rub together. I suspect I am named as executor and will be required to settle her affairs. Still, there may be something among her personal possessions to remember her by.'

Freddy glared at him. 'And why should she leave you anything, when it is I who is head of the family? *I* am the one who must make ends meet and pay all the damned bills, not you!' A hint of bitterness crept into Freddy's tone as he continued with his self-pitying rant. 'Yes, you can play and drink to your heart's content, Max, while I cannot enjoy a few nights of cards without you acting like my nursemaid.'

'A few nights?' Max's tone was sharp. 'Have there been other card parties?'

The Honourable Geoffrey made haste to clarify. 'Perfectly unexceptional, I assure you. Plank and I—that is to say, Lord *Burtenshaw* and I—have been indulging in a few practice rounds with a couple of other chaps, in preparation for this bigger party tonight.'

'I see.'

Have they been fleecing him? Freddy is certainly cloth-headed enough. Is he becoming a gamester?

'We shall play on, Max,' Freddy continued, 'for I have a feeling you are the cause of my ill fortune. You go. Yes, and you too, MacDonald. Geoffrey and I shall do very nicely alone with these chaps. I have a feeling my luck will change without my brother and his Scottish crony glowering at me. You may send the carriage back for me when you are done.'

There was little Max could do in the face of such a direct order. His face set, he muttered polite farewells, as did Angus, and they each gathered their modest winnings and made their way silently to the hallway to await the Burtenshaw carriage. Max was too mortified to speak of it when they were alone, but the look in Angus's eyes told him that his friend sympathised.

What a brother I have!

Instead Max made inconsequential conversation, asking Angus what his plans were for the morrow.

'Eilidh and I have been invited to the Sandison ball tomorrow night, so no doubt I shall be subjected to knee breeches and lectures from my sister on her expectations of me. Our first *ton* ball, and I cannot say I am anticipating it with any joy.'

Max gave a short laugh. 'Your sister is…formidable, Angus. I wish there were more like her.'

I am glad they have finally been invited to a ball, but all of it hastens the day when she must take her leave.

'Your own sister is fairly formidable, you know.'

He still likes her, and she him. And yet it cannot be. For he cannot leave Scotland and his people, and her place is here. What a tangled mess!

'She is, but she will submit to Freddy's demands for all that. We men have our troubles, but women too must suffer in other ways.'

Angus swallowed. 'Has she…has she made her choice, do you know?'

'She has not. It is down to Embury or Barnstable, I think, for Craven is likely to opt for the Bell girl, since Isabella has not encouraged him.'

Lord Embury was much older than Isabella, while the Honourable Geoffrey was entirely unsuitable.

A dotard and a dullard. What a choice!

'Barnstable! Surely your brother would not allow her to marry such a man!' Angus's shock was plain.

'You saw them tonight, Angus. Bosom bows, the pair of them.'

'I…yes, you are right. He does not seem to see Barnstable clearly.'

'He sees very little. It is one of his many limitations.'

'You would have been much more suited to be the elder son, Max.'

So he can see it too.

'I thank you for saying so, but what is must be. In my own way, I am as powerless as Isabella. The law demands and society upholds. It is ever so.'

They fell silent and around them an air of lowering pessimism grew and thickened.

I am powerless against Freddy. As is Isabella.

Their freedoms and choices all rested on the decisions of a limited, cloth-headed man-boy, who was even now frittering away more money on cards than he allocated to Max in a quarter. Wild notions of leaving Town surged through Max's mind. Perhaps he could sign up as an infantryman, or take work as a common sailor. At least then he would be free.

No.

Someone like Eilidh would never stoop to consider allying herself with such a man, he believed, and with his rational mind, he knew it was madness to even consider such a path.

Why am I even torturing myself with such thoughts? Soon she will be gone, and I can find peace again.

Chapter Seven

Friday 12th April

Eilidh awoke early, her head filled with half-remembered dreams—dreams that heavily featured Mr Maximilian Wood. She sighed, pushing herself up into a sitting position. Such occurrences were now much too regular. The man was haunting her. Clasping her arms around her knees, she considered the matter. While she could do nothing to prevent her fevered dreams, at the very least she could try harder not to think of him quite so much during her waking hours.

Worse, her waking daydreams consisted largely of kissing him and, honestly, she wished to do it more than anything. Despite her concern for the lifestyle given him by the *ton* and his seeming acceptance of it, the spark between them was strong.

Perhaps, she mused, *it is because I like him so much that I wish for him to be everything he can be.*

So why should she not experience his kiss just once in her life?

I could bring the memory back with me to Benbecula and treasure it always.

Angus had been out with Max last night, she knew, and Isabella's brother was likely to be at tonight's ball, for all of society was expected to be there. Her heart skipped a beat at the very thought of seeing him again. Their walk in the woods together had been magical—a chance for them to talk and learn to know one another a little better, unobserved by anyone. Dancing with him during their lessons had been exquisite torture, and even now, if she closed her eyes, she could recall exactly how it had felt to hold his hand, to turn under his arm, to feel his breath on her cheek.

Will he dance with me tonight?

Suddenly filled with vigour, she climbed out of bed and rang the bell for Mary. Isabella was due to call this morning, and before she took to her bed again tonight, she would have seen him.

Today will be a good day.

Two hours later, the two young ladies were seated in Eilidh's drawing room, enjoying a comfortable coze. Isabella was gently hinting that Eilidh and Angus might once again meet with some coldness tonight.

'There may be some high sticklers who would not have invited you, Eilidh. It seems they view any Scot with suspicion, and a ball is considered the highest of events outside of Court. So even some who may have been agreeable towards you at less formal events may not be so courteous tonight.' She bit her lip. 'I should not like for you or your brother to feel insulted, or to think it is anything about you or him personally, for indeed it is not!'

Eilidh waved this away. 'Never fear! In Scotland too the doings of our grandfathers and great-grandfathers still echo today, and to be fair, in some settings an Englishman might be looked on with the same suspicion.' She smiled. 'No, we can only hope that the invitation has a positive impression on Lord Burtenshaw, for my brother means to speak with him very soon.'

'I have the same notion myself. Oh, not about your estate. Freddy does not believe women have the minds for matters of business, and so if I dared to mention such a thing, it would only work against you, I am afraid.' She lifted her chin. 'I mean to speak with him about my marriage.'

Eilidh's eyes widened.

She still likes Angus, I know. Does she think he might offer for her?

'Indeed? Does he still insist you marry this Season? For there are not many weeks left.'

'He does, but I mean to ask him if I can choose a husband next Season instead. My reasoning is that there are not very many eligible bachelors at present, and I do not fancy Lord Embury or the Honourable Mr Barnstable.'

Next Season. So not Angus, then.

Perhaps this is her way of gaining some distance from my brother before choosing—a sensible notion.

'No, indeed! But what of Mr Craven?'

'I expect him to offer for Miss Bell, if he has not already done so.'

Eilidh grimaced. 'I had wondered about that. Is there an understanding between them, then?'

'Not that I know of. But Mr Craven grew tired of my disinterestedness, I think.'

'Ah.' Unspoken between them once again was the probable reason for that disinterestedness. 'Surely your brother will see that neither Embury nor Barnstable would be a suitable husband for you? Next Season there may well be better choices for you.'

'Yes, and I mean to offer to promise faithfully to

Freddy that I shall do my duty without complaint next year.'

'That seems more than fair.'

'I hope my brother agrees with you!'

The door opened, admitting Angus. His face lit up on seeing Isabella, and Eilidh suppressed a frown.

This will not do...for either of them.

Yet she could not judge them, for was she not forming a similar attachment herself? An attachment doomed to end in disappointment, for there was no way she or Angus could stay in England, and no way that Isabella or Max would leave their home to live far away in the Hebrides.

'Good day, Miss Wood!'

'Good day, Mr MacDonald,' Isabella replied formally, although Eilidh knew they had been using first names for some time. 'Are you looking forward to your first ball in London?'

He grimaced. 'I am and I amn't, I must confess. I am not sure it will make much difference to my business with your brother, for if he has not as yet formed an impression of my character, then why should one ball make a difference?'

Eilidh tutted. 'Yes, but as Isabella and I have just been discussing, being invited at all is significant.' She shrugged. 'Besides, we have come this far. We might as well go to the ball with the possibility it might have some influence.' She grinned. 'As well as the possibility we might even enjoy it!'

'I fully intend to enjoy it, Eilidh, I assure you!' He turned to Isabella. 'And may I speak up now for two dances with you, Isabella? Your choice of dance. I understand that I must not dance with any lady more than twice, is that correct?'

'Yes, for it might look as though…' Her voice faltered.

He nodded. 'As though I was singling her out for particular attention? I should not like to draw the attention of the gossips to any young lady.'

'Especially as the gossips will be watching your every move, Angus,' Eilidh interjected tartly. 'Yes, and mine!'

'So tonight might be both ordeal and pleasure at once?'

'I hope,' Isabella offered, 'that it will not be an ordeal at all!'

'That remains to be seen,' said Eilidh rather grimly. 'Still, our course is now set. We must see it through to its conclusion.'

Conclusion.

There was a feeling of finality in the air. They had surely done enough to enhance their reputation by now. Following tonight's ball, Angus would speak to Burtenshaw and soon afterwards they would leave London for good, with or without the deeds to Lidistrome.

Max sat in the lawyer's office, trying to concentrate on what the man was saying. The thought of tonight's ball filled him with the usual *ennui*, although this time there was also a stomach-clenching anticipation. Eilidh would be there and he would dance with her, and he would then suffer another night of disturbed sleep and impossible dreams. Wondering idly how much money Freddy had lost at cards last night, his mind drifted from there to Angus, and back to Eilidh again.

Freddy thinks himself better than others simply because of our name and English title. Yet Angus and Eilidh are each worth ten of him.

'And this one, sir.' The solicitor handed him another paper. His Great-Aunt Morton had named them both as joint executors—hardly a surprise, as she had had no one else who took an interest in her. Thankfully the lawyer had already completed much of the paperwork, although Max was required to sign various documents, which he was currently doing while half-listening to the solicitor's instructions. Swiftly, he ran his eye over the latest paper—another set of household bills to be settled. Having been keeping a tally in his head, he now knew he would need to approach Freddy for the funds to settle even these small accounts.

Damnation!

'Then there is the will itself,' said the solicitor. 'I assume you are aware of its contents?' He lifted a parchment and waved it in front of Max.

'Actually, no. We did not discuss such matters.'

Has she asked for a pension for her maidservant? It is the least we can do, for the woman served my great-aunt faithfully to the end.

Recalling Freddy's treatment of Cooper, his jaw hardened, for he knew a hard battle lay ahead.

The solicitor's eyes widened. 'I see.' He sat up straighter, adopting a formal tone. 'Then it is my duty to inform you, Mr Maximilian Wood, that Mrs Morton has bequeathed everything to you.'

'Everything? All her debts, you mean?' He grimaced. 'Never fear, I shall ensure they are all settled.'

'Debts?' The solicitor looked bewildered. 'No, sir. Apart from these small domestic bills, there are no debts. There is the house in Mayfair, as well as forty thousand in the bank and substantial investments in the Funds. Mrs Morton was a very wealthy woman.'

Max's jaw slackened and there was a roaring in his ears.

This cannot be.

'There must be some mistake. My great-aunt lived in a state of near poverty. Why, I needed to give her servant small sums regularly for food and fuel for the fire!'

The solicitor was smiling. 'Your great-aunt, sir, was a singular woman. A little eccentric, to be sure, but perfectly rational, I assure you. She saw no necessity to spend money on anything she did not need. I and my clerk witnessed her will, and I had no concerns about her state of mind.'

'The sly old fox!' A slow smile broke across Max's face as the news began to sink in. 'I can scarce believe it!' His heart was thumping and his palms were suddenly slick as his mind began furiously working out the implications.

What does this mean? For me, for my life, my options?

An hour later, having signed further papers completing the transfer of his great-aunt's entire fortune to him and promising to return on the morrow to complete the business, Max left the lawyer's office feeling as though he had been kicked by a horse. Everything seemed not real, distant and strange. There was the street, filled with horsemen and jarveys and carts, just as it had been earlier. There was the same pile of horse dung he had avoided trampling in on his way into the office. Stepping neatly around it, he was aware that he needed time to understand what this news meant.

I shall tell no one yet, until I have had an opportunity to deal with this in my own head.

Yet as he made his way towards his club, he was beginning to realise that his life would never be the same. Today a new day had dawned, and things that were impossible yesterday were now...

* * *

The Sandison ball was an absolute crush. Eilidh looked about her in some bewilderment. Everywhere she saw glittering jewellery, sumptuous silks and satins, and false smiles and jollity. Her own gown was green silk chiffon over a tartan underdress, and she wore a simple string of creamy pearls—a legacy from her mama—about her neck. The noise was deafening—chatter, laughter, the clink of fine glassware and, somewhere in the background, music. Since their arrival a few moments ago, she and Angus had been wandering through the crowds, but so far no one apart from their hostess had deigned to speak to them.

'Angus!' It was Max, looking suave and handsome in full evening dress. Eilidh swallowed, unable to pull her gaze away from him. Her heart was pounding and her mouth was suddenly dry.

Lord, how does he manage to do this to me?

They exchanged greetings, Max paying her an outrageous compliment about her gown.

Does he even mean it?

Following him and Angus through the crowd, Eilidh was conscious of a strong feeling of disorientation. For the first time since their arrival in London, she felt truly lost—as though she were an outlander, someone who did not belong here at all.

Max brought them to where Isabella was standing with Lord and Lady Burtenshaw, and as they made their curtseys, Eilidh felt again a sense of *otherness*. Everything was wrong. Even the people she thought she knew were strange and different. Burtenshaw and his wife were stony-faced, even more so than usual, Isabella's gaze was vacant and Max had a distracted air, his eyes bright and his attention seemingly elsewhere.

Have they quarrelled?

Something had certainly changed since her comfortable chat with Isabella earlier.

Well, whatever it was, none of them seemed willing to acknowledge it. Instead they all made small talk as best they could amid the deafening din. Exchanging a quick glance with Angus, she could tell that he also had noted something was amiss. The conversation continued, although Isabella was remarkably quiet.

She looks pale.

There must surely have been some sort of quarrel or falling-out among them all. Various acquaintances came to speak with the Burtenshaws and Max, each of them no more than polite towards Eilidh and Angus.

We are still not fully accepted then—and Lord Burtenshaw will note the way they behave towards us.

'Observe, Prudence!' Lord Burtenshaw suddenly stood straighter. 'The Beau is here!'

He was looking at a gentleman who had, it seemed, lately arrived. The man looked vaguely familiar, but just now Eilidh could not recall where she had seen him. Max undertook the explanations. 'The Beau is a close friend of the Prince Regent, and an arbiter of fashion. His approval can be the making of a man or lady, and his disapproval a blow from which no one has ever recovered. His attendance tonight is something of a coup for the Sandisons.'

Eilidh responded instantly. 'And are you intimate with such an *important* man?'

This entire ball is false, as are the people, and even Max—whom I had thought better of—bows to a man who has influence because he has opinions on fashion, of all things?

Eilidh's disappointment was acute. She had thought her friends capable of more depth than this.

Max was visibly bristling. 'No, although everyone here knows who he is. And I do not say he is important, though I am certain many here would think it.'

They eyed one another for a second and Eilidh was again struck by a sense of disconnection.

Where has my Max gone?

The man before her *looked* like Max, but his distracted air and cool gaze made him in that moment a stranger. And why should she think him in any way hers? Once she was safely back home, she would surely never hear from him again.

'Hush!' admonished Lord Burtenshaw. 'For he is walking this way! Oh, my Lord, what if he means to speak to us?'

'Stand up straight, Isabella!' Prudence hissed, as Lord Burtenshaw adjusted his waistcoat, an uncertain smile on his face.

'Good evening, ladies and gentlemen.' The man joined them and they made their bows. Lord Burtenshaw stammered a few words about it being an honour and a pleasure to enjoy a moment of the Beau's time, and the man then turned to Angus.

'Mr MacDonald!' The Beau bowed deeply, his tone genuinely warm. 'I thought it must be you.'

'Mr Brummell! I am glad to see you here, for I have missed our walks these past few days.'

Ah! That is why I recognised him. He is our neighbour—the man who has daily walks with Angus.

She stifled a grin at the astonishment on Lord Burtenshaw's face.

'I too. I have been out of town with Prinny. Perhaps tomorrow?'

The Beau stayed for almost ten minutes, laughing and talking with Angus, and clapped a hand on his shoulder on making his farewell, clearly indicating to the gathered assembly that Angus was not simply to be tolerated, but embraced. Burtenshaw's eyes nearly popped from his head at such an affirmation.

'Well!' Prudence was first to recover. 'Mr MacDonald, you have acquired some fine friends in London.'

Angus shrugged. 'I did not know that he was a notable figure. I simply enjoy his company, for he has wit and humour. He might almost be a Scot!'

'I think not!' Burtenshaw retorted. 'The very notion!'

Angus's eyes met Eilidh's, and his were brimming with humour at Lord Burtenshaw's clear inability to allow any compliment to the Scots to go unchallenged. Her gaze moved on to Max and she was disconcerted to discover that his attention remained elsewhere. Stung, for she was becoming quite accustomed to Max sharing the same humour as herself and Angus, she pretended to be busy with her fan and the moment passed.

The effect of Beau Brummell's endorsement was not long in becoming clear. A train of people took turns to greet Angus and Eilidh, laughing at their every utterance and declaring them to be refreshingly different and entertaining. Eilidh's cynicism deepened.

I have nothing against Mr Brummell, who seems perfectly sensible. All this falseness, however, is too much.

There was no time to consider it fully, for her concern for Isabella was growing. Her friend remained pale and silent, her eyes still dead and vacant and an air of deep distress about her.

What on earth has happened?

Suggesting they go together to the ladies' retiring room, on emerging she lost no time in asking directly.

'Here, sit with me!' Eilidh indicated a nearby sofa which had just been vacated by two middle-aged ladies. 'Please, tell me what ails you. Are you unwell, my dear?'

'Unwell? Yes, I suppose I am. But I shall never be well again.' Isabella spoke slowly, as if the very act of speech took tremendous effort.

Eilidh took both her hands, deeply concerned. 'Tell me what has happened.'

'I am to marry Barnstable. It is all signed and agreed.'

Eilidh gasped.

Barnstable!

'No! I never thought you would choose him.'

'I did not. Freddy chose him. I am not even to have a say.'

Eilidh's heart sank as Isabella's shocking words sank in.

No wonder she is distraught.

'But that is… I cannot understand it!'

'Nor I. But he is my guardian, and so I must submit.' Isabella's response was delivered in a flat tone.

They will force her? Or has she accepted her fate?

Eilidh quizzed her a little more, expressing her outrage in no uncertain terms, but eventually there was nothing more to say.

'Shall we return upstairs?' Isabella asked placidly. Unnatural placidity.

She must be experiencing a severe shock. Indeed, Isabella should not even be out tonight. *How dare they do this to her?*

'Are you well enough to be here, Isabella? Should you not go home?'

Isabella simply shrugged, and they began making their way through the crowds towards the main staircase. 'It matters not whether I am here or at the house. I have no home.'

'There you are, Isabella!' It was Lord Burtenshaw, a smile on his face that did not quite reach his eyes. 'Look who is here to see you.' He stepped aside to reveal the Honourable Geoffrey Barnstable, who instantly bowed and took Isabella's hand to kiss it. Shuddering, she snatched it away and Eilidh's jaw dropped.

'Good evening, ladies. I hope you are well.' He bowed to Eilidh, who ensured both hands were busy with her fan as she curtseyed in response.

I do not want that wretched creature to even touch me. Oh, why are they forcing poor Isabella to marry him?

'Yes, well,' declared Freddy, rubbing his hands together. 'Is this not delightful?'

Isabella eyed her brother in mild confusion. 'How so?'

'Step aside a moment,' he stammered, propelling Isabella to his right and jerking his head towards Barnstable.

Eilidh, still in shock at the revelation that her friend was to marry the most obnoxious man in the *ton*, could not hear what passed between them but after a moment Isabella swept away from the two men and made for the staircase, Eilidh on her heels.

'How dare Freddy do this to me?' she muttered as they made their way through the crowds.

They reached the upper floor just as sets were forming for the first dance, and both young ladies were immediately taken off by their promised partners, Eilidh gritting her teeth in frustration.

Afterwards she searched, but could not find her friend. Craning her neck during her dance with Max, she was relieved to find he did not quiz her on her agitation.

At least I now know what has been happening today.

How could she even broach such a subject when she herself was struggling to take in the enormity of it? How on earth must Isabella feel, being forced into marriage with the Dishonourable Geoffrey?

The music was loud, the chatter of the people in the ballroom oppressive. Eilidh had no urge to speak, simply making her way through the dance, her mind racing. Max too was entirely distracted, but they managed the dance reasonably well regardless. As they began the final figure, Eilidh's fear and shock began to give way, revealing a burning anger at Isabella's fate.

Why did Max not put a stop to this?

Unable to prevent herself, she could not help glaring at him as they bowed and curtseyed at the end of the dance.

Surely he could have prevented such an outrageous betrothal?

His eyes widened but before he could say anything, she had spun away, hiding herself in the crowd of mostly taller people.

I cannot speak to him of this yet, for I might speak too harshly.

Thankfully, she had no partner for the next set, so now was her chance to again try to find Isabella. Having searched the ballroom while consciously evading Max at the same time, she wondered suddenly if Isabella had sought solitude on the terrace below.

The notion had no sooner occurred to her than she was away, squeezing past people and making for the staircase. Hopefully she could find her friend, and would attempt to offer whatever comfort she could.

This whole society is poisoned, she was thinking as she descended.

Lord Burtenshaw forcing his own sister into an abhorrent union. Max standing by and allowing it. All of them showing off their jewellery and their falseness.

The sooner we can leave London, the better.

There she is!

Catching the briefest glimpse of tartan and green, Max fixed his eyes on the distinctive gown. Amid a hundred ladies he had struggled to find her, but now he was on the scent. Making his way through the crowds in her wake, he realised she was going downstairs and he pursued her with purpose. Whatever she had meant by the scathing look she had thrown him at the end of their dance, he was determined to discover it. He had certainly been rather distracted tonight and was concerned that he had come across as rude to her.

Everything seemed peculiar tonight. Isabella seemed upset about something, and Freddy was in an obstinate mood.

They must have had words earlier.

He foresaw that he would have to smooth things over—whatever the issue was—and support poor Isabella. Freddy could be difficult, critical and demanding towards both of them, and perhaps Isabella had received a tongue-lashing from their elder brother today for some reason.

Having needed time away from his family to consider the momentous change in his circumstances he had kept to his club all day, returning home briefly to change for dinner at the club before making his way to the ball. Despite having had a few hours to consider the matter, he was no nearer to accepting and understanding that he was now—suddenly and abruptly—extremely wealthy. He had choices. No longer was he beholden to Freddy. No longer would he have to obey his brother's strictures.

He shook his head again, bringing his attention back to the present. He had no idea what his newfound freedom meant for his future, or for his fixation with Eilidh. Such matters were too large and complicated to be considered in haste. He only knew that she was angry with him, and that would not do. Having reached the ground floor, he watched as she walked straight past the chamber set aside for the ladies' comfort, making for the terrace.

Following her out, he glanced left and right, realising the area was entirely empty. She was directly ahead, and as he watched she descended the three broad steps into the dimly-lit garden.

What on earth is she doing? Some harm might befall her out here all alone.

Lengthening his stride, he caught up with her just as she paused amid the shrubbery.

'Eilidh!'

She jumped, whirling to face him, her face lit by one of the flambeaux that had been placed at intervals around the gardens. 'Oh, it is you, Max. I am looking for Isabella. Have you seen her?' Her expression was closed.

She is certainly cross with me. But why?

'I…no. And why would she be out here?'

'Because of what has happened. I wonder that she is at this ball at all—it was cruel to force her to attend!'

He frowned. 'What do you mean?'

Has Isabella confided in Eilidh about whatever it is

that came between her and Freddy today? Did Isabella not wish to attend the ball for some reason?

'What ails Isabella?'

Her lip curled. 'As if you do not know! Your brother has done a heinous thing, but he at least has the benefit of being an *amadan*, with little between his ears! You, though, you know better—or you *should*, leastways. You have a brain, Max. And a heart. You are simply too much of a coward to use them!'

For the second time that day a roaring sound filled his ears as he struggled to take in her words.

This is what she thinks of me?

He shook his head.

Something is not right here.

'I have no idea what you are talking about! Explain!'

Her brow furrowed, but to his relief, she answered. 'As of today she is betrothed to the Dishonourable Geoffrey—a man who disgusts every lady he meets. How could you possibly not know this?'

His jaw dropped. 'Barnstable? *Barnstable?* Outrageous! What the devil is Freddy thinking?' He put a hand to his head. '*Barnstable!* That man is the last person who should win Isabella's hand!'

Her brow cleared. 'Then…you truly did not know?'

'I did not! So that is why Isabella is so wan, and Freddy so…so belligerent tonight.' He groaned. 'And you thought I knew of it! No wonder you are angry.'

She bit her lip. 'I am sorry, Max. I made an assumption, and I was wrong.'

He sent her a cynical look. 'But your assumption is based on your opinion of me. Is that not correct? You think me cowardly.' His tone was flat.

'No! At least…I have sometimes wondered why you

do not…' Her voice tailed off. 'I cannot walk in your shoes, Max. I cannot know what it is to be you.'

'Yet still you see fit to judge me?' Dimly, he realised his words were fuelled by hurt—the same hurt that had been festering since the night at the theatre. This lady found him wanting, and she was the one lady whose opinion mattered.

'No! I…I like you, Max. You must believe that!' She laid a hand on his arm to emphasise her point and he felt the warmth of her skin permeate his sleeve through her thin glove.

Like? She likes me?

Such words were as nothing to the flames that burned within him when he thought of her.

Damned to mediocrity.

He wanted more than 'like' from her. Much, much more. Along with her hand on his arm, Eilidh's choice of words proved his undoing. With a groan, he gathered her into his arms, ready at an instant to release her if she showed even the slightest resistance. He was not in the habit of compelling unwilling women. To his relief she showed none. Instead her arms swept around him, pulling him close, while at the same time she lifted her face to receive his kiss.

The first touch of his lips to hers was hesitant, tentative. Never had he felt so nervous about a kiss before. But this was Eilidh, and that made all the difference. His eyes closed as his lips met hers, and instantly he was lost. Her lips parted and he tasted the sweet nectar of her mouth, their arms tightening about each other as their tongues danced and explored. Dimly, he half-listened for any sound that might suggest someone approaching. But the darkness was a warm blanket of privacy around them, and they made the most of it. How many times they kissed he afterwards could not say. But for the first time in his sorry existence, he experienced a desire of the heart alongside the body, and the combination was like nothing he had ever imagined.

He was not a man much given to flowery thoughts or spiritual reflection, but the feeling that came over him as he held her, her head now tucked under his chin and their breathing gradually slowing, was one of utter peace.

This is right.

His hands were gently stroking her back, from the smooth silk of her gown up to the silky smoothness of her skin. She quivered, and he felt a sense of wonder at this clear evidence of her desire for him.

If only...

Abruptly, he halted the usual fatalistic direction of his thoughts. He need no longer mourn for a wished-for life. He was now a man of means. *If only* could become...

Might it be? Could it be? But how? How?

His mind awhirl, he could only gaze at her helplessly, drinking in the sight of her as she leaned back to look at him.

'I am glad I did that,' she muttered, and there was a fierceness about her that deprived him of breath. 'There can be no future between us, for your place is here, and mine is in Benbecula. But I shall treasure the memory of tonight.'

A maelstrom of emotion swirled through him at her words.

She feels it too! Or does she?

His mind raced. Was this for her simply a pleasant interlude, a memory to be kept in a box and relived occasionally, something without deeper meaning? Her words echoed in his ears, in his mind, in his heart, and each syllable was a stab of agony.

'There can be no future between us...'

Oh, he had always known of her desire to return to Benbecula, and truly he could not imagine being so selfish as to remove her from her home, and her people, and Scotland, just because he...wanted her. And yet the notion that in order to win her, to keep her, he would be forced to leave behind everything and everyone he knew...

No!

It was incomprehensible.

'...treasure the memory.'

'I too,' he replied softly, knowing it was true. 'If things were different, in another life...' For now, it was as much as he could give. Bending his head, he pressed his lips gently to hers, and the sweet sorrow in it almost proved his undoing.

Swallowing hard, he took a step back, offering her his arm. Together they walked in silence amid the stars and the garden scents and the blanketing darkness until they had reached the terrace. There they separated, standing a decorous distance apart.

'Be assured—' he eyed her directly '—that I intend to raise the matter of Isabella's betrothal with my brother on the morrow.'

She inclined her head. 'I do hope you will meet with success, for—' She grimaced. 'And I apologise again for my harsh words earlier. I always seem to be—'

'Please, do not say any more on the matter!' He shook his head. 'I would rather hear your true opinions, whether I agree with them or not. You do me honour by speaking plainly. I would not wish you to rein in your tongue when you have something to say!' This earned him a smile, which he pocketed with gratitude. 'Now, I suggest you go inside first, and I shall follow after a little time. We would not wish to set tongues wagging!'

He bowed, and she made a slow, elegant curtsey before turning to the doors. As he watched her walk away into the light, drinking in the beauty of her auburn hair, her graceful walk, the smooth skin of her shoulders, his heart felt full to bursting with warmth and pride, and… something else that he could not quite name. His mind beset by conundrums and riddles on all sides, still there was a place of endless peace within him. A place with her name on it.

Chapter Eight

Saturday 13th April

As she had once before, Eilidh sat by the window in her drawing room, keeping an eye out for Angus's return. Today her brother was meeting with Lord Burtenshaw, and very shortly she would know whether this entire trip to London had been pointless.

Catching the direction of her thoughts, she pulled herself up. Pointless? Decidedly not. Even if Burtenshaw refused to sell the land—and Eilidh had a strong suspicion that he would refuse—she had gained much from her trip to England. She had learned of a different place, an entirely different way of life. Moreover, she had learned about herself. There had been many challenges along the way—managing an elegant London townhouse, with staff she barely knew. Finding her way about Town—the safe places and the areas where she should not venture, the interesting and historical locations, the places where bargains were to be found. Already three crates of supplies for the people of the Broch had been shipped to Benbecula, along with a box of personal gifts she had selected from the bazaars and emporiums of London.

And then there were the people. Acquaintances like the Bells and the Sandisons who had been friendly towards them. The many others who had been reserved, clearly wary of Scots—or at least of Highlanders not associated with His Majesty's forces. Lord Burtenshaw, who might even now be dashing the hopes of hundreds of Islanders. His dour wife, who seemed never to hold an opinion of her own. Darling Isabella—her heart wrenched—currently under threat of coercion into what surely would be a disastrous marriage.

Finally, she allowed herself to think of Max, and instantly a wave of warmth surged through her. *Max!* Their kisses had been sweet and wonderful and fiercely passionate and deeply sensual, all at once. Even now, she was filled with a heady mix of fiery desire and wonder, just from allowing herself to remember and, in a way, relive the experience. The way he had looked at her… Her heart turned over at the memory. Never had she experienced such a response to any man—and, she acknowledged, this had been building long before last night's kisses. Something about him just called to her, and her soul answered to his.

Yet somehow she needed to protect her heart, for in a matter of days, irrespective of Burtenshaw's decision, they would be on their way home and she would never see him again. Squeezing her eyes tight against the sudden rush of emotion, Eilidh tried instead to fix the memories in her brain, for she knew that they would weaken with time. Max bending his head to kiss her. Max with that warm appreciative look in his eye. Max as he had looked when he had bowed to her last night— the last image she had of him.

How many more times would she be in his company before they left? Two? Three or four even? Certainly no more than that, for it would be wrong to waste any more of their money on being away from home. Inside, she was fiercely glad she had kissed him, for soon she would say goodbye to him forever. Indeed, it had been the reason she had allowed herself to do it. Max was... Max. Quick-witted, kind-hearted, devastatingly handsome. He was also a *ton* gentleman, a second son who spent his days as a wastrel.

Idly gazing at the street below, she straightened at the sight of Angus's familiar chestnut hair.

What will the answer be?

She did not have to wait long. Within minutes, he was in the drawing room, delivering the worst news. Burtenshaw would not sell. Because the Lidistrome estate had been gifted to his grandfather after Culloden, Burtenshaw held it to be a matter of family pride that he *must* not sell—particularly to Clan MacDonald, from whom the land had originally been confiscated.

'So that is that then,' Angus finished, and Eilidh embraced him, unsurprised to find tears in her eyes.

'We tried. You could not have done more, brother.'

He shrugged, clearly unconvinced. 'I am meeting with Searlas shortly, to make arrangements for our journey home.'

Eilidh nodded. 'I shall call the housekeeper this instant, to begin our packing.'

In the doorway, he paused, as if he would say something more. Then, giving a vague gesture, he left, shoulders slumped and a heaviness about his tread that echoed the sadness in Eilidh's heart.

Failure.

Sunday 14th April

With the benefit of a decent night's sleep, despite vivid dreams involving a certain flame-haired Scottish lass, Max realised he now felt ready to begin to consider his future options. Having spent most of yesterday with the lawyer, it had been something of a relief to have so potent a distraction. Today, though, reality must be faced. He must stop trying to avoid thoughts of Eilidh and he must tackle Freddy about his preposterous agreement to Barnstable's suit, as well as raising the vexed question of the estate in Benbecula.

Eilidh.

As he made his way downstairs to his brother's library, he was recalling vividly how he had followed her down the Sandison staircase and out into the night. He had relived their kisses a hundred times already it seemed, and the potency of the memory had yet to wane.

'Yes? What is it, Max?' Freddy looked and sounded irritated, bringing Max abruptly back to the present.

'I hear you declined to sell the Lidistrome estate to Angus.'

'I did. I had my reasons.' The chin was up, the lips tightly pressed together.

Max suppressed a sigh. 'And would you sell it to me? I should like to make you an offer.'

I could gift it to Angus, or sell to him for a token amount. Lidistrome should never have been taken from them in the first place.

Freddy laughed. 'To you? Even if you could afford it—which I know you cannot—no, I would not sell to you.'

'I see. Any particular reason?'

'None that you need worry about. Now, was there something else?'

Gritting his teeth at his brother's patronising tone, Max simply asked, 'Is it true that Barnstable has made an offer for Bella?'

Freddy nodded. 'More than that. It is all agreed.'

All agreed? Surely not.

There must be some way to make Freddy see sense. Abandoning for now the topic of Lidistrome, Max gave his attention entirely to the vexed question of the proposed betrothal. Having given some thought as to which approach might work best, given Freddy's pride, Max had decided to be blunt and straightforward. Sometimes it was the only way to ensure Freddy plainly understood.

'But Freddy, you must know the man is a reprobate! He brings only disgrace and pity to our family.' His brother did seem to be listening, so Max went straight for the angle that might land most effectively with Freddy. 'I thought you wished for her marriage to *add* to the consequence of our family name?'

'Nonsense! He is perfectly respectable, and his family have a long and distinguished history.'

'Well, his own history consists of ogling debutantes and fondling serving maids against their will!'

'Says who? I'd wager the serving maids were delighted to receive the attentions of so highborn a man!'

Max shook his head. It was like attempting to reason with a horse. 'You know Isabella detests him—hardly an auspicious start to any marriage. I presume the first banns have not yet been read? We have time to discuss this further as a family, come to a considered agreement.' He kept his tone light, not wishing to force his brother to close down the matter entirely. 'Another solution can surely be found.'

Freddy's gaze dropped, and he cleared his throat. 'That will be impossible, I'm afraid. Isabella must be married, and soon. There are reasons...' His jaw hardened. 'I do not wish to discuss this further at present. I am extremely busy, as you see.' He indicated the papers before him, a set of routine household accounts as far as Max could make out.

A strategic retreat then, and the chance to consult with Isabella to agree the arguments they could use. Biting his tongue, he left.

'Where is my sister?' he asked the nearest footman, making for the breakfast room when the man confirmed her current location. As he passed the servants' staircase he spotted a familiar figure. 'Cooper!'

'Well, Max! Your yacht is safely moored in St Katherine's Dock, in a nice safe spot. But tell me—' his brow creased '—they are saying below stairs that Isabella is to be married immediately. Is it true?'

'Not immediately, no,' Max replied then stopped. 'Actually...' Freddy had neither confirmed nor denied his assumption that the marriage would take place following the traditional four weeks of the banns being read. Immediately? Surely not?

But that would require—

A dreadful realisation came over him, and he turned on his heel. 'Excuse me!'

Marching straight back to Freddy's library, he barged straight in. 'When is the wedding to take place? Have you secured a special licence? *When?*'

Freddy shuffled to his feet. 'Now, Max, do not be hasty. I must act as head of the f—'

Max had had enough. Grabbing his brother's cravat, he hauled him up against the wall. 'When. Is. The. Wedding. Happening?'

'I demand that you release me!' Freddy's face was slowly purpling with outrage.

Max remained ice-cold. 'And I demand that you answer me. We are at an impasse, it seems.' He pressed harder into his brother's chest—enough to cause him only a little discomfort. 'I still recall the beatings you gave me as a boy, Freddy,' he added conversationally. 'You had nine years on me, you know. We are more evenly matched now, I think.'

'Today!' Freddy almost shrieked the word. 'She will be married today, and there is nothing that you can do about it, for I am head—'

'Head of the family. Yes, I am aware,' Max replied lightly, as fury built within him at his brother's revelation.

How could he?

Releasing Freddy's cravat, he adopted a boxing stance. 'Fair warning, Freddy. I am about to hit you.'

'Why you, you…*upstart!*' Freddy's face was mottled with rage, his mouth twisted in an angry snarl. Still, he drew up his fists, dropping into a defensive posture, before lunging wildly at Max. Unperturbed, Max easily ducked Freddy's attempted swing before landing him a single resounding punch to the side of the head.

'Ow!' Freddy was rubbing his left ear vigorously. 'You shall pay for this, Max, believe me!'

'Honestly, I care not,' Max replied frankly, his mind already on more important matters. 'That you would do such a thing to your *own sister*—!' He made a face. 'Sometimes, Freddy, I am ashamed to be related to you.'

Wrenching open the door and scattering the assorted footmen and serving maids who had clearly been listening in the hallway, Max made straight for the breakfast room.

There she was, his beautiful sister. Pale, motionless, and with no sign of herself in her eyes.

Max felt a dreadful sickness in his stomach. 'Is it true? Freddy tells me you are to be married today!'

Surely it cannot be true.

'Bella, is it true?'

For answer, Isabella nodded mutely, seemingly incapable of speech.

'I had known him to be foolish, but I had not thought him capable of such cruelty!' With a muttered expletive he departed abruptly, calling for Cooper. When the man appeared he bade him quickly confirm with the servants all the known details of the planned nuptials, then yelled to the footman to procure them a hackney and to find his boots. Max might not be able to marry the girl of his choice, but perhaps, with quickness, a little ingenuity and a dash of courage, Angus might!

'Where to, sir?' the hackney driver asked ten minutes later, as he and Cooper climbed inside.

'Chesterfield Street and make it sharp!' He sat back in his seat, adding for Cooper's ears only, 'For we have a wedding to stop.'

Chapter Nine

The dreadful banging on the door reverberated throughout the MacDonald residence. Indeed, such a racket could probably be detected in the next street, so loud was it. Eilidh paused in the act of folding a gown for packing, murmuring to her maid, 'What on earth is that? Such a clatter!' Leaving the chamber, she leaned over the banisters a little in an attempt to discern who was there, and why they were behaving in such a dramatic manner.

Someone had just entered the hall below from the street. 'Where is he? Angus?' The voice was familiar to her, and her heart leapt. *'Angus!'* Max called again. 'Where the devil are you, man?'

'Max!' Untying her apron as she walked, Eilidh made her way swiftly down the wide staircase. 'What has happened?'

He took both her hands. 'Where is Angus? Isabella's wedding is to take place at noon today!'

Curling her fingers around his, she drank in the sight of him, even as she responded to his words. 'Noon today! So soon? Why, it is almost eleven already!' Shaking her head, she added, 'Angus is walking in the Green Park, trying to clear his head.' Withdrawing her hands from his, she swiftly removed her apron completely. 'Just give me one moment.' She turned slightly, calling, 'Mary! My boots and cloak, if you please!'

'Ah, but you are astonishing!' His eyes shone. 'No unnecessary questions or requests for information that might slow us. Your quick mind has already divined what must be done.'

'Well, I cannot claim to know all of the detail, but I assume you wish to disrupt the wedding. Thank you, Mary.'

A moment later they were in his hackney and he was introducing her to his friend, Cooper—an older man who, Eilidh remembered, had served the Wood family for many years. Cooper, it transpired, was originally from Islay, an island in the Inner Hebrides, and he promptly expressed delight at being able to speak his native tongue with her, even briefly. Conscious that Max was listening intently, she translated the gist of their brief conversation for him while Cooper smiled broadly.

The man looked decidedly familiar and she wondered if he simply had an 'Islander' look about him or if she had perhaps come across some of his relations at home. The thought warmed her heart, recalling to her mind a myriad conversations in Benbecula figuring out the genealogy of newcomers with connections to the island community.

There was no time now for genealogical discourse, however, as the jarvey had pulled up at the gate. Max bade him wait, then they split up inside the park, Cooper taking the path to the left while Max and Eilidh proceeded straight down the main thoroughfare, her hand tucked into his arm and both of them vigilantly looking about for any sign of Angus.

They talked too as they made their way briskly down the path. Isabella was dreadfully ill, Max explained, and Freddy seemingly determined to go through with his plans regardless. Drastic action was needed, and Angus might wish to play a part in it. He glanced sideways at her. 'You do not mind?'

She knew exactly what he was asking.

Should Angus marry Isabella and take her to Scotland, if she wishes it?

She considered the matter, and all of the barriers and challenges Angus and Isabella would face if they did marry. The alternative, however, was for poor Isabella to be condemned to a life with the Dishonourable Geoffrey. Back and forth she went, until her mind was whirling and she could no longer make sense of anything—including what such an outcome might mean for her too.

In the end, she simply sighed. 'I just wish for them both to be happy. And while I imagine it would be unusual for a young woman to reject a suitor at the altar, I believe Isabella has the right to do so.' She frowned. 'Such a situation would be unheard of at home. No one must marry unless they sincerely wish to.'

Having now reached the bottom of the path, they turned left as one, intending to continue until they reached Cooper, at which point they would begin to search in a different section of the park.

'I think I prefer your way of marrying,' he murmured, setting a thousand butterflies fluttering in her stomach, and reawakening the memories of their kisses in the darkness. If Angus did marry Isabella, then at the very least Max might some day visit his sister in the Islands...

Wrenching herself away from a whole host of daydreams, Eilidh sternly reminded herself that no such future was fixed. Indeed, until twenty minutes ago it would not have even seemed possible.

'Max, Miss MacDonald, I have found him!' It was Cooper, Angus by his side.

Instantly, Max and Eilidh increased their pace, hurrying towards the two men. 'Thank the Lord!' Max's relief was clear. 'Quickly, to the carriage, for it is almost noon!'

Angus frowned. 'Why, what is amiss?'

Cooper has not yet told him.

'Freddy means to marry Bella to Barnstable today. And she does not want him.'

Angus's face sagged in shock. He glanced at Eilidh, and she gave the smallest of nods.

Yes, it is true, she was signalling. *And yes, I shall support you if you intervene.*

He straightened. 'Not if I have anything to say about the matter!' Anger had thickened his accent, and Eilidh felt a sudden rush of pride in her brother.

Max hit him a brotherly slap on the shoulder. 'I knew it! We shall need to make haste though!'

'Lead on, Max,' Angus declared, 'for I have had my fill of English manners. It is time to show these fine gentlemen how we do business where I come from!'

The journey from the Green Park to the church was a little less than a mile, but their progress was impeded numerous times by farm carts, costermongers and even by a group of horsemen racing one another up Piccadilly. Max had offered to pay the jarvey twice the usual fee if he made haste, and the driver edged his carriage deftly amid the London bustle and busyness that never seemed to let up. Finally, the white portico and high campanile of St George's, Mayfair, came into view.

Max checked his pocket watch, conscious that his

heart was racing. 'A quarter past noon.' He grimaced. 'I pray we are not too late.'

They had no plan, save to disrupt the wedding, preventing the marriage from taking place. The wedding ceremony, though, would be fairly brief, and Max briefly wondered if he should have handled the thing himself rather than racing to find Angus. He stole a glance at his friend. Angus's visage looked as though it had been carved in granite, although Max spied the tic of a muscle along his set jaw.

No, it is right that he is here. This is his fight too—perhaps even more than it is mine.

'I shall wait outside,' said Eilidh, and Max's gaze swung to meet hers. She was a little pale—and why should she not be, given the extremity of the action he and Angus were about to take? 'No violence, boys!' she advised them sternly. 'Just bring Isabella to me as quickly as you can.'

Max nodded tersely, and their eyes remained fixed on one another for just a second too long. He could almost *feel* her unspoken message to him. Isabella must not be condemned to a life as wife to Geoffrey Barnstable. The notion was unthinkable.

The carriage was still moving as Angus opened the door and leapt down lightly, Max following in his friend's wake. Angus was already running, pushing open the outer door and entering the church, Max at his heels.

Max could see them all at the foot of the altar.

Isabella and Barnstable.

The vicar.

Freddy standing nearby.

Prudence seated in the front left pew.

Barnstable's family in the same spot to the right.

'Stop!' Angus bellowed, striding up the aisle. 'Stop this wedding!'

They all turned to look, shock evident on every face. Angus addressed the vicar directly, passion in his tone.

'This woman is being forced against her will to marry an unsuitable man. Surely the church should not condone such a thing? This wedding must be stopped instantly, or annulled if needs be!'

Nicely done, Angus.

His friend had been clever enough to appeal to the priest's sense of morality. Now, would he be heard?

'You!' Freddy glared at Angus, his expression one of utter loathing. 'How dare you interrupt a private family event?' His brow creased. 'And how did you even know—?' His face twisted in anger as he spotted his brother. 'Max! You did this? You would work against your own family?'

He truly sees my intervention as treachery against the family?

Max suppressed a strong desire to lash out, saying only, 'I have done what I believe to be right. Our sister's welfare matters more than your pride.'

'This is an absolute outrage!' Geoffrey Barnstable had found his voice. 'Plank!—Burtenshaw, I mean— we have signed a legal agreement for this marriage—an agreement that also entails the settling of your gaming debts!'

Gaming debts?

The card games!

Max could scarcely believe what he was hearing. This was why Isabella had been given to such a man? Out of the corner of his eye, he noted that Isabella and Angus were looking at one another, and that Bella's eyes were shining.

Freddy visibly paled. 'Barnstable! We agreed to keep such matters confidential!'

Max's stomach felt sick. Even the additional layer of secrecy spoke of the depth of Freddy's dishonour.

'Only if I got the girl! Our agreement is now void, and I expect full settlement of your debts *today*!'

Got the girl? This is how he speaks of my sister?

Max's right hand formed a fist. At present, he had no idea which of the two reprobates before him deserved it more—Freddy or Barnstable.

No violence.

Reluctantly, he loosened his hand.

Freddy, aghast, managed to stutter, 'But…you know I cannot…that is to say my c-current circumstances do not allow… Perhaps we might come to some arrangement?'

Isabella, who had been looking from one to the other, found her own voice. 'Debts? You agreed to this marriage in exchange for the settling of your gaming debts, Freddy? And you *dare* to speak to me of honour and duty? You have *sold* me—or tried to. There is no other word for it.'

Well said, Bella.

Max was quite ready to take a hand in matters when needed. For now, he was content to see Freddy expose his dishonour so completely to everyone present.

'That is a very ugly word, Isabella.' Puffing out his chest, Freddy elaborated. 'As Head of the Family my responsibility is to address all matters, including financial matters. Wedding settlements are normal.' He turned back to the priest. 'Please proceed with the ceremony. All else can be addressed later.'

Oho! So the deed is not yet done?

Aware of a dawning sense of satisfaction, Max folded

his arms and waited to see how the priest would respond. Surely, he could not persist now, given the revelation about Freddy's sordid deal with Barnstable.

The vicar stepped forward. 'Most of you seem to be aware of the law of the land, which does indeed allow a guardian to choose a husband for a young woman.' Isabella gasped, but Max was encouraged by something in the man's tone. 'However,' he continued, 'I should like to educate you a little. Are any of you familiar with the *Decretum Gratiani*?'

Max's attention was entirely focused on the priest.

We may yet have to prise Isabella from here with force.

Not that Barnstable and Freddy could possibly withstand himself and Angus, if it came to that.

No violence.

Everything depended on whether or not the vicar continued with the wedding.

'It is a twelfth century textbook of Canon Law that stands to this day,' continued the vicar, 'and it has much to say with regard to marriage. Under civil law, it is enough for the couple to simply be present. Under *church* law, however, both parties must consent, and consent freely. So, you see, I *cannot* continue with the ceremony, and nor would I wish to. Now,' he added briskly, 'I must ask all of you to leave this place. Any further discussion between you should take place outside the church. There will be no wedding this day.'

Yes!

Isabella and Angus were grinning at one another like ninnyhammers, but despite their victory in halting the wedding, Max knew they were not out of the woods yet. The fact remained that Freddy was Isabella's legal guardian.

'Outside, where *he* may contrive to carry her off to Gretna, and ensure my humiliation is complete?' Freddy jerked his head towards Angus, his face still twisted with anger. Angus did not even deign to look at him.

Gretna? Yes, it may come to that.

'Outside,' the priest repeated firmly, and slowly they turned and began walking towards the heavy wooden doors at the foot of the church.

Freddy took Isabella's arm, his clear intention to propel her down the aisle, but she simply stopped, waiting until he removed his hand with a muttered expletive. 'Shocking language, Freddy,' she murmured. 'Father would be most displeased.'

Max suppressed a smile. The empty-eyed Isabella from earlier had gone and in her place was his darling sister Bella, in all her opinionated glory.

She and Eilidh are so alike!

For a moment, he tried to imagine Angus attempting to compel Eilidh into a marriage she did not like. He grinned inwardly.

Not a chance!

'Father? *Father?*' Freddy almost choked on the word. 'But he is not—' Clamping his mouth shut, he stomped off, leaving her to follow. And follow she did. But she walked on her own terms and with her head held high. Freddy and Prudence were in front of her, Angus and Max behind. Barnstable and his family were still currently remonstrating with the priest who was, Max thought sympathetically, having a very trying day.

Outside, Eilidh was waiting, her brow furrowed. Her eyes flew to Max, who sent her a happy nod, signalling that they had managed to prevent the wedding. With a strong sigh of relief she wrapped Isabella in a fierce hug, whispering something in her friend's ear. Cooper was next, and he hugged Isabella with great warmth, his expression clearly signalling his relief.

'I might have known he had a hand in this debacle,' commented Freddy bitterly to Prudence, clearly referring to Cooper.

No! In this mood, Freddy would seek to lash out at anyone he perceived to be unprotected.

It is time for me to intervene.

'This "debacle" is entirely of your making, Freddy,' Max declared tersely. 'You did not need to do it.'

'You have no idea, Max. No idea of the burdens I must bear.'

Not this again.

'Like gaming debts to Barnstable?'

Freddy recoiled, but managed to mutter, 'Any man might have a run of bad luck at the tables. I must pay my debts.'

He never seeks counsel of me. No, not even when faced with a challenge so great as this one.

Rather than judge, he decided to question his brother. 'And why did you not speak to me of them? Why, eh?'

Freddy shrugged. 'There is no one who can help me. This is my riddle to solve.'

Still managing a reasonably calm tone, Max continued. 'Freddy, yesterday I offered to buy from you a certain estate in Benbecula. You declined my offer. If you had accepted it you would not have needed to bring Isabella here today.'

Freddy gave a short laugh. 'You forget, Max, I know your income almost to the penny. No doubt you had good reason for making such a foolish offer, but as you now know, my situation has an added urgency.'

'Indeed, it does.' Geoffrey, who had followed them outside, now marched up to them. 'I am decided. If your debts are not settled by midnight, then I shall declare you to be a scoundrel lacking in honour, and I shall ensure the *ton* knows of it!'

'But…but…be reasonable, man!' Freddy was aghast.

'You think me unreasonable, after the insults delivered to me today by you and your family? No, it is clear who is lacking in honour here, and all of society shall soon know it. Good day!'

With this, he departed with his family, and without looking back. They climbed into their carriage and were gone.

'Oh, Lord!' Freddy was wringing his hands, now genuinely agitated. 'Oh, Lord…oh, Lord…oh, Lord.' He turned to Isabella, his face twisting. 'Now see what you have done! We are ruined, ruined!'

He blames everyone but himself.

Before Max could speak, Prudence, who had remained in the background the entire time, stepped forward. Placing a hand on her husband's arm, she declared calmly, 'All will be well, Husband. If you will permit, I should like to play a part in this situation.'

'Yes, do, Prudence, for I am at my wits' end. How am I to possibly find such a sum by midnight?'

She nodded and turned to Max. 'Does this concern your Great-Aunt Morton?'

A gleam of admiration lit Max's eye. 'Well deduced, Prudence. Yes, the old lady's penury was apparently self-imposed, for she had a fortune in the Funds which she never touched.'

'And she left it to you?'

'Every penny,' he confirmed.

Eilidh, who had been watching silently the entire time, gasped. 'Then—'

Max nodded to her, his expression solemn. 'Here

is my chance to see what sort of man I may be. That should please you, Miss MacDonald.'

Her eyes locked with his, and he was conscious of holding his breath. 'And your first act was to offer to buy the Benbecula land?' Eilidh shook her head slowly. 'This surprises me, I admit.'

A pang went through him. Her surprise was no more than he deserved, perhaps, but he had thought she had been coming to know him a little.

Angus sent him a keen glance, referring to a comment Max had made with respect to Lidistrome. 'The ace you had to play, Max?'

Gathering himself, Max turned to his friend. 'Indeed. Freddy turned me down, which is hardly surprising since I did not disclose to him that I was my great-aunt's heir—a fact I have only recently discovered myself.'

'Wait.' Freddy was finally realising what had occurred. 'She left you a fortune? *You*, the useless second son? But—'

'I should be careful who you insult today, Freddy.' Max's tone was mild, but inwardly he felt as though he were made of iron. For the first time in his twenty-eight years, he had the upper hand over his brother. Freddy might call him useless, but Max would now have a chance to prove him wrong. 'You have already made some gaffes today,' he continued softly. 'I should not like to see you miss your last opportunity to avoid social ruin. Now tell me, what is the sum of your debt to Barnstable?'

Freddy looked uncomfortable. 'I shall whisper it in your ear, Max, for such matters should never be discussed unless strictly necessary.' He named a sum that would have seemed impossible to settle just a few days ago.

Thank the Lord for Great-Aunt Morton!

'I should be eternally grateful if you could see your way to…' Freddy's voice tailed off. He swallowed. 'Any disgrace will reflect upon your reputation just as much as mine.'

'No. For I care less about such things than you do,' Max replied calmly. 'We were never the same.' Ignoring his brother's puzzled look, he added in a louder tone, 'Now, Freddy—' he glanced towards the others '—you know that I have the means to mend this. Sell me the Benbecula land—or sell it to Angus—and use the money to pay Barnstable.'

Freddy's jaw dropped, and he looked from Angus to Max and back again. He closed his eyes, groaning. 'I…I cannot. No, not even to avert Barnstable's threat. Our family name is everything to me, and I cannot bear the thought that our prize for service to the Crown will leave the family and go back to the Scots from whom it was confiscated! No, not even to save my own reputation will I do it!'

What madness is this? What can possibly be more important than his precious reputation?

'If I sell it to you,' he continued, his tone that of a man tortured, 'then you will simply pass it to *him*. And that cannot be.'

Max tried to reason with him. 'But our family name will be more directly destroyed by Barnstable's tattle than by your selling a small estate in Scotland, even if it *was* given to the family by the King.'

Freddy stuck his lower lip out mutinously. 'Perhaps people will not take Barnstable seriously. Perhaps…'

He will not change course. He was ever thus.

There was only one thing to be done. Max sighed, then nodded. 'Very well. There is only one option. Sell it to me and I shall promise not to sell it to Angus—or indeed to any Scot. I vow to keep it in my ownership all my life.'

This way, Freddy can settle his debts and I can bequeath the estate to Isabella's children.

Freddy thought about it for a moment, then nodded. 'Very well. I will sell it to my own brother, with his word he will not sell it on. I think my grandfather would be content with that.' He stuck out a hand, and Max clasped it.

They stepped aside then to agree the practicalities of deeds and agreements and quickly accessing some of Max's new wealth in the Funds in order to settle the debt before midnight. Meanwhile, Angus and Isabella were quietly talking, while Eilidh stood to the side, her eyes following Max intently.

What does she make of all of this?

'Eh? What's that?' Freddy abruptly seemed to notice for the first time that Angus was holding Isabella's hand. 'Unhand my sister, sir!'

Angus opened his mouth to reply, but Isabella forestalled him. 'It is for *me* to decide who will hold my hand, Freddy. Not you. As the vicar made clear, consent is necessary for a marriage to take place. I shall choose my own husband, and I hope you will support my choice.' Without so much as glancing sideways, she added, 'I hope that he does too.'

Freddy shook his head. 'As your guardian, I must also have a say. Church law may be on your side, but the law of the land is on mine.'

Oh, Lord, why can Freddy not let it go? It is as plain as a pikestaff that Isabella has chosen Angus!

Before he could once again intervene, Angus spoke up. 'English law,' he stated flatly. 'In Scotland, a woman of your sister's age may marry without the consent of her guardian.'

Isabella gasped and turned to him. 'Then—?'

He took her other hand. 'Isabella, would you do me the very great honour of becoming my wife?'

She caught her breath. 'Are you asking because you believe you must rescue me from Geoffrey? For that threat is gone, and I believe I rescued myself!'

'You did that, but if it is not Geoffrey today, it will be some other man in the future. And I strongly believe that no one must marry you but me.'

'Why, Angus?'

'Because I love you, *mo leannan bhoidheach*. And I have some hope that you might love me too.'

'Well, of course I do!' She smiled up at him. 'What do those Gaelic words mean?'

'They mean "my beautiful sweetheart". Now, kiss me and say that you will.'

'Oh, I will, I will!' She kissed him with enthusiasm, ignoring Freddy's disapproving noises. Grinning, Max could not resist glancing towards Eilidh. She too was delighted, judging by the smile in her blue eyes.

Naturally, Freddy was less impressed. 'Isabella! Have some decorum, please!'

'I am sorry, Freddy.' She tilted her head to one side, reflecting on her own words. 'Actually, I am not in the least sorry for kissing Angus, and I warn you I intend to do it again shortly, but I am sorry that you do not approve of my choice.'

'I most certainly do not! In fact, I cannot allow my sister to marry a Scot!' he declared venomously. 'I have only just averted the threat of some of our family lands going to them!'

'Angus is my choice,' she declared firmly, but Freddy was not having it.

'You cannot expect me to stand in a church and condone it, Isabella, for it goes against everything I was raised to hold dear.'

'Then give us your blessing and we shall wed in Scotland.' Angus's voice and demeanour were entirely calm, in contrast to Freddy's purpling outrage. 'You need not be there.'

'Never! I—' He broke off as Prudence once again laid a hand on his arm.

'Let them go, Freddy,' she said softly. 'It is for the best.'

His wife's intervention seemed to shock him, for he paused and they gazed at one another for a moment. Prudence remained still, eyeing him steadily, and after a moment he exhaled slowly, all the fight seeming to go out of him.

'Very well, but our agreement stands, Max. You are not to sell the land to MacDonald, even if he is Isabella's husband.' He glowered at Angus. 'Come to see me in the morning, and we shall go through the wedding agreement.'

Angus bowed. 'With pleasure!'

Stomping off while Prudence had a quick private word with Isabella, Freddy paused to say something to Cooper, whose expression did not change.

Isabella waited until their carriage was moving away before announcing, 'I declare he has forgotten about me!' She smiled, elated. 'I am as yet unwed and have nowhere to live!'

'Well, that is easily mended,' Angus responded, 'for

I shall repair to a hotel for a few days and you can move in with Eilidh while we prepare to go to Scotland.'

'An excellent plan!' Eilidh and Isabella hugged again. 'And we are to be sisters! I could not be happier!'

Max congratulated them. In truth, he had no qualms about placing Isabella's happiness in Angus's hands. The only difficulty was that she would be so far away. That they would all be so far away.

Abruptly, a notion came to him. A simple idea, and yet the maddest, most foolish idea he had ever had. Fanciful to be sure but, to his mind, beautiful.

'We have begun to pack anyway,' Eilidh was saying, 'and although I dread the weeks on the road, it will be wonderful to be back in Benbecula again.'

Weeks on the road…

Adapting his idea to take into account Eilidh's words, he heard himself cough mildly. They all looked his way. 'As to that, I have a suggestion.' He turned to the former servant, believing that Cooper would grasp his intent. 'Cooper, would you mind?'

Cooper grinned. 'I understand you, Max, and I think it an excellent notion. But are you certain you wish to do this?'

Isabella was looking from one to the other, mystified.

Ah, Bella, you are not normally so slow-witted. I daresay Angus's kisses have temporarily frozen your brain.

He knew this because Eilidh's kisses at the ball had had exactly the same effect on him.

Perhaps they wield some sort of magic, these Islanders.

Aloud, he said only, 'This is my opportunity, and I intend to take it!' The expression on Cooper's wise face indicated approval. Turning back to Isabella, Angus and

Eilidh, he declared, 'We shall sail my yacht to Benbecula, and I shall accompany you!'

I shall see my sister married and take time to consider what I shall do with my life.

In the ensuing melee of exclamations and questions, Max managed a quiet word with Eilidh. 'Well? Will you mind very much having me visit your home?' Inwardly, he was hoping for an indication that she might welcome him for his own sake, and not simply because of his sister.

She hesitated, her expression shuttered, and his heart sank. 'No, not at all,' she replied politely. 'My brother made the invitation many weeks ago, and we are always delighted to welcome visitors to our hearth and home.'

Damnation!

He might have known she would not want him. Not really. Well, why should she? By reading more into their kisses than she had intended, he had committed a fatal error. For him, she was beautiful, unattainable, someone far above him in merit. The logical reverse from her perspective was that she also sensed the differences between them and knew she did not wish to encourage him.

No doubt there were better men than he in the Islands, men who all their days had choices and opportunities, the chance to know themselves and prove themselves. A dilettante second son whose greatest achievements had been made in the boxing ring and at the card table could have nothing to offer such a woman. It was foolishness to think it, even for a moment.

'I shall certainly prefer travelling by sea rather than by road. Our journey to London was arduous indeed!'

'Then I am happy to ease your pain,' he replied formally. 'You are our friends after all, and we are soon to be related.' Every word he uttered acknowledged the distance she had put between them.

I understand you, he was trying to say. *I accept your rejection of me.*

Protocol kept his words neutral, his face expressionless, yet inwardly his heart was sore. Yes, he would go to Scotland and see Isabella settled. And afterwards he would leave again, knowing that Eilidh would some day wed another.

I am reaping what I have sowed.

All those years of hedonistic pursuits—wasting his time on drinking and gambling, courtesans and horse races. Knowing he should be doing more—*something* more, yet never managing to find a way. The only achievement he could lay claim to was some proficiency at sea, and that could be laid at the feet of his Scottish mentor.

Rejection was a new experience for him, delivered at the hands of a woman. With his fine face and gentlemanlike manner, he had charmed his way into the beds of nearly a dozen widows and high-flyers over the years. His error was to assume that a discerning lady could be similarly charmed. Oh, he had managed to get some kisses from her, it was true. Even at the time, he had sensed how precious a memory their encounter in the velvety darkness would be. And he had not been trying to seduce her. A highborn unmarried lady was simply not available for bed sport. So what on earth had he been playing at? And why had he allowed her opinion of him to matter to him so much?

Great-Aunt Morton's legacy had allowed him to secure Isabella's happiness. It had helped rescue her from Freddy's clutches and send her on her way to a new life with Angus. It had opened doors for him too and yet just now he found his newfound freedom to be more burden than boon. Now there was nowhere to hide. He could not simply reassure himself with old litanies of all the things he could not do. He felt exposed, vulnerable.

What sort of man am I?

One thing was for certain. The trip to the Hebrides, suggested on the spur of the moment, would mark a turning point in his life. By the time he returned to London, he would hopefully have had the opportunity to learn, to grow and to consider his next steps.

Cooper's words returned to him now, from a time when he had been dreaming of a life as a lawyer, a vicar or an army captain.

'You do not like your current life, but you have no clear calling to another. Until you know for certain, best to keep your powder dry.'

Very well. He would begin this new stage in his life with a short stay far from home. He would ponder and consider until he understood the life that called to him. Some day perhaps there would be another lady who might capture his heart as Eilidh had.

And next time, he would be worthy.

Chapter Ten

Scotland, Monday 29th April

Eilidh gripped the rail as the yacht speared its way up the Minch towards Benbecula, the scene lit by a glorious sunrise to her right. *Nearly home!* The journey along the south coast then up the Irish Sea had taken a little over two weeks, and Eilidh had both loved it and hated it.

Angus and Isabella were blissfully happy, and sickeningly in love, and Max's yacht was far too small to avoid them entirely.

Sickeningly? Eilidh frowned at her choice of word, then nodded. *Yes, sickeningly.*

The pair were constantly embracing in corners, much to the amusement of the crew Cooper had hired.

Searlas, Angus's secretary, and Mary, Eilidh's personal maid, who had accompanied them to London, had said not a word, but Eilidh could tell they both approved of Isabella. They kept themselves to themselves, and Eilidh wondered if there was a connection developing between them too.

I am surrounded by lovers!

Even when Angus and Isabella were not kissing and

embracing, they were sending one another meaningful looks, laughing together in lowered tones or simply being exuberantly *happy*. Eilidh and Max were constantly rolling their eyes at their siblings' antics and she had grown accustomed to the way Max's mouth would quirk up at the corners in a wry smile when the lovers were nearby.

Eilidh's views of Max were changing by the day. When he had first declared he would travel with them to Scotland, she had been horrified. How on earth could she protect her heart from him? The only reason she had allowed herself to kiss him that night was because she had believed they would soon part, and she had wanted the memory to take home with her and treasure long after she had seen him for the last time.

His decision had turned everything on its head. He would be in Benbecula—in Broch Clachan itself! While he had stated he intended only a short visit to see his sister married, it would prolong the propinquity that threatened her peace of mind. Her heart, she knew, was already in danger from him, and she had hoped to turn him into a memory—a disturbing, wonderful, regret-filled memory, but a memory nevertheless.

Now that Angus was to marry Isabella, she was forced to rethink the finality with which she had viewed her connection with Max. He would be Angus's brother-in-law, uncle to her own future nieces and nephews, and might well choose to visit the Islands on occasion, given his love for sailing. He also was now the owner of Lidistrome, a fact he had not mentioned since London.

Has he even thought about what it means?

Would he simply abandon the Islanders—be an absentee landlord like his forebears? He certainly had not been raised to understand the responsibilities he now carried.

Glancing to her right, she saw that Max was helping adjust the lines to take full advantage of the nice westerly current buffeting the yacht. He and Angus had ditched their formal wear for garb more suited to sailing, and she had been enjoying the sight of Max's fine frame displayed to advantage in soft buckskin breeches and simple linen shirts open at the neck. Neither gentleman had worn a cravat since they had made their last landfall to purchase supplies two days ago, and Eilidh could not disapprove.

Having recovered from the initial shock of Max's announcement outside the church, Eilidh had decided that the best way to protect her heart from him was to ensure coolness between them. Being pleasantly polite to keep him at a distance had worked reasonably well at first, but her plan had disintegrated the moment he had begun talking to her of his childhood.

At the time, they were spending a night in Burtenshaw House—an impressive pile between Newhaven and Seaford—in order that Isabella might pack a trunk of winter clothing and childhood treasures to bring with her to Scotland. She might never again return to her childhood home, and they all knew it. Max had taken Eilidh for a tour of the house and lands and had shared something of his ambivalence about the place.

'Mama and Cooper ensured that Isabella and I had a good childhood,' he had revealed as they walked away from Cooper's boathouse. 'We spent most of our time here or out on the water, while Freddy and Papa would meet with the steward. I know now that Mama was deeply unhappy.' He had shaken his head, his dark eyes closing briefly at some remembered pain. 'Papa took his duty very seriously and expected much of Mama—of all of us.' His face had twisted briefly as another memory had returned to him. 'His way of imposing *duty* involved little other than criticism and, for me, beatings. He positively disliked me. I never understood why.'

'I am so sorry, Max.' Eilidh had briefly touched his arm, her heart sore, seeing the anguish of the child he had been. He had brushed it away with a self-mocking comment but that conversation had haunted her. The notion of 'heir and spare' was a common one in the *ton*. A gentleman apparently always needed two sons—the second to be held in reserve in case something happened to the first. Held in reserve and given education on estate matters, but never allowed to act, to lead, to grow. They were expected to be dutiful and compliant, to support the heir and blend into the background. Men like Max were the result.

He laughed now at some comment from Cooper and she could not tear her eyes away from the sight of his relaxed features and strong frame. Seeing him at sea, watching him work hard with the crew, had impressed her. Here he was active, energetic, purposeful—the exact opposite of his demeanour in the drawing rooms of London. At the same time, he seemed more carefree, less troubled.

Circumstances had thrown them together and every day they would spend hours in one another's company while Angus and Isabella sought time alone together at the other end of the yacht. Hours of talking, of assisting the crew, or simply reading in silence together on the deck. And every day, every hour, Eilidh knew, forged a stronger bond between them—a bond that would be forcibly broken when Max returned to England.

There had, naturally, been no repeat of the wonderful kisses they had shared at the ball. Like her, Max seemed wary of overtly demonstrating that kind of warmth, and truthfully Eilidh did not know whether to be glad or sorry.

Perhaps he too is wary of suggesting anything more meaningful than a few kisses and a warm friendship.

Yet underneath everything—their conversations both serious and teasing, their companionable shared humour and their silent time together—it thrummed like a distant storm. Occasionally, when Eilidh observed him without his knowledge, or when their eyes met, her heart would pound, her breath caught and a burning sensation would grow in her chest, so fierce that she felt as though it would consume her. Did he feel it too? She had no way of knowing. Perhaps such things were commonplace.

As the yacht continued to glide smoothly up the coast, he came to stand alongside her. 'So where are we now?'

She pointed. 'That is Ruadh cam nan Gall, and the inlet beyond is Loch a' Laip.' Feeling the familiar cadence of the Gaelic words in her mouth was a blessing. Seeing known places come into view was raising her spirits and at the same time causing a hard lump of emotion to lodge painfully in her throat.

Home!

She took a breath, then continued. 'Soon we shall pass Maaey Glas and Maaey Riabhach, and then we shall make the turn into Loch Uskavagh.' She sent him a sideways glance. 'I was speaking to Angus earlier. We have decided to land at Lidistrome.'

His eyes widened. 'Lidistrome? Freddy's—I mean *my*—estate? Is it far from Broch Clachan?'

He still thinks of it as belonging to Freddy, then.

She shook her head. 'Your estate marches with ours.

Your western boundary forms the eastern end of the Broch Clachan lands.'

It will do no harm to remind him that he, and not Freddy, is now responsible for Lidistrome and its people.

'We wrote home to let them know roughly which day we would arrive, but we shall have to send someone from Lidistrome to fetch the carts from Broch Clachan.' She shrugged. 'It will take an hour or two for them to come for us. You can stay on the yacht if you wish, or we can walk about Lidistrome.'

There was no hesitation from him. 'Let us explore then. Although—' he frowned '—I think it would be better if no one knew of my…involvement with the estate. At least not yet.'

'Very well. You should tell Angus and the others, in case someone should accidentally reveal it.'

Inwardly, she identified a sense of trepidation. How would the people of Benbecula react to two English people being landed in their midst? Particularly when it became known they were part of the hated Burtenshaw family? And especially since Max clearly had no idea of the responsibility he had taken on. Isabella would, she was sure, eventually win them over with her kind heart and her love for Angus. Max, however, was an altogether different prospect. A man—an *Englishman*—the new owner of Lidistrome? She shuddered inwardly.

Max's decision to not reveal himself was definitely the sensible option, even if his reasons were different from hers. For now—and perhaps throughout his stay. It was not up to her, but there might well be advantages in keeping his identity secret until after his departure. Not because he would be in any danger—Angus, as Laird of Broch Clachan, stood his friend and his safety was therefore guaranteed. But Eilidh could not predict what unpleasantness might occur if the tenants realised who he was. Yes, best for everyone if he was simply Mr Wood, Isabella's brother.

Max stood by Eilidh's side, watching with avid interest at the land unfolding before him. A strange feeling lurked in the pit of his stomach, quite unlike anything he had ever experienced.

The past fortnight had been exquisite torture as he and Eilidh had spent almost every waking hour together. Occasionally, the ladies would go off together to converse, leaving Angus and Max—and often Cooper—to their own entertainment, and they tended to retire to their cabin earlier than the gentlemen, who would linger on deck on milder evenings, drinking brandy, playing cards and speaking of nothing, while the stars twinkled and the sea whispered and murmured. The entire journey had felt like a world apart, with no connection to humdrum reality.

If I could, I would stay here forever on this boat, with these people.

Yet reality was once more bearing down on him and he had a sense of standing in a doorway between the past and the future. Great-Aunt Morton's legacy had given him endless choices where once he'd had none, and this journey was a welcome opportunity to reflect and consider his options.

Unfortunately, it was also binding him ever more firmly to Miss Eilidh MacDonald, who was out of reach. It was plain to him that while she valued his friendship, and even held some warmth towards him at times, he could never meet her requirements for a husband. While the notion was lowering, he could hardly blame her, for he entirely agreed with her assessment.

He thought of her now with the same fatalism he had until recently considered his lot as a second son of the *ton*. A sense of powerlessness had been his sorry existence for most of his life—except at sea, where he could work with the waves and the wind to go where he wished.

These past two weeks had been an idyll, a never-to-be-repeated sojourn with Eilidh, Isabella, Angus and Cooper—the four people in the world who were most important to him. And two of them he had met only this year. He shook his head slightly, recognising it felt in his heart as though he had known the MacDonalds forever. And with Isabella soon to be married and Cooper let go, everything was changing.

This journey had been deeply personal in so many ways—not simply his affinity with his companions but also the timing, coming so soon after his unexpected inheritance. His life was at a crossroads and he needed time to consider his options.

There was also Lidistrome. Having wrested the estate from his brother's careless possession, he had given little thought to the implications. While he had promised Freddy not to sell in his lifetime, he had every intention of bequeathing the place to Angus and Isabella's children, if that would be the right thing to do. He had also briefly discussed with Angus his willingness to send funds for any necessary maintenance. Angus, he recalled, had given a wry smile, saying only, 'As to that, you must make your own assessment about what is needed, for you will visit the estate soon.'

Not this soon.

Max had had no expectation that they would make landfall in the place itself. Eilidh raised an arm, pointing to the head of the bay.

'Lidistrome,' she said simply, and Max's gut twisted. His eyes tried to take in everything at once—the bronze and green landscape, the vegetation a mix of spring grass, heather and bracken. Cottages and barns huddling near the small slipway. A large yellowish manor house standing proudly behind them, on a slight rise. 'That is An Taigh Buidhe,' Eilidh added softly. 'The Yellow House.' A smile danced in her eyes. 'We are nothing if not plain speaking in Benbecula.'

'Max! A hand, if you please!' It was Cooper, distracting him from the spell of Eilidh's humour-filled gaze. 'We shall drop anchor here and take the rowing boat through the shallows.'

Working with Cooper, Angus and the crew, they soon had the yacht anchored and secured and the rowing boat lowered over the side, along with a ladder of wooden slats and strong rope. Cooper gave the three crewmen one final lecture about the quiet traditional community they were about to mix with, including a stern warning about avoiding drinking, swearing or any notion of propositioning the respectable, virtuous young ladies of the island. The crew would continue to sleep in the yacht, taking turns to go ashore during the day. Angus had invited Cooper to the Broch as his guest, and Max marvelled again at the easy mixing of the classes. Naturally, he saw Cooper as an equal—he always had—but for a servant to be the guest of a laird was remarkable.

Max descended to the rowing boat, then assisted Isabella down the unsteady ladder. Thankfully the time they'd spent on boats over the years under Cooper's tutelage served them well and there were no mishaps. Angus and Eilidh followed, and soon they were approaching the slipway at

Lidistrome. The locals were out in numbers, and Angus and Eilidh were greeted with smiles and clear affection.

Angus switched to English. 'May I introduce Calum Bán Laing and Donald Iain Laing, both of Lidistrome. Their family has fished these waters for generations. These are our new friends from England, Mr Maximilian Wood and Miss Isabella Wood. And this is John Cooper, an Islay man who has spent some years in England.' He beckoned more people forward. 'Max, Isabella, Cooper, here is Mrs MacKinnon and her son Alasdair. And this is Ronald MacLean and his wife Kenina. And may I also introduce you to…'

Max smiled, and bowed, and desperately tried to remember at least some of the names of the fishing families. Thankfully, years of practising *la politesse* in drawing rooms and ballrooms had sharpened his attention to such matters, and he and Isabella acquitted themselves creditably. Cooper, an Islander himself, was immediately quizzed at length in Gaelic, and Eilidh whispered to Max and Isabella that the locals were exploring Cooper's lineage and connections.

Not so different from the ton, *then.*

They made their way up the slipway and towards the cottages, leaving Searlas and Mary to supervise the unloading of the trunks. Calum Bán explained in English that his other son, Calum Óg, had gone to alert the Broch of their Laird's return, and that the other fishermen were currently out at sea. After supping tea and eating fresh oysters and freshly baked oatcakes with delicious yellow butter, all the while exchanging pleasantries with the Lidistrome folk, Angus suggested they take a walk about the area to stretch their legs, since they were still swaying from two weeks of being mostly at sea.

This was met with both humour and understanding, and soon afterwards the five of them set out with Angus leading the way, everyone ascending a narrow path up the grassy hill in single file. Reaching the top, they turned first to gaze towards the water, the vista before them spreading for miles in all directions. The narrow natural harbour with Max's yacht moored halfway out. The land enclosing it on both sides, as if in a welcoming embrace. The grey-blue sea beyond melding into a huge, cloud-plump sky.

'It is so beautiful!' Isabella murmured. Angus took her hand, responding that he had hoped she would find it so.

Max himself found he was quite speechless. Never could he have anticipated a vista so exquisite. The colours—mainly greys, blues, browns and greens— merged in a palette of perfection. The sounds of nature surrounded them—the call of birds, the susurration of the gentle breeze and the endless murmur of the sea below. And the scents! A salty ocean tang mingling with sweetness and sharpness from the spring vegetation and rich soil all around them, and occasionally a whiff of smoke from the cottages below. The Islanders had explained their fuel was dried turf, not wood, and as Max looked about he understood the reality of Eilidh's previous comments about the lack of trees on the Islands. There was nothing taller than a waist-high bush, and yet the whole place was teeming with colour and life.

As he watched, a heron flew past, flapping lazily and with perfect grace. Following it with his eyes until it disappeared to his left, he was aware of a contented stillness within him—a novel feeling, and profoundly welcome.

Vaguely, he became aware that Eilidh was watching him. His gaze met hers. 'You like it?' she asked softly.

He swallowed, nodding, then cleared his throat. 'I knew it would be beautiful, but I never expected—' his arm swept out to indicate the view before them '—this.'

Cooper also seemed to be particularly moved, which was hardly to be wondered at. 'I cannot tell you how happy I am to be back in the Hebrides after so long,' he declared huskily, 'and in the company of you two!'

At this, Isabella spontaneously wrapped the older man in an embrace and Max, moved beyond measure, joined them briefly, wrapping his arms around them both.

'Your mother would be delighted,' Cooper murmured, his voice slightly muffled, and Max's heart burned with…*something*. Something unexpected.

Eilidh. Cooper. This place.

It was causing strange feelings within him. Things he had never felt before. Things he could not even begin to put into words.

Turning, they walked together in silence towards the Taigh Buidhe, Max looking all about at the rolling hills dotted with cottages, livestock and the same green-bronze vegetation. As they neared the house, what had seemed from a distance an impressive manor house showed signs of dilapidation. Broken windows. Lichen and moss. Holes in the roof.

That means damp.

Max grimaced. His head was telling him it would be a waste of money to rescue the place. And yet something within him—something illogical but heartfelt—wanted to do just that.

The house was beautiful—well-proportioned and solid, the colour not a bright yellow but a warm and mellow golden-amber, the hue of sunlit honey. There was a small portico over the front door and two rows of tall sixteen-paned windows.

It looks dejected, thought Max somewhat fancifully.

They walked around to the rear, Max noting all the signs of the lack of care that his brother had presided over. But Freddy had not needed the house, for he'd never intended to visit. It was, surely, not unreasonable to let it slide in the circumstances. And yet Max sensed a profound sadness about the place, mainly because it was easy to see how beautiful the house had been at one time. How beautiful it could be again with a little love and care—and money.

Behind the house were more buildings—cottages showing signs of habitation, as well as varied sheds and barns. The yard was neat and well-swept, and there was smoke coming from one of the cottage chimneys.

'Angus!' A man emerged from the cottage, his face creased with age and his shuffling gait denoting his advanced years. His clothes—full Highland dress like the fishermen—were neat as a pin, and he carried himself with quiet dignity. He added a question in Gaelic.

Angus grimaced, replying in the same language before adding in English, 'My friends, allow me to introduce Andrew Donald McIntyre, known as Anndra an Cú. He has lived here all his life and wishes to know if the…er…"Burtenshaw bastard" has given back the land. I have indicated that some progress was made, though there is more to be done.' He turned back to the elderly man. 'Anndra, we have brought some English friends, and another—a long-lost Islay man.'

Following the niceties, the conversation then inevitably diverted to Cooper and his connections, to Max's great relief. Of course he had known that the Burtenshaws would not be well-liked here, for Angus had explained that the needs of the Lidistrome people had not been met for a very long time.

'The Burtenshaw bastard...'

Looking about him, he could see the reason for their anger. While the area was well tended and clean, there were signs of neglect that only money could mend. Swallowing hard, Max suddenly felt a wave of...of *fear*, almost. Fear mixed with guilt. Acquiring Lidistrome had been in a sense simply a *move* to him—a trump in cards, almost. A chance for him to help his friends while pulling a fast one on Freddy. For the first time, he was understanding in his gut that this was a real place, and that real people now depended on him.

'Eilidh...' She was, as always, by his side.

'Yes?' Was that sympathy in her eyes?

Lord, I am a fool!

'How many people live in Lidistrome?'

'The whole estate? Including all the farmers and fishermen and their families?'

He nodded, almost dreading the answer.

'Not as many as twenty years ago. Not as many as even two years ago.' She thought for a moment. 'More than a hundred. Probably closer to a hundred and fifty.'

'A hundred and fifty people.' He closed his eyes briefly. He owned a yacht. He had owned a dog once— a dog who had lived to the ripe old age of seventeen before breathing her last on a sunny porch in Sussex. But he had never—*never*—been responsible for the welfare of another human being.

Can I do this? How can I do this?

He swallowed hard. 'Very well. I should welcome your advice. Yours and Angus's, if you are willing to give it.'

She squeezed his arm. 'We are more than willing, Max. You are not alone in this.'

He nodded, his eyes meeting hers. A silence charged with meaning passed between them, making his breath catch and his heart thunder.

Blinking, she shook her head, adding lightly, 'And you need not do anything today.' She made a face. 'The problems in Lidistrome have built up slowly over many years. Another week will make little difference.'

'Lidistrome... The word does not sound very Gaelic.'

She raised an eyebrow. 'An astute observation. Some of the place names in the Islands are Gaelic, while others were given to us by the Norsemen.'

'Vikings? Truly?'

She nodded. 'When the seas were the highways, the Islands were strategically important.' She shrugged. 'Now the rest of the world sees us as unimportant, and often forgets our very existence.' She swept a hand towards the back of the house where the render was peeling in places, displaying raw stone beneath, like skin and bone. 'As you see.'

Isabella had wandered across to a large stone building and was peering through the small window. 'What is in here, if I may be so bold as to pry?'

'That is the fancy furniture from the house, *a chaileag.*' Anndra made his way slowly across, the others following. 'Once the roof started to leak there was nothing for it. I could not let all of the fine stuff decay—it just would not have been right, and this barn is still watertight to this day.' There was an air of pride in his tone, and Max joined in the general praise for the old man's achievement in protecting the furniture. 'Everything is covered in dust sheets,' Anndra continued, 'and gets checked and cleaned once a year. I clean three pieces a week, I do. It is good to keep busy, even though sometimes there seems to be no point in it.' He sighed. 'I am old now, and there will be no one to look after it when I am gone. Both my sons are gone to Canada, you see. Nothing for them here.'

Angus placed a hand on his shoulder. 'Things may change, Anndra. Keep the faith, and I shall call back to see you in a few days.'

The old man eyed him keenly. 'I have heard that before, *a thighearna*. I shall believe it when I see it with my own two eyes.'

'What is his income?' Max asked as they walked towards the gardens. 'What I mean to say is, what is the *source* of his income?'

'Burtenshaw,' Angus answered tersely. 'That is to say, *you* now. The McIntyres stayed on as official custodians of An Taigh Buidhe after their laird was stripped of his ownership, their aim being to preserve the possessions and traditions of their chief, but over the years they were worn down. Anndra pays no rent and is supposed to have a wage as caretaker, but Burtenshaw's factors have reduced the wages almost every quarter. He lives on a pittance now, and the fisher families down below bring him food.'

Max shook his head. That any human being should be reduced to such penury—never mind such a wise and dignified person as Anndra—was shocking. That such injustice had been meted out by his own brother, whether conscious of it or not, left him feeling sick to his stomach. 'He called you something like *aheerna*. What does that mean?'

'*A thighearna*.' Angus corrected his pronunciation a little. 'It means laird. I may not be *his* laird, but he knows me well.'

Anndra had bid Angus take his guests to view the gardens, such as they were, and once again Max felt a sense of sadness to see how rundown the whole place was. Anndra grew vegetables for his own consumption in the field behind the cottages, but everywhere else was a tangle of overgrown bushes and plants, signs of a once-beautiful series of gardens. There were chrysalises aplenty beneath the leaves, hinting at plentiful butterflies in the months to come, but the more delicate plants had been swarmed out by their more robust neighbours. Even in this one area alone, there was a clear need for radical work, sensitively done, a need to thin the plants without harming the cocoons.

At one side was a south-facing double wall, which Angus explained had contained furnaces for the cultivation of exotic fruits such as oranges and lemons—a luxury that the locals could now only access through paying outrageous sums to growers in mainland Scotland. Recalling the extensive orangery at Burtenshaw House and the ease with which Max had enjoyed the availability of citrus fruits, Max felt a little shamefaced at how much he had taken such luxuries for granted.

'Can you not grow oranges at Broch Clachan?' Isabella asked, and Angus shrugged.

'I suppose we could build something like this but, honestly, there is never the time for such a project.' He sent Max a wicked glance. 'Far better if An Taigh Buidhe restored their hot wall!'

Max opened his mouth, then closed it again. His mind was awhirl, and he had absolutely no idea how to respond. Soon afterwards, calls from below let them know the carts had arrived, so they called to bid Anndra farewell, then made their way carefully down the slope. Their trunks were already being loaded on to the three carts and they each hopped up into seats, greeting the drivers with warmth. Angus, naturally, helped Isabella up beside him in the lead cart, while Cooper jumped up on the second cart with Searlas and Mary, leaving Max and Eilidh to travel together in the last vehicle.

'Carts?' he asked with a raised eyebrow.

She shrugged. 'We do have a carriage, as does our cousin Alasdair, but carts are more stable for short journeys like this. The roads, as you are about to discover, are fairly poor in places, particularly in—' She broke off.

'In Lidistrome?'

She gave no answer, but eyed him steadily. Shaking his head, he could not prevent a sigh.

'But today is not the day to worry about such matters. I simply want to show you Benbecula. May I do so?'

He agreed, pushing his worries to the back of his mind. To be fair, the next hour was delightful. They traversed the track at a steady pace, Eilidh pointing out landmarks along the way, including Rueval, the tall hill to the north, leaning protectively over Lidistrome and the Broch Clachan lands. 'My cousin Alasdair lives to the north-east,' Eilidh explained. 'He married an English lady last year, and they are expecting their first baby in the summer.'

'An English lady, eh?' He sent her a sideways glance. 'So Angus will not be the first?'

'Indeed, no! Two such marriages in a row, after generations of Islanders marrying no one who was not Scottish.' She thought for a moment. 'I suspect Alasdair's marriage to Lydia meant Angus gave himself permission to act when Isabella was threatened with forced marriage to the Dishonourable Geoffrey. In that sense it was *precedent* rather than coincidence, you know.'

He did know, and they talked again about their hopes that Isabella would settle well in Broch Clachan. 'I shall visit regularly, you understand,' Max murmured, 'for Isabella is dear to me.'

She flashed him a smile. 'I know. It is one of the many things I like about you. Your closeness with Isabella is very like me and Angus, I think.'

Many things?

'So there are things you do like about me?' he asked lightly. Then, fearful of her answer, he quickly added, 'How soon will the wedding be, do you think?'

Her eyes danced. 'If I am not mistaken, Angus intends to have the banns read for the first time this very Sunday, which means they can wed in a little over four weeks.'

'Not long, then.'

And afterwards, I must leave. Return to my real life.

'No, but still a lot more civilised than your brother's rushed plans for her,' she retorted.

He frowned. 'I meant no criticism, Eilidh. They may marry as soon as they wish, with my blessing. But will it be long enough for the people here to know her?'

A slight colour had flushed her cheeks. 'I know not. But she will have years for that.'

'The rest of her life.'

She nodded, and Max was conscious suddenly of just how remote this place was. Would Isabella truly manage, so far away from the *modistes* and ballrooms of London? Why, she could not enjoy so much as an orange or some lemonade—a commonplace treat among the *ton*.

Eilidh raised an arm. 'There it is. Broch Clachan.' Her voice broke with emotion, and abruptly his own throat was tight as he understood how moved she was. The building—in fact a cluster of wings and outbuildings around a massive, thick round tower—looked as though it had grown from the landscape itself. If An

Taigh Buidhe had been built to stand out, then surely the Broch had been designed so as to blend in. It must have been constructed from local stone a very long time ago, for it melded into the rocks and stones of the island as though it were part of nature itself.

'How old is it?'

'We have honestly no idea. Old.'

She said no more, clearly overcome by strong emotion. It took great self-restraint, but Max managed not to cover her hand with his. A few moments later, they drove beneath a stone archway into a busy yard. Dozens of people were milling about and the place was alive with activity. There were sheep penned in one corner and chickens underfoot. The contrast between the Broch and The Yellow House could not have been stronger. Here was life. An Taigh Buidhe was, if not quite dead, then in a very deep sleep.

Jumping down, he offered her a hand. Ahead, Angus was embracing various people, shaking the hands of others and generally being welcomed like the Prodigal Son. The same crowd then descended upon Eilidh, and Max could not help grinning at the delight and genuine warmth with which the MacDonalds were being greeted.

The main door to the tower was open and a moment later a couple emerged, the lady clearly expecting a baby. Max's assumptions about their identity were confirmed a few moments later when Angus introduced them as his cousin Alasdair, Laird of Ardmore, and his wife, described as Lydia MacDonald, Lady of Ardmore. Lydia wrapped Eilidh in a long hug and, when they parted, both sets of eyes were suspiciously bright.

This woman is important to Eilidh.

'Oh, stuff!' the lady declared inelegantly as Angus gave her full title.

She is English, of course. Max recalled.

'Call me Lydia,' she continued, 'for Angus in his letter described you as friends, and his friends are my friends!' She made her curtsey with surprising grace considering her condition, but there was clear speculation in her gaze as she eyed Max and Isabella. 'Angus, Eilidh, we have been here for four days, as we did not know exactly when you would return. I am desperate to know if your quest met with success!'

Angus glanced briefly at Max, who shrugged. 'Let us go inside, for I am aching for the sight of my own hearth!' He kept up a running commentary as they entered, then paused to formally greet his housekeeper, senior manservant and steward.

'We received Searlas's letter, *a thighearna,*' the housekeeper declared calmly, having followed Angus's lead and switched to English. 'I have prepared rooms for your guests, as required, and organised baths for the ladies—we have already begun bringing the water upstairs. You gentlemen will need to wait until tomorrow. Dinner at six?'

'Perfect!' Angus was beaming with delight. He turned to the others. 'May I suggest we meet in the dining room just before six? No doubt we are all ready for some solitude and the chance to freshen up.'

There was general agreement, and Max allowed himself to be taken away by a serving maid who would show him to his chamber. Unable to help himself, he stole one last glance at Eilidh. She was looking his way and gave him a bright smile. It was good to see her happy.

This is where she belongs.

Chapter Eleven

*S*olitude.

Having enjoyed a strip wash and helped himself to the fine wine, fresh oatcakes and cheese awaiting him in his chamber, Max wandered again across to the window. His room was in the main tower and the outer wall curved slightly, the deep-cut window embrasure complete with a cushioned chair at exactly the right height to enjoy the magnificent vista before him. His view was to the east, with Rueval to his left and the sparkling sea in the distance. The land between was part Broch Clachan, part Lidistrome. This was the first time he had been truly alone in a fortnight, and his mind and heart welcomed the calm quietness within.

Over the years, he had attended many parties in country houses, and in some ways the routine was familiar—the housekeeper, the offer of baths, finding one's way about—yet never before had he looked upon a landscape so different from the wooded vales of England. Hearing Gaelic spoken everywhere was a reminder that he was literally in another country. Thankfully everyone seemed to speak English too.

I must learn some basic pleasantries in Gaelic.

Never before had he looked upon land he owned, was responsible for. Foolishly, he had avoided thinking of Lidistrome since acquiring it, being altogether more focused on Eilidh, on Isabella and Angus, and on enjoying a sea journey unfettered by gloomy reflections on his limited life.

In his head, he ran through the old options again. Lawyer. Doctor. Clergyman. Soldier. Strangely, all were now unnecessary, given his level of wealth. Once again he needed no profession, this time because—unless he was extremely foolish with his money—he would never need to earn a living. He was certainly wealthy enough to marry, and yet he had no desire to rush straight back to London to assess this Season's debutantes. The Marriage Mart held no appeal, and he knew exactly why.

I need to allow my fixation with Eilidh to run its course. He grimaced. *It will not be easy to forget her.*

Squaring his shoulders, he reminded himself of the truth. Despite his strong feelings towards her, she did not esteem him in the same way and, besides, she clearly needed to marry an Islander, for no man should be cruel enough to take her from this place. He sighed, turning away from the window. It was time to dress for dinner.

Eilidh made her way to the dining room a little early. As she walked along hallways and down solid stone stairs, she delighted in the well-loved familiarity of every nook and cranny.

Home!

Truly, there was nothing like it. Here she had been born, had learned to walk and talk and, later, to read and write. Here she had mourned the loss of her parents—first her mother, then a short few years later, her father. On that sad day, Angus had been ready to take on the mantle of Laird, a role he had been prepared for all his life.

Unlike Max. The man clearly had no understanding of his responsibilities, although, judging by his shocked reactions at An Taigh Buidhe, he at least understood that the situation had not been managed well by his brother as absentee landlord.

He needs to meet his tenants.

'Eilidh!' Alasdair and Lydia were already in the dining room and they all embraced again.

'It is so lovely to be home, and to be with you both again.'

Before Eilidh could respond the door opened behind her, admitting Max. After the exchange of greetings, Lydia took Eilidh's hand.

'You must tell me all about London,' she declared, her eyes shining. 'Was it different to your expectations? Did you visit some of the places I told you of?'

'I did! I know my way about Piccadilly, and the parks, and all of the bazaars. I have trunks full of shopping, I assure you! We also went to soirées, and the theatre, and even a private *ton* ball. And,' she finished with a flourish, 'we visited the Tower of London!'

Alasdair was frowning. 'But you are happy to be home? You have no intention of making London your home?'

Conscious of Max to her right, Eilidh spoke carefully. 'London is certainly a fascinating place, and we met some wonderful people there. But no, I could not survive away from the Islands, I think.' The very thought of it made her shudder. 'How Cooper lasted so long in exile I shall never understand.' She turned to Max, anxious to send the conversation in a different direction. 'Did he ever speak of it?'

Max thought for a moment, and she took the opportunity to observe him. He was dressed as for a formal dinner in England, and he looked so handsome that her heart turned over just standing close to him.

'He sometimes seemed sad, it is true, but he spoke little of his origins. Perhaps not every Islander is as connected to the place as you are?'

They all denied this, instantly and vociferously, and he was forced to concede, with hands up and a short laugh, 'Very well! I sincerely apologise for daring to suggest such a thing!'

His eyes were dancing with humour and Eilidh slapped him playfully on the arm. 'Do not do so again! You should know better, Max!'

Turning back to Lydia, she noted a speculative gleam in her friend's eyes and was powerless to prevent a slow flush coming over her. 'Anyway,' she said in a rush, 'How do you, Lydia? Are you well?'

'I am, and thank you. I was very tired for a couple of months, but now I am full of vigour again. And a good thing too for we are engaged on some major repairs to one wing of the castle. Another shipment of wood is due this week, and the hammering will begin again.' She rolled her eyes.

Max's gaze had sharpened with interest. 'I had noted the paucity of trees on the island. So you import wood when needed? From where, might I ask?'

Despite looking a little puzzled, Alasdair answered with alacrity. 'From a merchant in Ullapool. He has suppliers throughout the Highlands and can generally deliver a cargo of wood in a matter of weeks.'

Max nodded slowly. 'I see.'

Eilidh's heart was skipping.

Does he mean to take charge of matters himself?

During their brief conversation on the day that Isabella had almost been forced to wed, Max had indicated that he would pass money to Angus to address the needs of Lidistrome, but was he thinking twice about it? Angus could, naturally, do so, but it would be much better if he could concentrate on the Broch, with Max taking responsibility for his own lands and people. The tiniest spark of hope flared within her—a spark that hinted at miracles and impossible things.

Ruthlessly, she turned her attention away from it.

No! He is of the ton. *And, unlike Isabella, he is here for a short visit only.*

She needed to protect herself—protect her heart—as best she could, guard herself against the day when he would depart. A day that was only a few weeks away.

Isabella joined them then, as did Cooper. He was in Broch Clachan as friend to Max and Isabella, and here he was no man's servant. His status here would be equal to those he had once served, yet Eilidh was confident Max and Isabella would have no issue with it.

Finally, Angus bustled in, with apologies for keeping them waiting. There was much to be done, he explained, making it clear that many people had demanded his time and attention during the past couple of hours.

Eilidh had had a similar experience, having been accosted by both the housekeeper and the cook almost as soon as the initial round of greetings had subsided. Both were competent women who had managed perfectly well in her absence, but they had been keen to update her and seek her advice on innumerable household matters. After addressing their most urgent issues, she had promised them her full attention on the morrow.

Soon Isabella will take over from me as the Lady of Broch Clachan.

The notion was a little strange, but she was determined to ensure she allowed Isabella her place while supporting the new Lady as she grew into the role.

Heading to her chamber, Eilidh had enjoyed a warm bath, and had decided to leave her hair half-down for dinner—a perfectly acceptable coiffure for young island women, even for a formal dinner such as this. After months of having her hair constantly pinned up, it was a relief to let her riotous red curls fall free, and to secure only the side sections in jewelled combs.

I am Eilidh Ruadh again.

Red-haired Eilidh.

Already she had been greeted many times by her Broch name—a necessity to distinguish her from the other Eilidhs living here and throughout Benbecula.

When Max had joined them just now, she had noted the way his gaze had lingered on her tresses, how warm the expression in his dark eyes. It had lit a flame in the pit of her stomach.

This is how he looked at me when we kissed.

Unfortunately, she feared Lydia might have noted his expression too and anticipated some questioning later from her friend.

Dinner was a pleasant experience, with Alasdair and Lydia keen to hear of their London adventures, and to get to know the newcomers a little. Taking their time over each course, they sat together all through the evening, their conversation enhanced by wine, laughter and camaraderie. By silent agreement, they all skirted around the issue of Lidistrome until after the boards had been cleared, the whisky toast completed and the servants had departed.

In addition, Angus had yet to mention his intention to wed Isabella, but his plan seemed sensible to Eilidh.

Following a long evening together, Lydia and Alasdair could be in no doubt as to how delightful Isabella was.

They like Max too I think.

Well, how could they not? This evening he had demonstrated all his best qualities, as had Isabella—intelligence, wit, humour and kind-heartedness.

Once again, Eilidh was struck by how different Max and Isabella were to their older brother.

They favour their mother.

The former Lady Burtenshaw must have been a special person. And of course they'd had Cooper—an Islander—as a guide all their lives. Cooper had remained serene and composed throughout the evening, contributing to their conversation with dry wit and insightful commentary. Indeed, Eilidh could not recall ever seeing him agitated about anything.

He is a good man.

They sat on in the growing dusk, as candles flickered on whisky glasses and mellow yellow light draped them in contented affinity. Eilidh had been unable to resist meeting Max's gaze at times and it was not simply because he was seated opposite her, next to Lydia. A few times she had noticed her friend draw him into one-to-one conversation, as she had with Cooper, but she wondered if Lydia suspected Eilidh's partiality for him.

Partiality?

It seemed too small a word, too tame, for the way she felt about him. Thinking of him made her burn fiercely inside—with passion, with affection and occasionally with frustration. Why could he not have been an Islander? He was so *nearly* perfect. If he had been raised here, he would have…

Dragging her gaze away, she directed a comment to Cooper. There was no point in what-ifs. Max would not understand the pull of the Islands, was not born to be the true Laird of Lidistrome, could not be made to stay where he felt he did not belong.

Cooper seemed to sense her agitation. 'All will be well, lass,' he murmured. 'My Max and my Isabella are here now. Let it go. Let the air and the sea and the land work its magic on them.'

Before she could ask him to explain further, Angus cleared his throat, drawing all eyes to him.

'Alasdair,' he began. 'Lydia.' His tone was formal, garnering their full attention. 'As you know, I travelled to London with Eilidh in an attempt to persuade Lord Burtenshaw to sell us the land. We did not succeed in doing so, and yet things may work out in an unexpectedly satisfying manner. We met many people during our stay, some of whom we liked more than others. And we made some true friends—the three people you have met today. You already know that Max and Isabella are brother and sister. Well, I can tell you that their older brother Frederick is none other than Lord Burtenshaw himself!'

Alasdair's jaw dropped, while Lydia gasped in shock. 'But they are so amiable!' she declared, before flushing. 'My apologies, I did not mean to suggest…that is, I…'

'What my wife may be trying to say,' Alasdair managed, his expression shuttered, 'is that it is difficult to reconcile the treatment of Lidistrome with the demeanour and good sense clearly demonstrated by you and your sister.' His comment was directed at Max, who grimaced ruefully.

'Your observation is entirely justified,' he responded quietly. 'I cannot know what information my brother had, but I certainly had no notion of the true situation until very recently.'

'And may we assume from your decision to travel

here, that you mean to address these matters on your brother's behalf?' Alasdair, clearly used to taking a lead, wasted no time in coming to the point.

'Ah. To be fair, our decision to travel to Benbecula was related to—' he glanced at Angus '—another matter entirely. But now that we are here, I mean to assess the situation very carefully, and do what I may to put things right.' He eyed the Laird of Ardmore steadily. 'You should understand that my brother has allowed the estate to pass into my ownership very recently.'

'I see.' Alasdair's expression suggested that he did not see, not at all, but Eilidh was simply glad that the truth was out and that what Max said suggested he was aware of the responsibilities he now carried.

But he will be able to achieve little in a few short weeks.

She had no time to think further on this, for Angus had risen to his feet.

'As to the other matter Max refers to…' he began, nodding to Isabella, who rose to join him. 'I wish to let you know that Isabella has agreed to marry me. I count myself the luckiest of men.' He kissed her hand, and Alasdair and Lydia made haste to congratulate the pair.

They are concerned, Eilidh realised. *And why should they not be? They do not yet know Isabella as we do.*

'The banns will be read from Sunday, and we shall marry next month.'

Everyone had now risen from their seats and the next few moments were spent in embraces, exclamations and hand shaking. Max and Cooper, wearing identical grins, joined in the general hurrahs but, beneath it all, Eilidh knew they all had a long way to go to assuage Alasdair's and Lydia's well-meant reservations. Angus was to marry the sister of the hated Lord Burtenshaw, a woman he had known for only a matter of months.

Biting her lip, Eilidh recalled Alasdair's first marriage, contracted in haste while under the influence of infatuation. His young wife, Hester, had never adapted to island life and had died in a carriage accident while running away to Edinburgh, having abandoned Alasdair and their young daughter, Mairead. It had taken Alasdair a long time to recover, and even then, he had fought his attraction to Lydia, who had been Mairead's governess, for the longest time.

Lydia has proved it is possible to adapt, to become part of the community here.

And both Lydia and Eilidh would be by Isabella's side as she learned to adapt to island life.

Once again, Eilidh's fevered imagination began applying the same arguments to Max, and once again, she ruthlessly pulled her attention away from that subject. Max had no reason to even *try* to live in Benbecula long-term. It was clear he had not even given Lidistrome any thought before today.

They retired soon afterwards, Angus promising their English visitors a tour of the Broch lands on the morrow. Max bent over Eilidh's bare hand as they made their goodnights, and as she made her way upstairs, her skin tingled yet with the memory of his kiss. Foolishly, she refused to wash it off before bedtime, and covered the spot with her other hand as she drifted off to sleep. Max was here, in the Broch, and the knowledge brought her a giddy happiness that was as intense as it was inappropriate.

Tuesday 30th April

After spending the early part of the day with the female staff, Eilidh joined the ladies in the airy, comfortable morning room that was her favourite place in the

Broch. She had informed the housekeeper and cook of Angus's upcoming nuptials, as was proper, and they had promised to speak with Searlas and the steward to make all the necessary preparations. Lydia, citing her slow, ungainly gait, had declined the offer to take part in the tour, and so Isabella and Eilidh joined her for tea in the hour before they were due to set off.

'So tell me, Isabella, about your courtship with Angus, for I wish to enjoy all the details!' Lydia's warm smile invited confidences, and before long Isabella and Eilidh were regaling her with all the details, finally reaching the part where Lord Burtenshaw had informed Isabella of her upcoming marriage to a man she detested.

Lydia was shocked, and said so in the strongest terms. 'I am sorry to say so, Isabella, but your brother should not have done it. We women have little enough agency as it is. The very least we may expect is the freedom to choose a husband!'

Isabella grimaced. 'It pains me to criticise my own brother, but I fear I must agree with you. Freddy values duty and reputation above all else. My happiness or lack of it was of no relevance to him. And I could never have been happy with Mr Barnstable.'

'*Barnstable?* Never say he meant you to marry the Dishonourable Geoffrey!'

Eilidh's jaw dropped. 'You know Barnstable? Ah, perhaps from the time when you were a governess in London?'

'Know him? He propositioned me—tried to kiss me in front of my young charges. He had the effrontery to offer me jewels if I would become his mistress! The man is a menace!'

'Indeed he is!' declared Isabella. 'Quite why Freddy

thought he was an appropriate husband I shall never understand.' She grinned. 'I refused to say "I will" during the wedding, and soon afterwards Angus arrived to declare himself.'

Eilidh noted a slight crease on Lydia's forehead. 'I can see,' the former governess said carefully, 'how Angus was a much better prospect, even if he does live far, far away from London society.'

'Oh, please do not misunderstand me! I was already in love with Angus, but had given up all hope of ever being his wife. He thought it too much to ask of me to live here forever. He still does, to be honest.' Isabella bit her lip. 'He told me of Alasdair's first wife.'

Eilidh held her breath. The shadow of Hester's unhappiness hung over them all.

Lydia seemed to choose her words with care. 'Naturally, I never met Hester, but I believe she was deeply unhappy, and unable to adjust to the remoteness and harshness of life here. Perhaps she also struggled to see the beauty of this place, or to feel the warmth of the people.' She smiled. 'But Hester need not be your pattern-card, Isabella. I am proof that a person may indeed adapt. I do love it here,' she finished softly.

'Thank you!' Isabella's eyes were suspiciously bright. 'With both of you to assist me, I mean to do my very best to become an island lady. I shall work hard, and not complain about the lack of lemonade, and Angus is already teaching me some Gaelic. *Madainn mhath*,' she added carefully. '*Tapadh leibh. Slàn leibh.*'

Good morning. Thank you. Goodbye.

'Excellent!' Eilidh clapped her hands. 'I have no doubt you will learn quickly, for you have a good mind. Lydia has been here for less than two years, and her Gaelic is almost as good as that of a native speaker!'

'I should not go so far,' Lydia replied with a shake of her head. 'I shall be learning forever, I think. And we do occasionally buy citrus from the mainland, you know!' They laughed at this, then Lydia added in a more sober tone, 'Will you not miss your family and friends, Isabella?'

She frowned. 'I shall miss Max, of course. And Cooper, if he accompanies Max back to England. And while it will be strange not to see Freddy and Prudence and their children again, I confess it does not concern me overmuch. As for friends, you know well that I found little in common with the other debutantes, Eilidh. You are the closest friend I have had, and you will still be with me.'

'And I too,' Lydia declared firmly. 'We shall all be great friends, I know.' She took a breath. 'Now, tell me about Max, for he interests me greatly.'

Isabella's face lit up. 'He is the best of brothers! He has not been well-served by being a second son, but has recently come into an inheritance from our dear Great-Aunt Morton, who died a few weeks ago. It is how he was able to buy Lidistrome from Freddy.'

Eilidh was suddenly busy with her reticule, as she feared a tell-tale flush from Lydia's knowing glances.

'So will he sell to Angus, then?'

'No, for Freddy forbade it.'

'Forbade it? But why?'

Isabella explained in a halting manner, as the story once again did not show Freddy in the best light.

'I see,' said Lydia. 'So Max will retain Lidistrome for life. Does he mean to settle here, like you, Isabella? For if he is to restore Lidistrome he would be better living here.'

'Oh, no! At least, I do not believe so.' She cast a

glance at Eilidh. 'He has not had much time to consider his options, you understand.'

'I see,' Lydia said again, and Eilidh shuffled uncomfortably. Lydia saw far too much for her liking!

Thankfully, the clock on the mantel came to her rescue. 'We must go, for the gentlemen will be waiting.' Rising, she embraced Lydia, then she and Isabella made their way to the hall, donning outdoor boots and warm shawls while waiting for the gentlemen to join them.

Max had spent a fascinating morning with the two lairds. Having accepted Angus's invitation to join their meeting, he had remained largely silent as the men had discussed matters relating to their own estates, and to the island as a whole. Matters of finance, of support for tenants, of plans they had put in place over the winter and could be acted upon now the better weather was upon them. Alasdair's repairs to his own castle was one such project, involving the coordination of materials and craftsmen as well as significant disturbance to the members of the castle household who resided in that particular wing.

'We have had to find places for entire families to live for the next two months.' Alasdair sighed. 'Lydia has been wonderful in helping organise everything, but every nook and cranny in Ardmore, including all of the guest bedchambers, has been taken up by the displaced staff and their families.' He turned to Max. 'I should like to invite you and Cooper to stay once the work is completed, which should be in early July.' He grimaced. 'Then again, it might possibly be August.'

Max expressed gratitude for the kind offer, but inwardly he knew it was likely he would be long gone by then. His intention was—had always been—to stay until the wedding, no longer. So why then did he suddenly get the strangest urge to stay until summer, to visit Ardmore and enjoy a longer stay on Benbecula?

'Time to go,' Angus announced. 'The ladies will no doubt be waiting for us.' He led the way to the main hall, where Eilidh and Isabella were indeed ready to go. A cart pulled by the same breed of sturdy ponies as yesterday took them part of the way, but the land was so fragmented by myriad ponds and lochs that eventually they bade farewell to the driver and continued on foot. There were tracks to all the farms and cottages, Angus explained, but it was much quicker for them to cut directly across the moorland.

The next few hours were intriguing. Angus introduced his bride to all of his tenants, and Isabella was met with friendly warmth everywhere they went. Watching her, Max could not prevent an occasional stab of envy. She would have a home here, a community to be part of. The Broch staff had been just as welcoming to their new lady, and Max had the strong impression that Angus was a good leader, well-liked and seen as fair in his dealings. Freddy's tenants, in contrast, had always seemed fearful of him.

The cottages and farmhouses on the Broch lands were in a decidedly better state of repair than the fishermen's homes in Lidistrome, and Max once again felt rather ashamed at the actions—or, more accurately, the *inaction*—of the Burtenshaw landlords over at least the last two generations. Angus and Isabella were at the centre of everyone's attention, and Alasdair was clearly well-known to all of the families they visited.

It suited Max perfectly well to be relegated to the rear, where he walked in step with Eilidh. As they explored, she was constantly talking, pointing out land-

marks, naming the various birds, plants and wildflowers
and generally displaying pride in her homeland. He
found himself enthralled not just by the place but by
a new sense of seeing Eilidh fully for the first time—
as herself, far away from the pretension and pretence
of the *ton*.

'I hope you are not irritated by my prattling,' she remarked as they walked back towards the place where
the cart would meet them to return them to the Broch.
'Being here again after being away for so long…it is as
though I am appreciating its beauty anew.'

'I know what you mean,' he offered, looking at her
intently.

*Seeing her here, where she belongs, she is even more
beautiful.*

He shook his head slightly. Until this moment, such
a thing would not have seemed possible.

'You do?' She pursed her lips and he was conscious
of the need to restrain himself yet again, wishing for
nothing more in that moment than to bend and brush
those pink lips with his own. *Eilidh Ruadh*, they called
her here. Red-haired Eilidh.

Shaking himself, he made haste to answer her. 'Er…
yes. Yes, I do. I believe you are seeing it all with what
might be described as fresh eyes. The eyes of someone
who has never seen it before. *My* eyes, perhaps.'

'That is true—' she nodded slowly '—and yet for
me there is also the added layer of meaning because I
know it so well, and it is my home.'

'I can only imagine what it must be like, to be able to
call such a place home.' He gave a cynical laugh. 'The
nearest thing I have to a home is Burtenshaw House or
Freddy's townhouse and, despite my childhood memo-

ries, I no longer belong in either of those places. They are Freddy's now.'

'Your memories are not lost, Max, for they live within you.' Reaching out, she squeezed his hand and instantly he twisted his around to capture hers. They were once again at the back of the group and no one could see, and she allowed her hand to rest in his for almost half a mile. The conversation continued and Max played his part, but his consciousness was almost entirely directed to the woman by his side, and her warm hand in his.

If only this moment could be made to last forever.

By the time they were back in the Broch, Max had made a decision. 'I know we talked of climbing Rueval on Thursday, and I remain committed to that, but…I should like to return to Lidistrome tomorrow,' he announced to the others, 'if it might be arranged.'

'Yes, of course!' Angus was beaming, and was there a glint of approval in Eilidh's eyes?

Only Alasdair's expression remained inscrutable. 'Lydia and I must return to Ardmore, I regret to say. We have been gone long enough. But we can accompany you part of the way.'

The arrangements were confirmed and the conversation then moved on to other matters. For Max, though, as he went through the day and into the evening, at the back of his mind was a constant itch. This was different to his constant awareness of Eilidh, which he would characterise as something between admiration and longing.

This was…this was more like *worry*. A feeling that he was failing the people of Lidistrome. It was an entirely new sensation and, while he disliked it, he recognised it was intimately connected with his new responsibilities. The contrast between the rundown, uncared-for buildings of Lidistrome and the well-maintained dwellings and barns of the Broch families had been striking.

Yes, Anndra and the fishing families kept their homes and areas clean and spruce, but there had been a general air of tiredness about Lidistrome. Tomorrow, with the Broch fresh in his mind, he would visit Lidistrome again—including many of the farming families—and he knew already that what he would discover might prove challenging. He foresaw that after returning home to London, he would have to send money to Angus and Alasdair to make things right, and resolved to do so.

And yet something did not sit right with him, and he knew not what it was.

Chapter Twelve

Wednesday 1st May

Isabella had agreed to spend the day with the house-keeper, exploring the Broch and getting to know the staff a little. Despite Eilidh's attempted reassurance she had remained clearly nervous.

'I just want them to know that Angus did not choose someone totally unsuited to the role,' she had declared as Eilidh was departing to join Max, Angus and Cooper on the trip to Lidistrome. 'I do not speak Gaelic and I do not know your customs here, but surely the training I have had as a young lady may still be of use? I have spent years assisting Prudence with household matters—everything from staff squabbles to supplies and menus.'

'Of course!' Eilidh had made haste to reassure her. 'Our housekeeper is both open-minded and kind-hearted. All will be well.'

In truth, Eilidh was glad to be out of the Broch today, for Isabella needed her place, and time alone with the staff without the Laird's sister in the way. As the cart lumbered steadily towards Lidistrome, she recalled a calm amiability about Isabella during her first days here, despite her understandable nerves earlier. Her friend would do very well.

Isabella's brother was another matter entirely. She stole a sideways glance at him. While he seemed outwardly serene, currently engaged in looking about him, she sensed he was troubled or concerned about something.

I can only hope it is Lidistrome that vexes him.

Lidistrome *needed* to be vexing to the man who now owned it. He needed to feel responsible. To *care*. The wedding of Angus and Isabella was set for the first week in June, and Max would leave soon afterwards. So they had a little more than a month to try and help him to recognise and understand his obligations. While she had no expectation that he would live here, the very least Max could do would be to stay a while and supervise the initial works. Despite her affection for him, Eilidh could not forget he was a second son of the *ton*, abandoned to pleasure and self-indulgence.

Oh, but he could be so much more! I know he could!

For the next several hours, they went from farmhouse to cottage, visiting the Lidistrome tenants and hearing their most pressing complaints. The pattern had a depressing familiarity. The tenants worked hard but were barely managing to scrape together the rents demanded by Burtenshaw's agents. And in the meantime, their homes, barns and farmland became steadily more dilapidated as money that should have gone to essentials was instead diverted to rent.

Throughout, Max did not speak, but his expression grew increasingly grim. By mid-afternoon, as they approached the fisher families' cottages at the slipway, he looked pale, his jaw was set and he was sunk in reflection, speaking to no one and even avoiding glancing at the others.

Cooper had befriended the driver and was chatting away in Gaelic, but in the back of the cart, Max, Eilidh and Angus were entirely silent. Angus caught Eilidh's eye and she shrugged. However painful this was for Max, he needed to understand Lidistrome.

Her chest ached at her own stern thoughts. While the Burtenshaws were entirely responsible for the plight of the Lidistrome tenants, Max himself could not be held liable for the actions of his brother, father and grandfather. And yet her understanding of Max told her he would currently be feeling low, and guilty, and possibly even helpless.

'Max...' Lifting his head, his gaze met hers and the pain in his dark eyes seared her. 'The past is done. You are here now, and you may begin to put things right.'

He nodded, but the bleakness in his expression remained. She would have said more, but a shout from the cottages diverted them all. They had just crested the hill and had clearly been spotted. As they watched, a woman began running up the hill towards them. 'Something is amiss!' declared Angus as the driver spurred the horse into a trot. 'And there is a boat in the loch!'

It was true. A tall sloop was anchored in the deeper part of the sea loch, beyond Max's yacht. Eilidh half rose to see better. 'There is a new rowing boat at the slipway.' Whoever they were, they had already landed.

'*A thighearna!*' The woman, panting, had reached them. 'Burtenshaw's men are evicting Anndra!'

'What?' Angus looked as shocked as Eilidh felt. 'They are there now?'

She nodded, and the driver took off as fast as the horse would allow. Eilidh, holding on to the side of the cart, was horrified. Anndra an Cú had been born in that little cottage behind An Taigh Buidhe. How dare Burtenshaw evict anyone, never mind Anndra?

'What is happening?' Max looked frantic. 'Tell me! I heard her say Burtenshaw, I think.'

Eilidh shook herself, only now realising that Max would not have understood the Gaelic conversation. She translated, and Max's jaw dropped. There was no time to say more, however, as they were approaching the house. Jumping down even before the cart had come to a standstill, they raced behind to the yard.

The scene that met their eyes was one from a nightmare. Two burly men were engaged in removing Anndra's furniture from his little cottage while their overseer stood to one side in a relaxed slouch, a decided smirk on his face and a flaming torch in his hand. Clearly, he intended to burn the cottage once it had been emptied, to prevent Anndra's return. Two fishermen and a young boy were seemingly remonstrating with the overseer, who did not appear to be heeding them in the slightest. Anndra himself stood to one side wearing a dazed expression, as well he might. Eilidh could scarce believe what she was seeing.

'*A thighearna!*' One of them had noticed Angus. 'Thank God you are here. Please can you do something?'

The overseer had straightened and was eyeing them warily. 'Mr MacDonald,' he declared, a hint of sneering in his tone. 'We meet again. As ever, I am carrying out the lawful business of Lord Burtenshaw, who is master here. You may return to your own Broch if you do not wish to observe. You are not Laird of Lidistrome.' The man spoke English and Angus responded in kind, his tone tight and his expression twisted with anger.

'What "lawful" business could possibly include treating a valued tenant and employee with such disdain? Anndra has lived here all his life and has looked after the house and gardens as best he could, given the pitiful allowance he has received.'

The overseer shrugged. 'As to that, you may question Lord Burtenshaw. I am simply doing what was ordered.' He patted his greatcoat as if to indicate something held there.

'Let me see.'

Angus took the paper and ran his eyes over it before handing it to Max. 'Inglis!' he declared with loathing. 'I might have known!' He frowned. 'Let me see it again. I wish to check the date these orders were written.' An instant later he gasped. 'March Eighth. The very day I visited him in his office!' He looked at the overseer. 'These orders have not come from Lord Burtenshaw, but from his man of business, Mr Inglis.'

The overseer shrugged. 'It matters not, for it's Inglis I take my orders from. The thing is valid, and I am compelled to carry it out.'

Throughout, his assistants had continued to carry out Anndra's furniture and personal belongings. One had now found the man's chamber pot and set it on a chair in the yard. Anndra, clearly distressed at the indignity, looked at his feet.

Eilidh had been keeping a watch on Max. Surely he could see that he had to intervene? Surely he could no longer keep his responsibilities a secret?

She was not to be disappointed.

Squaring his shoulders, he stepped forward. 'Stop!'

The roaring in Max's ears was like thunder. Never could he recall feeling so angry, so outraged.

How dare they?

His anger was all-consuming, and while his current target was the loathsome overseer before him, along with his two subordinates, Freddy and his man of business, along with every Lord of the Burtenshaw line, were equally culpable. The letter from Inglis was outrageous. Anndra 'added no value to the estate', apparently, and his salary was 'a cost Mr Inglis has decided they could do without'.

No value? Who do they think they are?

'Stop!' Something in his tone must have alerted the villains for they both stopped, looking to their overseer.

'My name is Maximilian Wood, and I am the brother of Lord Burtenshaw.' Using every inch of hauteur he had learned in the vicious card rooms and ballrooms of London, he eyed the overseer as though he were excrement on his shoe. 'Your name, sir?'

'Er…Stephenson. Samuel Stephenson.' The man looked significantly less insolent than he had a moment ago.

'Well, Mr Stephenson, permit me to inform you that your orders are out of date and are superseded by new ones. Lidistrome is no longer owned by my brother, but by me, and I have lately arrived in Benbecula to inspect my estate.'

'I…I see,' declared Stephenson, then a sly look crossed his face. 'And how am I to know that you are who you say? This may be all a hum, designed to prevent me carrying out my lawful duties.' He stepped forward aggressively and his men, sensing the change in mood, left the cottage and moved forwards to flank him, chests out and malevolent expressions on both faces.

They would fight me?

Max felt another rush of anger flood through him. Vaguely, he was aware that Angus and Cooper had moved to flank him, mirroring Stephenson's henchmen and making it clear they too were not averse to settling the matter with fists if needed.

Still, the part of his brain that was still functioning recognised there was some merit in Stephenson's question—even if his intention had been nothing but obstructive. Sliding his signet ring from his finger, he reversed it to show the wax seal—an amended version of the Burtenshaw seal, with added symbols highlighting the sea and sailing. 'You will recognise this as being similar to my brother's seal. I should also inform you that the deeds are currently at Broch Clachan. I am happy to bring the matter before a magistrate if you prefer.'

'Sheriff,' murmured Cooper.

'Before the Sheriff, then. I am entirely at your disposal, Mr Stephenson.'

Grumbling, the overseer admitted defeat. Jerking a head towards his accomplices, the three of them stomped off, to jeers and cheers from the now sizeable crowd of farmers and fishermen. As soon as they rounded the corner, a great cheer rose up from the throats of the assembly—a cheer that made the hairs on the back of Max's neck stand to attention. In it he heard joy and relief, and echoes of a century of similar injustices.

Still gripped by anger and somewhat in a daze, Max found himself surrounded by Lidistrome people wishing to shake his hand or clap him on the back, congratulating and thanking him in a mix of Gaelic and English. Some had the glint of tears in their eyes, while a few were unabashedly crying. Angus too was being celebrated, Max saw. Their eyes met briefly, Angus giving a rueful shrug.

Somehow, Eilidh and Cooper had managed to remain close by, one on either side of him. That had meaning to him. At the far side of the yard, Anndra was being similarly feted. While Max was relieved to see that Anndra's possessions were already being moved back inside, and that the man himself was surrounded by well-wishers, he could not help but feel overwhelming guilt alongside the relief. Max himself did not deserve any accolades, for all he had done was prevent a clear injustice. Even as the thoughts were forming, yet more people were coming to thank him.

'Thank you, sir,' said one of the farmers he had met earlier, pumping his hand. 'We shall never forget this.'

A middle-aged woman he had never seen before then shook his hand before pressing a kiss on his cheek. 'I know not who you are,' she said, 'for I have only just managed to get here. But it seems you have sent Burtenshaw's man packing, and for that I am grateful.' She sent a grin in Cooper's direction. 'You should be proud of your son.'

'Oh, but I am not his—' Max began, but the woman had already turned away, making for Anndra.

'Your son.'

The words sank in, reverberating around Max's head, and abruptly his legs felt soft, as though they would not hold him up. 'Cooper?' he managed, turning his head to where the man stood. 'Cooper?'

Chapter Thirteen

In an instant, the entire world had changed. Everything Max had known or believed about himself. About Cooper. About Mama. His mind took only a moment to put together the hints and clues of a lifetime.

Mama and Cooper. Cooper and Mama.

'She loved you.' His voice was hoarse, his heart pounding.

The older man was pale, his throat working with strong emotion. 'Aye,' he replied croakily. 'And I loved her. I am sorry, lad. We could not tell you.'

'And my father? I mean…Lord Burtenshaw.'

Papa was not my father.

'Did he know?'

Cooper nodded. 'They became estranged soon after Freddy's birth. She locked her chamber door because he tried to force her. He said it was his right.'

Max grimaced. 'The law would agree with him. How did she manage?'

'Pride was everything to him. She threatened to make it known among her friends that his prowess in the bedchamber was not…er…' He shrugged. 'Anyway, suffice to say they ultimately agreed they would maintain a façade for the sake of society, but that she would have the freedom to stay at Burtenshaw House most of the time.'

'With you.'

'Eventually, yes. When I began working there, they were already estranged, and she was shaking off the force of his oppression. She always used to say that, like a butterfly, she was reborn.'

Max's mind flicked briefly to the cocoons in the gardens to his right.

Reborn.

'She was happier after he let her go.'

'She was, and I was honoured to know her.'

Max was still figuring everything out. 'So Freddy is my half-brother?'

Cooper nodded. 'And the spit and image of his sire, thank the Lord. Burtenshaw never doubted it, and blood meant everything to him.'

Max gasped as another thought came to him. 'Isabella!'

Cooper nodded. 'Aye. I shall speak to her when we return to the Broch. I do hope she will forgive me.'

'Forgive you? Whatever for?' Finally, reality was sinking in.

Papa—that dour, cruel, arrogant man—is nothing to me!

Instead he had Cooper—the wisest, kindest man he knew. With a muffled exclamation, he opened his arms for his father's embrace. They clung to each other, both overcome by unmanly emotion, and as they finally released one another, they both reached for their handkerchiefs. 'You have done nothing that requires forgiveness, Cooper.'

Eilidh, who all the time had been standing nearby,

gave a sound somewhere between a hiccough and a sob and Max turned to look at her.

'I am so sorry for listening,' she managed, 'but I was overcome and could not make my legs work to step away.' Dashing away a tear, she managed a tremulous smile. 'I am so happy for both of you. This is wonderful news.'

'Then…it does not bother you that I am a…that I was b-born…?' He struggled to find words that would not insult Mama and Cooper, and stuttered to a halt.

'Out of wedlock?' she finished. 'Not at all. It is not what anyone would *choose*, of course, but the important thing is that your mama found love after a marriage that had clearly made her unhappy.' She grinned. 'And we are far, far away from the *ton* and its judgements.'

'We are.' Max knew her words were important in some way beyond the obvious. He tried to grasp it, but the inkling slipped away like a silver fish in the sea. Gone.

'What's this? Is something else amiss?' Angus had crossed the yard to speak to them, a confused frown on his brow.

Before Max had a chance to respond, Cooper intervened. 'Angus, might we have a word? There is something I must say to you.'

They moved off to one side but Max had no opportunity to observe them, for it seemed others were ready to speak to him. Having been huddled together for private conversation, the Lidistrome people now turned to face him, Anndra stepping forward with intent.

'Sir,' he began, 'I must thank you for what you have done today. But I must ask you, is what you said true, or was it said to befuddle Stephenson?'

There was a sudden hush and all eyes were on him.

Around forty or fifty people were in the yard now and they were all eyeing him intently, awaiting his response.

It is time.

Turning his attention away from the astounding revelations of the past few moments, Max straightened to face the people of Lidistrome.

'It is true.' His words dropped like stones into a still pond, sending ripples murmuring through the crowd. 'I have lately bought Lidistrome from my…from my *half*-brother, Lord Burtenshaw.'

Hushed conversations broke out everywhere, all in Gaelic. Max simply stood, awaiting events. The glances that were being sent his way contained a mix of scepticism, anger and, heartbreakingly, hope.

I must wait and endure whatever they must say to me.

'The name Burtenshaw has been hated in Lidistrome for generations.' The speaker was a man in his middle years, with an intelligent gaze and decided scepticism in his tone. Like the others, he wore the traditional Highland dress, a blue woollen bonnet covering dark hair, liberally peppered with grey. 'Just because you stopped them evicting Anndra today, it does not mean you will not do the same yourself tomorrow, or next year, or in ten years' time. Landlords usually arrange it so they do not have to observe the human cost of their actions, preferring to work through cold-hearted tools like Stephenson and his lackeys.'

Max nodded. 'I understand that and I cannot ask you to take me at my word, for you know nothing about me. Therefore, all I can offer is action.' He took a breath. 'First, I shall take no rent from anyone for this year. Not a penny.' There were gasps at this, but Max was not done. 'Your crop fields shall be left fallow, apart from whatever food you wish to grow for yourselves. I shall also return any rent you paid in the past year.'

His gaze roved over the crowd. Everyone—men and women alike—was watching intently. Catching Eilidh's eye, he noted a similar rapt attention on her face. Swallowing, he continued.

'Secondly, I ask each of you—and any other Lidistrome people not present—to make a list of all the repairs needing to be done, and the tools and materials you need to carry them out.' He paused. 'I shall need someone to coordinate.'

'Alec!' someone called, and this then was echoed by others.

'Yes, Alec!'

'Alec would be your man!' They were indicating the spokesman who had stepped forward initially—the one with the blue Jacobite bonnet.

Anndra added his voice to the others. 'Alec is my sister's boy. He will do very well as your steward, sir.'

Max met Alec's gaze. 'Will you do it? Will you work with me to restore this place?'

Alec remained impassive for a moment, then nodded. 'Your words give us encouragement, but you will forgive us if we reserve judgement on you for a little longer.'

Max inclined his head. 'Agreed.'

'Then I shall be your steward.' He stepped forwards and the two shook hands.

There was an eerie silence for a moment, then a voice rang out from the back. 'But we shall not trust you easy, you being a Sassenach bastard!'

Max shot back instantly, 'As to that, you may with accuracy refer to me as a bastard, but I am proud to declare I have discovered I am but half English. The other half is from Kilchoman in Islay, my father being John Cooper of that parish.' He grinned at Cooper. 'And I am proud to be his son.'

Alec was frowning in puzzlement. 'So are you a Burtenshaw or not?'

'I am not, though I was raised in that family. My sister and I belong to the Coopers by blood, and I mean to discover more about them. And, as some of you are aware, my sister will shortly marry the Laird of Broch Clachan and means to settle here.'

'And you?' Alec's look was intent. 'Will you stay?'

In an instant, Max's world teetered for the second time that day. *Stay?* A vista opened up before him— new, and tantalisingly possible. Making a home of An Taigh Buidhe. Raising children with his own dark eyes—so like Cooper's as well as Mama's, now that he knew the truth—his dark eyes and Eilidh Ruadh's auburn curls.

Impossible. She would never have me. Nor would the people here. And yet...

He swallowed. 'I do not know, Alec. That is the truth.'

The man's eyes softened briefly. 'I appreciate the honesty.' He turned to stand by Max's side, facing the crowd. 'Right. I shall need an office. Anndra, I suggest we clean up the empty cottage beside yours—the one that was your son's. Is that agreeable?'

Anndra sighed. 'He is long gone, so yes, of course you may use it.'

'Then let us get to work!' Without further ado, the crowd swarmed into action, moving more of Anndra's belongings back inside and opening the cottage next to his. Max simply watched them, allowing his breathing to slow a little and his mind to focus on what was happening in that instant, rather than on any of the massive, life-changing topics that had come up in the past twenty minutes. Alec, having ventured inside the empty cottage for a few moments, approached to suggest Max return on the morrow, when they could properly discuss his requirements.

The arrangements made, Max turned back to his friends. For a moment they all just paused. Max. Eilidh. Angus. Cooper.

My love. My friend. My father.

Then, Angus grinned. 'If you want Isabella to hear the news directly from yourselves, I suggest we get going. It is hard to keep a secret on Benbecula!'

Eilidh's mind was racing, much like her pulse. The events of the past hour had left her reeling. As the cart rumbled on and the men talked of what had happened, she found herself unable—or at least unwilling—to take part in their conversation.

Cooper is Max's father!

Now that she knew the truth, it seemed obvious. Looking at them now, the similarities were plain to see. Inwardly, she recalled the feeling of familiarity when she had met Cooper for the first time, and the sight of him and Max standing side by side with identical grins when Angus had announced his upcoming nuptials the night they had arrived in the Broch. What might have seemed impossible now looked inescapable.

What will Isabella make of it?

To discover that your mother had a lover, that your father was not your father... Still, Isabella's true father was a good man. She eyed Cooper surreptitiously. He had, in his own quiet way, been as good a father to his son and daughter as he could have been. She swallowed, struggling to even try to imagine the pain the man had endured over the years, seeing his children grow yet never being allowed to acknowledge them as his own.

'Eilidh?' It was Max, and she looked at him... *Oh, now she was lost in his eyes.*

'Will you stay?' Alec had asked, and Eilidh's entire being had waited for the answer.

When it came, it had felt like a blow to the heart.

'I do not know.'

Well, of course he did not know.

The man has only been on Benbecula for a heartbeat.

But his actions today had been exactly right, and there was every possibility that he might stay, at least for a while. And maybe if he stayed a while, he might slowly get to like it, and then maybe—

She shook herself. Daydreams were only daydreams. If such an eventuality ever came to pass, she would welcome it. But she must not rely on it. That way lay danger.

'Yes?' she managed.

'Would you be willing?'

His look was boyishly earnest, and she wanted to simply say, *Yes. Whatever you ask me, I would be willing.*

Instead she frowned a little. 'Willing for what? Apologies—I was distracted.'

'Willing to come with me and Cooper when we tell Isabella the truth.'

'Me?'

'You and Angus. He will be her husband, while you—you are her closest friend.'

Eilidh shook her head. 'No. You are.' She gestured at the three men. 'You *all* are—in different ways.' Thinking for a moment, she added, 'I am her closest *female* friend, and it is true she may have need of me. I shall remain nearby, and will join you if needed. But Max, it is important that you and Cooper tell her yourselves. My knowing it before she does, watching her as she hears the news—it would not seem right.'

This they agreed and an hour later Eilidh found herself in a cosy room next to the salon where Isabella, Max, Cooper and Angus had been closeted for the past thirty minutes. Finally, the connecting door opened and Angus beckoned her in.

To her great relief, Isabella was smiling and holding Cooper's hand, though she had clearly shed tears too. 'Oh, Eilidh!' she exclaimed. 'Isn't it wonderful? But how terrible for my poor mama!'

Eilidh joined her and together they discussed the matter, recalling some cryptic comments that Isabella's mama's friend had made at a London soirée that now made sense.

'What's that? Did you say Mrs Edgecombe?' Cooper was suddenly alert.

'Yes, she was one of Mama's closest friends.'

'I remember her. She always suspected us, but your mama would never confirm it.' Cooper shook his head slowly. 'I wonder though if she came to the correct conclusion at some point, and even hinted at it. That may explain why young Burtenshaw—your half-brother— found out. When he dismissed me, he gave very clear hints that he knew your parentage. Indeed, I believe that was his reason for letting me go.'

Isabella gasped. 'He did? I wonder if that was partly why he wished to marry me off so rapidly? And, come to think of it, I believe he did know, for his comments about the Scots were most particular.' She gave a little laugh. 'Strange to think I am as much Scottish as English.'

Angus grinned. 'That aspect had occurred to me also, and I am glad of it. If it helps you settle here, even a little, then I shall welcome it.'

'How could it not help? I am half Scottish—half *Islander*. Oh, Cooper, I am so glad to have you as my true father!'

Eilidh could not resist a quick glance in Max's direction. He was lost in thought, a strangely arrested expression in his eyes.

I do hope he feels it too.

Being of island blood was in one sense meaningless, for people were always more than their family, their clan, their country. And yet Cooper's children could, if they chose, use their newly-discovered ancestry to open their hearts to the Islands. To Scotland.

If they chose.

Isabella's course was set. She would marry Angus, live out her days on Benbecula, and, please God, raise Islander children. Max was a different case entirely. A wealthy bachelor, every path in England was now open to him. He could pursue a profession if he wished. He could certainly marry and sire children. Would he really wish to leave the country of his birth—his mother's country—to settle in a remote island community on the edge of the Atlantic ocean?

Logic said no. Logic suggested that he would spend some money in Lidistrome, leave the day-to-day work to Alec and sail back to London or Sussex or wherever he desired, following Isabella and Angus's wedding.

'Will the Islanders judge me for being born on the wrong side of the blanket?' Isabella's forehead was creased with concern. 'The community here is a very traditional one, is it not?'

Angus made haste to reassure her. 'While such matters would be frowned on, the people here are not so naive. They will judge you for yourself, not your parentage.'

'I see. I have work to do then.'

'No more than before. And you are making a great start. How did it go with the staff today while we were gone?'

'Very well, I think.' She went on to talk about her day and, as the conversation continued, Eilidh once again allowed her mind to wander back to the yard behind An Taigh Buidhe, and Max's decision. While he had not indicated any willingness to take on his responsibilities on any long-term basis, he had done well today.

'I have not forgotten, Eilidh.' His voice was low at her side, and as she turned to him, the full impact of his dark gaze set off a trembling within her.

I can feel it even in my toes. How does he do that?

'Forgotten what?' The others were continuing to talk, so Max drew her aside a little, out of earshot.

'We had talked of climbing Rueval tomorrow, but I now expect to spend the day with Alec. Could we perhaps postpone the outing until the day after?'

'Friday? But Angus is promised to his steward on Friday, and Isabella planned to sit in with them, so—'

'So we can go without them. It will be just you and me. Is that permitted here?' His eyes were speaking to her. Different messages from the words his beautiful lips were forming, but messages nonetheless. Intent. Reassurance. Something else too. Something deep, and powerful and entirely wonderful.

She took a breath. 'It is permitted—our habits here are different to London, and men are trusted not to misbehave if they are alone with a young woman.'

'And do you trust me?'

She looked at him, and could not answer at first.
Yes. Of course.

Then she imagined them both, all alone, at the top of Rueval.

No.

'I do, and yet I also do not,' she offered carefully.

Something flashed in his eyes. 'Am I so untrustworthy—too much the London buck?' His face twisted in an expression that was now familiar to her.

Self-hatred.

Reading it clearly, she recalled its source. Years of criticism from Lord Burtenshaw—the man Max had believed to be his father. The possible reason for Burtenshaw's antipathy towards Max was now clearer—though nothing excused his blaming a child for the actions of his parents.

She could not allow his assumption to stand. 'It is not that. I know you to be a gentleman—a man of honour.' At his raised eyebrow, she put a hand lightly on his sleeve. 'Truly. You are a good man, Max. I think perhaps you are a better man than you realise.'

This earned a shake of the head. 'I did not ask because I sought your approbation, Eilidh. But I would not wish for you to feel uncomfortable with me.'

'But do you not see? I trust you. I do. But I do not necessarily trust *us*.' Her eyes danced, and thankfully, his expression lightened in response.

'Very well.' He leaned closer, speaking softly into her ear. 'I shall promise not to ravish you on Rueval. Will that suffice?'

She swallowed, as the notion of being ravished by Max was very dear to her heart. Outwardly, though, she gave him only a mischievous grin and a prim agreement. 'It will.'

Thursday 2nd May

Max suppressed a smile as he recalled the conversation between them.

I do not...trust us, she had said, and his heart had clenched as her meaning had registered with him.

So she is not indifferent to me yet!

Tomorrow's outing to Rueval would allow him hours of her company, and a chance to see the whole island from its highest point. But first, like his sister, he had work to do.

'Ready?'

He nodded to Alec, and the two of them set off again. Having spent the morning in Alec's new office discussing matters of business, they had achieved a reasonably good understanding, Max believed. Alec was quick-witted and fair, and seemed dedicated to the well-being of Lidistrome and its people. They were now visiting some key locations and people within the estate, and Max was becoming used to saying the same things at every cottage and *clachan* they visited. Yes, he was the new owner. No, he was uncertain if he would stay. Yes, it was true they were to pay no rent for a year.

Alec would then lead the part of the conversation where Max's tenant would identify necessary repairs and materials, jotting down the details in a leather-bound notebook. Max had also asked that an assessment be made of the various roads and tracks crossing the estate, and indicated his determination to improve them. Realistically, it would take years.

Currently, they were visiting a settlement belonging to the Morrisons, a farming family whose cluster of cottages and barns was almost two miles from An Taigh

Buidhe. Alec had explained the island was around seven miles wide, and around the same from north to south.

Such a small place, Max had thought.

And yet their sense of community was fierce. Being surrounded by water would create that.

Their business with Calum Morrison completed, Alec suggested they visit the women in the waulking barn, for the Morrisons were renowned as the leading weavers of Lidistrome. Max had already noted signs of cloth-making all about—washed fleeces stretched out to dry on the heather, skeins of wool in different colours sitting ready for weaving in Calum's second barn, three spinning wheels in the back room of Calum's small house. As they approached the larger building, Calum pointing out the rusted hinges on the main door which needed to be replaced, Max heard the sound of women singing. They stepped inside and Max blinked as his eyesight adjusted to the dim light.

Eight women were seated on benches either side of a wooden table and they were pushing and kneading a long length of tweed between them, moving it around in a clockwise direction. The cloth was a simple brown with a thin line of red—a colour combination Max had seen being worn by many of the fishermen and farmers. As the women worked they sang, the song rhythmic and repetitive.

'This is called waulking the tweed,' Alec explained, his voice raised to ensure Max could hear. 'It softens the wool and makes it ready for wearing. This cloth can be worn by most Lidistrome people, for it contains only two colours.'

'The number of colours is significant then?'

The women had noticed them and come to a stop. Calum introduced his wife, Mina, and she in turn introduced the others, mostly their daughters and daughters-in-law, although there were two young women from a neighbouring farm helping with the waulking.

'We were just speaking of the number of colours in the cloth,' Alec offered, and Mina nodded.

'Aye—one for a servant, two for a farmer or fisherman.' She shrugged. 'We don't have much call for the others around here. It would be three for an officer, five for a laird, six for the poet and seven for a king or queen. But they defeated our Bonnie Prince, and there's no self-respecting Scot would weave for Elector George and his breed. They care nothing for us, nor we for them.' Her look was level, her comment clearly a challenge.

Max met her gaze. 'And absentee landlords failing in their duty?'

Pursing her lips, she made an expression of distaste. 'Aye. Them too. Now, let me show you our loom.' Leading the way to the rear of the barn, she indicated the device, showing him where the wool was inserted and how, with a single sweep of the shuttle, an entire row of plain could be merged with columns of colours. A length of cloth was already being woven—black, with a thin line of bright blue as contrast. The blue was a single bobbin at the bottom of the loom, the other bobbins all containing the black wool. 'It is very basic, of course—nothing like the fancy looms they have up in Lewis. But we make do. The men work the loom, and we women do the cleaning, dyeing and waulking, and there is enough cloth for every man, woman and child in Lidistrome.'

Max was fascinated, and said so. Calum and Mina went on to explain the process of cloth-making in some detail, and in the end it was Alec who bade them depart for, he said, they still had a number of clans to visit.

As they made their way down the track away from the Morrison *clachan*, Max commented on the poverty he saw everywhere.

'They sleep on straw mattresses, Alec. And while their houses are kept clean, the smell of fish-oil lamps is oppressive. Can you add to your list better mattresses, lamps and candles for everyone, please? Plus we need to order more wheat flour so everyone can enjoy bread as well as oatcakes. And...' he thought for a moment '...I should like to know more about these fancy looms in Lewis. Are they actually better? If so, how? And how much would it cost to buy one?'

Alec's eyes gleamed. 'Yes, sir,' he replied, scratching a note with his pencil. 'I shall write to my cousin in Stornoway on the morrow, to see what I may discover.'

Max suppressed a grin.

He is warming to me, a little.

That 'sir' had not escaped his notice, being the first time Alec had bestowed any sort of honorific on him. Strange to think how unlike London this place was. As a London gentleman he took 'sir' for granted, hearing it dozens of times each day. Here, it was earned, not given. And while Alec might be coming round, Mina had been decidedly sceptical.

They continued, visiting home after home, farm after farm. Some of the people were entirely welcoming, thanking him so profusely for assisting Anndra that he felt a fair degree of discomfort. Others were wary, almost afraid to hope he had meant what he had said yesterday. Max listened and observed, and spoke little, while the list in Alec's notebook grew ever longer.

'I shall begin ordering materials tomorrow,' he declared once they had returned to the office cottage behind the main house. 'Now, what of An Taigh Buidhe itself?'

Max frowned. 'I am not certain. The priority is the homes and farms of the Lidistrome people and, since I do not yet know how long I shall stay, I must not be diverted into a project that suits only vanity.'

Pride. My half-brother's flaw. I must not let it tempt me.

Glancing out of the cottage window at the faded walls of the house, he sighed. 'Let us explore the house on Saturday, when I return. I have another commitment tomorrow.'

As he spoke a cart pulled into the yard—the Broch Clachan driver returning for him as arranged. 'Is that the time?' Max was conscious of a slight feeling of shock.

How has the day passed so quickly?

As the cart rumbled back towards Broch Clachan, he reflected that he had rarely experienced a day so tiring, so productive, so satisfying. Helping Cooper caulk boats or mend his boathouse had been similar, but with one crucial difference: if he had wished, he could have walked away from assisting Cooper.

Lidistrome was different. For the first time in his life, he was shouldering true responsibility, and the notion was both terrifying and exhilarating at the same time. The satisfaction of having completed a good day's work was new to him, and he found that he liked it very, very much.

And now he was nearly at Broch Clachan, and would spend the evening in anticipation of a day with Eilidh tomorrow and good company tonight.

Good company? The best.

Eilidh, Isabella, Cooper, Angus. If he could choose

his company from anyone alive in the world, he would choose these four.

My Eilidh. My sister. My father. My friend.

A glow of affection burned in his chest, and yet the flame of it was too wild for mere affection. He *loved* these people. Loved them with a heart that was true, and fierce and full of hope.

His thoughts returned to Eilidh. His love for her was different to the rest. It was the same and yet…more. He burned for her with a passion he had never hitherto experienced. She epitomised what he was now learning about Benbecula and its people. Loyalty. Caring for others. A deeply ingrained connection to others, to the place, to the land itself. Beauty. Grace. Humour. Kindness.

Another conversation with a farmer returned to him now. Murdo MacInnes had been explaining that wheat would not grow in the Islands, so they grew mainly oats. 'Hence the porridge, and the oatcakes, and the oatmeal. And potatoes and vegetables, of course. All good food.' The problem was that without the ability to leave fields fallow every few years the crop returns were slowly falling. 'Over in Ardmore or in Broch Clachan they can afford fallow fields and healing fields. We cannot. Or at least we *could* not, until you came.'

'Healing fields?' Max had asked. 'What are healing fields?'

'Every farm should have at least one,' Murdo had explained. 'We plant yellow hay rattle to start with—though we have to keep it out of the usual fields—and after a while the healing field is full of wildflowers. It is where we put a sickly cow, or a nursing one. It makes them better.'

It makes them better.

He was not a sickly cow, and feasting on wildflowers would not heal him, yet he felt as though his short time in Benbecula had given him healing of a sort.

Perhaps this whole island is one great healing field, he thought somewhat fancifully. *I must make the most of it while I am here.*

Inside the Broch was an air of great excitement. 'The *seanchaidh* is here!' someone called to Max and the driver as they pulled up in the yard.

'What does that mean?'

'Ah, the *seanchaidh* is the storyteller. He comes only a few times a year. It is a great honour to have him.'

'I see.' But Max did not see at all.

A storyteller? Someone telling stories for a living?

It made no sense. At dinner, Eilidh explained it to him and Isabella.

'He is our bard. He can sing and tell stories, and play the harp and the fiddle. It is always exciting when he comes. They are making the Great Hall ready, and we shall all gather there in an hour or so.'

'How exciting!' Isabella's eyes were shining. 'I declare there is never a dull moment here!'

'Oh, please do not expect too much of him!' Angus laughed. 'He is one man, telling tales. I would not wish for your London expectations to be dashed.'

He is anxious about disappointing her.

'Never worry about that!' she replied instantly. 'I am yet to be disappointed by anything here—except perhaps the lack of lemonade.' The last was said with a grin, making it clear to her future husband that she was not in earnest.

'As to that, Lidistrome must save us! Max, have you started work yet on restoring the hot wall?'

'Not yet, but be assured I intend to give it my fullest attention.' In truth, he had discussed the matter with Alec, who had thought it an excellent notion. 'We could sell oranges, limes and lemons throughout the Hebrides,' he had said, 'should the hot wall help us produce enough.' He had added it to his list, sighing. 'I see that I shall have to travel to the mainland. There is nothing else for it.'

'And I shall accompany you. I need to find a man of business in Glasgow or Edinburgh who can link with my lawyer and banker in London.'

'I know the very man! A distant relative of Calum Morrison. He and his son are solicitors in Glasgow— that branch of the family left Lidistrome when it went to the Burtenshaws—begging your pardon, sir—and have done very well for themselves.'

'Splendid!' He and Alec had exchanged a grin. Strand by strand, they were weaving a new cloth together. A new future for Lidistrome.

Returning to the present, Max knew he needed to tell them of his plans. 'I must inform you all that I plan to travel to Glasgow next week.'

'What? But why?' Isabella looked a little upset and, beside him, Eilidh's hand was currently gripping her fork tightly. 'You said you would stay for my wedding!'

He made haste to clarify. 'Of course, and I intend to keep my word. Alec and I shall visit lawyers, bankers and merchants, in an attempt to organise building materials and other matters.'

'Ah, I see,' said Isabella. Her eyes narrowed. 'How are you finding it, Max, this business of being a Laird?'

He shook his head. 'I am no Laird. I am simply the man responsible for Lidistrome.'

'As good a description of the role as I ever heard,'

murmured Cooper. 'It is about responsibility, not power. Or pride, for that matter.' They exchanged a glance, the shadow of Freddy and his father passing between them.

Max shrugged. 'Nevertheless, I was not born to it.' The last thing he needed was to start thinking of himself in that way. He could never be a true Laird to them. All he could do was make some small gestures to counter generations of neglect from the Burtenshaws. 'So tell me,' he added in a determined change of topic, 'will the bard perform in Gaelic or in English?'

Chapter Fourteen

As she helped move benches and tables in the Hall in preparation for the bard's performance, Eilidh's mind returned time and again to the conversation earlier, and that moment when she, like Isabella, had assumed Max was planning to leave Benbecula earlier than expected.

The feeling of shock had been acute. Shock compounded by disappointment. No, that was too weak a word. *Devastation* was nearer the mark. Only now could she acknowledge how quickly and deeply her hopes had grown. Hopes that Max would someday love her. Love Benbecula.

He is open to it, I think.

Then common sense had intruded. Even if he had a *tendre* for her, he seemed to believe himself to be unworthy of belonging here.

He cannot love Benbecula—or me—until he truly loves himself.

Quite how she knew this, she could not say.

'*I was not born to it,*' he had replied, as though that mattered to anyone but Max himself. Yes, it helped that Cooper was Scottish—and a Hebridean, no less—but the people of Lidistrome would judge Max on his actions, not his bloodline. And, so far, Max's actions had been flawless.

Yet his long-term plans had not changed. After the wedding he would go, leaving matters in Alec's hands. Eilidh knew Angus's view on the matter—that a Laird should leave only when he must, and stay away for as short a time as possible. The difficulty was that Max had not accepted that he might stay.

Give him time.

Perhaps the magic of the Islands would work on him, perhaps it would not. In the meantime, all Eilidh could do was to ensure he saw the good things about Benbecula—like the entertainment tonight, and their trek tomorrow.

There he is!

Standing in the doorway, tall and handsome, his English clothing a stark contrast to the Highland dress everyone else wore... Her heart drummed its usual tattoo on seeing him. She waved, and his face cleared.

He made his way across to her. 'How can I help?' he asked simply, his eyes soft with admiration.

Ignoring the flush that was no doubt growing on her face, Eilidh resisted the temptation to bid him sit and let others do the work.

I must treat him as part of the family, not as a guest. He needs to understand that he belongs.

So she asked him to help her move another table and before long he was immersed in the preparations, working with everyone to help arrange the furniture in the best way to maximise everyone's view of the small dais where the *seanchaidh* would perform. The bard's harp was already there—a thing of beauty, the wood worn smooth by hundreds of hours of playing.

The kitchen staff began serving drinks—beer and

ale mostly, along with pure spring water and creamy milk. There was also wine for those who preferred it. Eilidh filled Max's cup with fine white wine—one of the new cases Angus had bought in London—and their fingers brushed briefly as she passed it to him. Thank goodness ladies need not wear gloves here!

The room was filling nicely and Max and Eilidh took their seats, side by side. The *seanchaidh* and his grandson were currently in Angus's library, where he and Isabella were awaiting their procession into the Hall.

'There will be formalities to start with.' Eilidh leaned forwards to ensure Max could hear her above the chatter. He turned his head slightly, and she caught her breath at his nearness.

'Formalities?' he prompted, but his gaze had dropped to her mouth.

'Er…yes.' She could almost feel his kiss, soft on her lips! Her body certainly believed he had actually kissed her, judging by her racing pulse. 'Angus will enter last, with Isabella, and then he will call for the *seanchaidh*.'

No sooner had she spoken, the doors at the back were flung wide, and the assembled company rose to greet their Laird. Eilidh stood with the rest, Max beside her, and kept her eyes on Isabella. Her friend glided forwards, her hand on Angus's arm. There was a hint of nervousness about her but her demeanour was generally calm. She looked elegant but not haughty, smiling at various people she now knew a little.

'Oh, well done, Isabella!' Eilidh murmured, and Max flashed her a grin.

'I do not believe I have ever seen my sister so happy.'

Eilidh looked again—past the performance, past the image of the Laird and his Lady. Isabella was glowing with happiness. She swallowed. 'Isabella deserves every moment of joy, after everything she has been through.'

Cooper slipped into a space beside them. 'I can second that!' he declared. 'I was at the back, for I could not find you amid the throng.' Finding an empty cup on the smooth wooden table, he poured himself a generous portion of wine. 'I must admit I am looking forward to hearing a *seanchaidh* again. It has been a very long time.'

'You stayed in England because of us.' Max's tone was flat.

'Of course, and I did not regret it for one instant. Scotland is part of who I am, but home is wherever your people are. There was no question of me leaving your mother, or leaving the two of you.'

They eyed one another, father and son, and Eilidh once again felt the privilege of knowing them.

Two good men.

It seemed an age since she had known Max only as a *ton* dilettante—a man of the card room and the ballroom. Now he was so, so much more to her. When she looked at him now, she saw honour and strength, and depth of character. And she also saw at times the boy he had been, bewildered as to why the man he believed to be his papa disliked him so.

There was a silence. Resisting the urge to ask Cooper what he would do after Isabella's marriage, when he would be forced to choose between remaining with his daughter or returning to England with his son, Eilidh instead focused on the oddly arrested expression in Max's eyes. His notions of home, and family, and belonging, were being turned on their head, it was clear.

Let him be. He needs to figure it out himself.

Angus rose to speak, beginning in Gaelic then

switching to English. He formally introduced his bride-to-be, expressed his great joy at being home again and then, finally, called upon the bard.

'I call,' he declared in Gaelic, 'Duncan MacDonald, Donnchadh mac an Tàilleir, to come and tell us all a tale!'

There was a great roar from the crowd and in the bard came, his grandson in his wake, to great acclaim, applause and the banging of metal cups on tables. He began with a song, a rousing air which got the crowd tapping and swaying in their seats, then he and his grandson—also called Duncan—played a selection of jigs and reels on the fiddles. Max was smiling and moving along with the rest, and it did Eilidh's heart good to see it.

The bard then pulled his stool to the harp, and a hush came over the crowd. 'I tell the tale,' he began in Gaelic, 'of the King who is over the water.' As he spoke his low, mesmerising tone was beautifully echoed by the contrasting sweetness of the notes he was plucking from the harp.

'He is telling the story of the Old Pretender,' Eilidh whispered to Max, 'and of his son, the Bonnie Prince.'

Max nodded thoughtfully, and as the tale went on his attention seemed equally divided between the bard and the crowd. When the tale was done, he leaned his head close to Eilidh's again to say something.

Loving the proximity, she inclined her head to his and tried not to be so distracted by his warm breath on her cheek that she could not take in what he was saying. 'Culloden was over sixty years go,' he was murmuring, 'and yet it brings tears to these people's eyes even now.'

She nodded. 'I believe we spoke of this in London. This is not simply history, for it affects us yet. When the commissioners—the *parcel o' rogues* Burns spoke about—sold our nationhood for English gold, the Bonnie Prince was our last hope. Our Scottish Parliament lies empty, our throne bare. Kings and Queens and Lords mean little to the common man, except when they forbid our Gaelic tongue and our Highland dress...' She tailed off, unwilling to name the third injustice, but he knew it already.

'Or when they confiscate Scottish lands and give them to absentee English landlords who care nothing for the people or the place.'

'Yes.' Their eyes met, his filled with concern and determination and...something more.

'Now,' the *seanchaidh* continued in English, 'my grandson will tell the tale of MacPhie of the black dog, and the twelve men who lay in *Airidh na h-aon Oidhche*—the sheiling of the one night!'

There was a murmur through the crowd. She leaned into Max again, welcoming every opportunity to feel his warmth, the power of his gaze. 'Listen, Max, for this is a truly frightening tale. It happened right here in Benbecula—indeed, I shall bring you to the place tomorrow, for it is on the lower slopes of Rueval!'

The grandson, a handsome lad in his mid-twenties, stepped forward. *'S' fhada, s' fhada,'* he began, his tone formal, mournful and compelling. 'Long, long ago, MacPhie, who was known as MacPhie of the Black Dog, *Mac a Phi a' Chu Dhubh*, built an *airidh shamhraidh*—a summer shelter—south of Stairaval.' Eilidh glanced at Max. His attention was completely fixed on the storyteller. 'When he was done,' Duncan continued, 'he and his twelve men lay down there, and every man among them said that he wished for his *leannan* with him.'

'*Leannan* means sweetheart,' she whispered, and Max repeated the word, looking directly at her.

'*Leannan.*'

Her heart skipped.

The storyteller continued. '"Ah, that is a bad wish to have brought upon us," said MacPhie, and he flew out of the *airidh* in a rage, and the *chu dhubh*, the black dog, after him. He was hardly out the door when twelve witches in the form of women but with *goib-chnamha*—that means beaks—flew in upon his dog and himself.'

Although the crowd had heard the story many times, there were gasps at this. 'God help them!' said one woman, crossing herself.

'He set his black dog on them and managed to get away. Running all the way to his house, he bade the folk there bar the doors. "Put four dishes of milk outside the door," he said, "but do not let the black dog inside." Well, the dog soon came and lapped the first dish of milk until it was empty. He drank the second, then the third, but when he drank the fourth he grew enormous in size. He was raving mad and not a hair on him. Then he burst and was seen no more.'

'Lord save us!'

'The mad black dog!'

'Raving, he was!'

The comments rippled around the room, the crowd, including Max, completely enthralled by the story. His left leg was touching Eilidh's right one, and she sensed him bring his hand beneath the table, searching for hers. She gave it willingly, and as his fingers closed around hers, she felt a powerful sense of *rightness* at his touch.

Glancing about briefly, she assured herself their hand-holding would go undetected by the crowd in the candlelit Hall. The need for secrecy was an added thrill, and her entire body seemed to tingle at his touch.

'Early in the morning,' the young bard continued, 'people rushed to Airidh na h-aon Oidhche to ascertain the fate of MacPhie's twelve. They found them there, and every one of them dead. Not a drop of blood left in their bodies, and no wounds save the peck of the *goib-chnamha*, the bone-beaked ones. Since that day, the *airidh* was abandoned and never more used and a new one had to be built nearby. And there ends the tale of MacPhie of the *cu dhubh* and the *goib-chnamha*.'

He bowed, and ringing applause broke out around the room. Eilidh and Max joined in, as keeping their hands secreted beneath the table at such a moment would have been remarked upon.

'What a tale!' said Max once the noise had died down a little. 'I declare the hairs on the back of my neck were standing to attention.'

'Aye, and well told too,' agreed Cooper. 'Now, *isht*! For here comes the bard again.'

It was true. The bard was stepping forward, fiddle in hand, with a smile for his grandson as they changed places on the dais.

'*Isht?*' Max looked puzzled. 'You always said that to us as children when you wanted us to hush. Is it Gaelic?'

'It is,' Cooper confirmed. 'Means *be quiet*. Now, *isht, a bhalaich*! Hush, boy!'

Max looked astounded. 'I have been listening to Gaelic my whole life, and I never knew it!'

There was no time for more, for the bard began to sing a series of Jacobite songs, including the rather bawdy 'Cam Ye O'er Frae France', which poked fun at George I of England and his mistress. When this was explained to Max, he took it in good part, laughing at the wit and taking no offence. 'I declare I am feeling less and less English the more this night goes on!' He grinned as he spoke, and took another sip of wine.

'We have nothing against individual English people,' Eilidh told him earnestly, but he waved this away.

'Of course! You told me this before, I believe. And I do not believe that my English blood means I must take responsibility for everything that nation has done. Or may do,' he added.

The night was long, and Max stayed until the very end. Long after the bard had finished. Long after those with children had left to tend them. Long after the wine was replaced with fine whisky, and Isabella and Angus joined them at their table. They sat on, enjoying the company and the whisky and the cosy darkness, until finally they all agreed it was time to retire. Max kissed Eilidh's hand with a gallant flourish, and she caught her breath at the look in his eyes. Floating on a cloud of joy all the way to her bedchamber, she reminded herself that tomorrow they would spend the day together. Happiness was hers. Happiness and hope.

Friday 3rd May

Max awoke early with a blinding headache and a feeling of hopelessness. Quite where it had come from, he was unsure. The hopelessness, that was. He knew very well where the headache had come from.

Normally, he was reasonably skilled at judging how much alcohol to imbibe. Enough to feel that welcome sense of distance from reality. Not so much that one would feel seriously worse for wear the next day. Well, whatever it was that had been in his cup last night, he had clearly miscalculated. Headache, dry mouth, even a hint of nausea. Lord, it reminded him of his wild days in Oxford! Closing his eyes tightly against the blazing sunlight peeping around the edge of his curtains, and willing himself to not wake fully, he managed to fall asleep again.

The next time he woke the headache had eased a little. The hopelessness, on the other hand, had strengthened. Last night he had allowed himself to become caught up in the event, and carried away by the island community. Foolishly, he had briefly allowed himself to believe he could be part of it. As he washed and dressed, he acknowledged the depth of emotion he had experienced last night. Feelings that he had never known were possible.

Oh, he had loved Eilidh in London. If it were possible, he loved her even more now. But it could never be. Yes, they had seemed to welcome him. Everyone had been kind and warm. It had seemed—temporarily— as though he was truly welcome, as though perhaps he could find a home here.

Last night, holding Eilidh's hand, with Cooper by his side and Isabella betrothed to their Laird, anything had seemed possible. But he, more than anyone, bore the responsibility for what the Burtenshaws had done. He, who had purchased Lidistrome without a moment's thought for the people whose home it was. He was no better than any Burtenshaw, and it did not sit well with him to be treated with such undeserved kindness.

In a whisky-induced haze, he had allowed himself to dream. To imagine he could be part of something. But the Benbecula people all knew each other—had known one another all their lives. Nay, their families had known each other for *generations*. While he…he did not even know their *songs*, much less their language.

How could he possibly imagine he could simply waltz in and become an Islander? It was clearly unfeasible.

There was only one thing for it. He must try to maintain some sort of detachment. His home was in London. If he belonged anywhere, it was London. To leave Eilidh and everyone behind would be a tremendous wrench, but a necessary one. His only protection was a cool head and a cool heart.

At the same time, he felt raw, exposed. It would take time to set his defences, to do what had to be done. And so, when they set off walking from Broch Clachan and Eilidh asked him what was the matter, he could with a fair degree of truth speak of his feeling under the weather following last night's excesses.

'Ah, that would be the whisky!' Her eyes danced, and a dimple peeped in her cheek. Fascinated, he could not tear his gaze away. 'It is much stronger than most people realise, and must be taken in moderation.'

'But I am no lightweight!'

'No, indeed.' She laughed. 'Still, you must give yourself the chance to become gradually accustomed to *uisge beatha*. The Gaelic for whisky literally means "the water of life", you know.'

'Water of life? You jest, surely?' He groaned. 'I could do with a restorative, although at this precise moment the very notion of alcohol is anathema to me!'

She laughed. 'I see I shall have to treat you gently today. Still, a brisk walk in the fresh air may clear your head, perhaps.'

He grunted noncommittally, and she laughed again. 'I am glad to be causing you such amusement,' he said sourly, but in truth he was storing up the memory of her tinkling laughter for the years ahead.

At least his self-inflicted ailment gave him something to think about other than Eilidh and how wonderful she was, and how beautiful was her island home. They made their way through neat fields and heather-rich moors, then eventually began to climb, Rueval looming impressively above them. Sometimes they spoke and sometimes they walked in silence, calmly enjoying the company, the walk and the sights, sounds and scents of Benbecula.

On the southern slopes, Eilidh showed him the ancient ruins associated with the tale he had heard last night. 'Rather than being an *airidh*—a shelter—it is more likely a burial cairn,' she explained. 'There is an actual *airidh* just over there—' she pointed '—and it *is* known as the one-night *airidh*, but only because it is used by travellers going between the Uists. You need low tide to cross to Benbecula, then you must wait a full day for the next low tide to travel on. So, one night!'

'No black dog then? Or beaked witches?'

She smiled. 'It always amazes me how scary the stories are when the *seanchaidh* tells them, and yet how innocuous these places are in daylight.'

'True. The reverse is also accurate. When we visited the Tower together, it looked a pleasant place, with grass and trees and pretty buildings...'

'And yet hundreds have been executed there.' They eyed one another soberly. 'London seems so long ago already, so far away.'

'Well, it *is* far away.' She rolled her eyes at this, and he had to chuckle. 'I do understand you, I think. It is like another world. London and Benbecula could not be any more different.'

'Exactly. It was why I thought Angus and Isabella could never be together. He would never leave the Islands.'

'And we yet cannot know if she will be able to adapt to the life here.'

'You think she will struggle?'

He shrugged. 'I did not say that. She has arrived in late spring, with flowers blooming and the kindest of weather. And she is newly in love. What she will make of it after a long cold winter, we cannot know.'

She was frowning, and he knew she did not wish to hear what he was saying. Still, it had to be said. Not for Isabella's sake, but his own. And Eilidh's.

They climbed on, the next part being particularly steep, and both of them were rather breathless by the time the hill evened out a little. Eilidh had had to raise her skirts slightly so she could watch where she was placing her feet, and Max was careful to avoid trying to glimpse an ankle. To be caught looking would make him feel as dishonourable as Geoffrey Barnstable—a man he had not, he realised, thought about in weeks.

'I wonder if Mr Barnstable has managed to overcome the disappointment of his wedding day,' he offered as they walked on.

She sniffed. 'I sincerely hope not, for the man deserves as much disappointment as fate may bring him. As does your brother, I am sorry to say!' She bit her lip. 'I mean your half-brother. How is it, knowing Cooper is your true father?'

He thought about this for a moment and she spoke again, her face creased with concern. 'I apologise, Max. I do not mean to pry.'

'I do not mind your question at all. I am simply trying to formulate an answer.' Glancing upwards, he saw they were near the top. 'I think the most surprising thing is how…how *unsurprised* I am. It feels *right* to know that he is my father, and it makes many puzzles from my childhood clear. Even the fact that Isabella and I are so different from Freddy. I understand now that we are a mix of Mama and Cooper—two of the best people I have ever known. That makes me proud. Yet I am beginning to hear new stories, some of them difficult to hear, although Cooper is as yet reluctant to be fully open. The habits of almost thirty years are not easily overcome. I always knew Mama had a difficult life with Papa—with *Burtenshaw*—until he left her alone. But I did not know the half of it.'

'I am sorry, Max.'

He shrugged. 'You have nothing to apologise for. The Burtenshaws, on the other hand…what he did to Mama, what the family did to Lidistrome—these things are unforgivable.'

What he did to you.

Burtenshaw's cruelty had left Max feeling unworthy, unlovable, filled with self-loathing. It was clear as day to her. She frowned, but kept her thoughts to herself.

A few paces more and they had reached the summit, a wide flat area with—

Max gasped. 'Such views!' Turning slowly, he made a complete circle. In every direction the vistas before him were astonishing. Benbecula surrounded him in all its raw beauty. Lochs and inlets dotted the landscape— indeed, from here the place looked to be as much water as land. From this distance, the green-brown land and the blue-black waters melded into the perfect scene of natural beauty. Beyond the island itself, the scene was framed by the silver sea and an endless sky.

He turned again, this time more slowly, as Eilidh pointed out landmarks. Ardmore Castle. Broch Clachan. An Taigh Buidhe. The buildings mere dots on the wild landscape. Never had he seen a place like it. The island chain lay before him, stretched out like a necklace with Benbecula at its heart.

'It is…solid,' he offered, trying to articulate the feelings within. 'Beautiful, and *real*, and reassuringly solid.' Gesturing towards the Atlantic, sparkling in the midday sunshine, he added, 'As a sailor I know the sea is beguiling but treacherous. Benbecula is a dark haven amid its hazards.'

'The Gaelic poets called Benbecula *An t-Eilean Dorcha*—the Dark Island.' Her voice was low, and he turned his head to look at her. Her eyes locked with his and he caught his breath.

'Dark and beautiful, like the night,' he said, and she nodded, her gaze dropping briefly to his mouth. 'And yet up close it is bright and glorious, and rippling with colour.'

As he spoke, he could not help but feel that, in his heart, she was an essential part of the beauty of the Dark Island. There she was before him, the most beautiful woman he had ever known. Auburn curls cascading over her shoulders in all their unruly glory, blue eyes shining. Her gown today was green, and she had teamed it with a woollen shawl—warm grey striped with grass-green lines.

Only one thing could make the moment perfect. Sensing that she wanted him as much as he wanted her, he raised a hand to trace the curve of her face. Her skin was soft beneath his fingers, and as he watched she closed her eyes, leaning a little into his hand.

'Eilidh,' he murmured, bending his head to brush her lips with a feather-light kiss. Lifting his other hand, he cupped her face with both hands and deepened the kiss.

As he closed his eyes, he felt as though he was entering a magical world. A world of darkness, of sensa-

tion, of communion with Eilidh. His body was on fire
with desire for her, his heart on fire with love. In that
moment, she *was* the island, and he belonged.

Never had he felt so rooted in a place, so entwined
with another person. Her arms were around him, en-
veloping him in her womanliness, and he stood tall
and strong, a man in his own right. Not Burtenshaw's
whipping boy. Not Freddy's shadow. Himself. His feet
were firmly planted on the island ground—at the top
of Rueval, the centre and highest point. His hands were
now on her back, stroking the soft wool of her gown,
and noting the way she trembled at his touch.

Eilidh!

In this moment, all doubts were gone, all thoughts
of the future irrelevant.

Her arms tightened about his lower back, bringing their hips more tightly together, and he could not
prevent a groan of need escaping. Their tongues were
dancing, his head was awhirl, and he wanted nothing
more than to lie down with her here and now in a bed
of purple heather, beneath that clear northern sky. The
impossible thought pierced the magic, and with all the
strength he had, he paused the kiss.

The sound of their noisy breathing melded with the
thunder in his heart and the Rueval breeze. Leaning
back to look at her, it seemed to him that she shared
the sense of magic.

Could this possibly be...?

'That was wonderful,' he managed. 'You are wonderful.'

Her eyes widened briefly, then a shadow crossed
them. Taking a deep breath, she took a step back from
him. 'As are you, Max,' she said softly, and he was
conscious of a wish to freeze time. Somehow he knew

that he would not wish to hear whatever she said next. 'You are very special to me,' she began, 'and one of the people I c-care about most in the world. But your plan is to leave here, is it not?'

He could not answer.

Yes. Yes, it is. It must be.

'We have become very close, I think, and so there may be hurt when you go. For both of us.'

This time he nodded.

Love is here, but I am not ready—I cannot tell her.

His heart soared at the instinct within that sensed her feelings for him. But he was still unsure who he was, what his future would be. It would be pure selfishness to claim her heart, to offer her his, when his mind was in disorder and he had no idea whether his future was in London or in Benbecula.

'I agree,' he managed before his throat closed up completely. A moment later, by unspoken agreement, they began their descent. By the time they had traversed the steep parts, they were speaking again— mostly about where they should put their feet, given the slipperiness of the ground in places. By the time they had reached the ancient cairn, they were making more normal conversation—about the upcoming wedding, about the myths and legends of the Gaels, about Max's upcoming trip to Glasgow.

'Cooper and Alec plan to accompany me,' he declared, 'and I intend to hire a new crew for the yacht when I reach Glasgow—men who do not mind working locally. Men from Scotland.'

'I see,' she replied, but she was frowning. 'But the wedding will be in just a few weeks. Would you not be better keeping your English crew until then?'

He shook his head. 'I plan to stay in Lidistrome for a

little while—at least until the materials have arrived and the work is underway. I expect I shall leave for London around the end of June. I can hire a new crew then, for there will always be men for hire at the Glasgow docks.'

She nodded, her face tight.

I had no intention of hurting her.

Grimly, he came to a decision. 'I shall be staying at Lidistrome, in the cottage next to Anndra. Now do not suggest,' he added in an attempt to lighten the mood, 'that I am too soft for such accommodation, when you have recently spent weeks at sea with me! Indeed I can manage with very few comforts!'

And I must sacrifice the delight and comfort of seeing your beautiful face, for to become ever more closer to you will increase the heartbreak for both of us.

To his relief, she played along. 'But who shall polish your boots, Mr Wood?'

Indicating his spoiled footwear with a gesture, he grimaced. 'My *ton* boots are long gone. These are now Benbecula boots, Rueval boots. I need footwear now that is serviceable, not fashionable.' A thought occurred to him. 'Wood is the Burtenshaw family name. When you said it just now, I confess it felt strange. As though I were an actor playing a role.'

It is all one—I know not who I am.

'You are still you, Max.' A thought seemed to occur to her. 'Who chose your given name? Did Lord Burtenshaw have a hand in it?'

'A good question.' He gave it some consideration, then grinned. 'Since the meaning of the name is "the greatest one", with a nod to the Roman Emperors, I suspect not. I imagine Mama chose it, and that Pa—that Burtenshaw—hated it!' Shaking his head at his mother's audacity, he added softly, 'As he hated me.'

She squeezed his arm briefly, and it was all he could do to resist covering her hand with his. As they walked towards the Broch, Rueval solidly at their back, he resolved to savour every moment left to him in her company, on the island. Should he feel unable to stay, he would need the memories for the long, lonely years to come.

Chapter Fifteen

Monday 3rd June

The day of Angus and Isabella's wedding dawned bright and mild, with a southerly breeze and the occasional scent of wildflowers drifting from the *machair* to the west. The bride wore the same cream silk gown she had worn during the attempted wedding to Barnstable, declaring that she now had only good thoughts of that fateful day.

'It was the day when I found my voice,' she declared to Eilidh and Lydia as they helped her dress. 'And the day Angus decided he wished to marry me. It is only right that I wear it today. Besides,' she added with a twinkle, 'it is a very pretty dress, and I feel pretty when I wear it!'

'Pretty? You are *beautiful*, Isabella,' Eilidh declared, and Lydia chimed in to agree. 'Now, are you ready to go downstairs?'

'I am, and thank you—thank you both for being my maidens today!'

'We are honoured to stand with you, Isabella.'

Eilidh meant every word, yet foolishly her mind was

running on two tracks at once. One, real life, where they were descending the main staircase, admiring the decorations of boughs and flowers festooning the Broch, and now entering the chapel on the ground floor, where the congregation was rising at the bride's entrance. Cooper met Isabella at the back of the chapel, escorting her up the aisle with pride, while Eilidh and a heavily-pregnant Lydia followed.

The other track continued throughout—a constant refrain in her head of *What if it were me and Max?* Her fancies were not dispelled by the sight of the man she loved standing at the altar with Angus and Alasdair, looking grave and handsome and...careworn, somehow.

As the ceremony began, Angus and Isabella stepping forward to take their vows, Eilidh stole another glance at Max. Having seen little of him since he had moved to Lidistrome the day after Rueval, she drank in every detail—the way his hair curled on his collar, his strong profile and absurdly long lashes, his solid masculine frame. He was the only man in the chapel wearing English clothing.

I should like to see him in Highland dress, just once, she thought, and her heart skipped at the notion.

'I will,' said Angus, bringing Eilidh's attention back to the matters in hand. Watching Isabella as she listened to the bride's vow, she could see only happiness shining out of her friend.

'I will,' Isabella declared, her voice clear and firm. Ah, surely there was nothing better than a wedding which was a true love match!

We could have had that, was the sobering thought that followed. *Max and I.*

They still could.

It must still be possible, she told herself.

He loved her, as she loved him. She was sure of it—although it would have been good to hear it confirmed from his own lips. That day atop Rueval she had felt it with every part of her. Her body, her mind, her heart and soul.

But he was troubled yet, and unsure of his path. His entire sense of history, of *himself*, had been rocked by the revelation that Cooper was his father, and he had already felt torn about Benbecula, about Lidistrome. Burtenshaw's antipathy towards him now had an explanation, and yet his childhood wounds remained.

Eilidh was wise enough to know the man needed time to understand it all. This was not something that could be resolved by a declaration of love—even if it was mutual. To speak of their feelings would add to Max's burdens at present, not relieve them. She only hoped that when the fog surrounding him lifted, he would choose her. Choose to become an Islander. Choose the rich, fulfilling life he could have here. She sighed inwardly. To do so, in a sense he would have to let go of much that had been important to him. His entire life until now had been immersed in London society, in being a second son of the *ton*, in playing at sailing to escape the *ennui* of a lively mind adrift in a purposeless existence.

Although she had missed him dreadfully these past weeks, she could only hope that he was learning to feel part of Lidistrome, learning to love the people and the place. He came to the Broch occasionally for dinner, and Eilidh's heart would be full of him every time he did so. His conversation was filled with timber and tools, and a new loom he had ordered, but the enthusiasm he displayed was a balm to her troubled heart.

This is what I want for him!

On the other hand, she had frequently had the rather lowering notion that his distance from her was perhaps a signal that he was guarding his heart, that he did, in fact, intend to choose London, and that he was confident his heart would recover.

For her part, Eilidh was unsure if she would ever recover. Seeing him here, seeing how seriously he was taking his responsibilities, how hard he was working with Alec and the Lidistrome people, just made her love him all the more. They had brought back an initial cargo of timber and tools from Glasgow and the Lidistrome community were working at great pace to make repairs to their houses and barns. According to Cooper, who had been spending more than half his time there, he and Max were labouring along with the rest, and Max was developing calluses and blisters in entirely new places.

While at the Broch, Max never mentioned such details and spoke only in general terms about the purchases he had made and the effect on the people. The new loom had caused great excitement even in Ardmore and Broch Clachan, and the Morrisons were already inundated with work—work which meant they had coins in their pocket and a desire to spend them.

'It really is the most extraordinary thing,' declared Max at the wedding breakfast. He and Eilidh and Cooper were seated together just beside the dais where the Laird and Lady of Broch Clachan were enjoying their first meal together as man and wife. Lydia and Alasdair, along with Alasdair's young daughter from his first tragic marriage, Mairead, were at the same table, but Lydia seemed to Eilidh to be unusually quiet.

'All of the families already barter with each other for items they do not have, but the introduction of a relatively small amount of wealth into Lidistrome has had an effect that is rippling through the whole community.'

Fascinated, Eilidh could not take her eyes from Max. It was not just the things he was saying, which were genuinely interesting, but the *way* in which he was saying them. His eyes were bright, his demeanour filled with vigour. He was as different from the listless London buck as it was possible for him to be.

'The Morrisons have been buying extra items,' Max was continuing. 'More fish from the Laings and the MacGregors, more eggs from the MacIntyres, who had a surplus, and extra cheeses from the MacKinnons. In turn, those families have been able to buy more items from others. It is as though the same few coins are moving around the entire estate, bringing comfort to everyone. It is like magic!' He grimaced. 'Or economics, perhaps. But to *see* it happen is astounding.'

'And this is why,' Cooper interjected, 'money that sits in a bank for fifty years does no good for nobody. I am not saying we should not have savings—not at all. I know myself how diligently I saved my shillings over the years, knowing that Burtenshaw or his son could turn me out whenever the notion took them. For me, the question is: how much money is *enough* for a man? Where does security end and morality begin?'

They talked on then, of Adam Smith and of Hume, and of the Enlightenment ideas they had all explored in different ways. Throughout, Lydia said little, which was most unlike her. Eilidh knew her friend had a lively mind and would normally have delighted in such a conversation.

Watching closely, Eilidh noticed that she was gripping the table edge, at the same time breathing deliberately and slowly. The hairs on the back of Eilidh's neck stood to attention as she realised what might be happening. Waiting until Lydia returned her gaze, she signalled with a subtle jerk of her head a question as to whether Lydia might accompany her to the retiring room. Lydia nodded, and they rose together, making their polite excuses. Alasdair, Eilidh noted, watched his wife intently.

Once safely in the retiring room, away from curious eyes and ears, Eilidh lost no time in questioning her friend.

'What is it, Lydia? Is the baby coming?'

'I do not know. Perhaps.' She shrugged. 'I have been getting curious tightenings—' she rubbed her stretched belly '—and sometimes they are quite painful, but then they go away again.'

'For how long? When did they start?'

'This is the third day. Mrs MacLeod, our housekeeper, tells me it is entirely normal, and it means the baby will come soon. She called it false labour.'

Eilidh's eyes grew round. 'How soon? Today?'

Lydia shook her head. 'This week some time. Alasdair is watching me like an owl with a mouse, and they did suggest I stay at Ardmore, but I was determined not to miss the wedding. Alasdair and Angus are more like brothers than cousins, and it would have killed Alasdair to miss it.' She grinned. 'And me too. I am much better here than sitting alone in Ardmore, sighing over what I was missing!'

Feeling reassured that the baby would not make its entrance any time soon, Eilidh extracted a promise from Lydia that she would let her know if anything changed, and they returned to the celebrations. Alasdair's daughter Mairead, who was seven years old and delightfully inquisitive, had lost no time in befriending Max, and

Eilidh was bemused, though unsurprised, to see the child questioning him about London, and Isabella, and why he had no kilt.

'It seems strange that you are wearing trews when you do not have to, Max,' she said earnestly. 'Does everyone wear trews in London?'

He was laughing, his face open and relaxed. It made Eilidh's breath catch in her throat and her heart turn over. 'All the gentlemen do,' he replied. 'And I think only Scots get to wear Highland dress.'

Mairead was frowning. 'Your voice is English, like Mama-Lydia. But she can speak the Gaelic now, and if she were a man I think she could wear the kilt if she wanted to. Would you not, Lydia?'

'I already wear the MacDonald tartan sometimes,' Lydia confirmed, 'although I am English by blood.'

'How hard was it to pick up Gaelic?' Max asked, and Eilidh's heart skipped again. Trying desperately not to show how interested she was in their conversation, she pretended to half-listen to Cooper and Alasdair's discussion about the new Prince Regent in London, while unashamedly eavesdropping on Lydia telling Max she had found it relatively easy to pick up Gaelic, simply by being immersed in it. Sadly, after just a few minutes, Mairead claimed Max's attention again, and his conversation with Lydia about learning Gaelic was lost. Hopefully Lydia had been able to reassure him, yet the very fact he had asked at all was surely significant.

Or perhaps he is simply being polite, and I am being fanciful.

Still, she could tell he was enjoying the wedding day. As the bride's brother and the new owner of Lidistrome, he was a notable figure in the gathered throng, and as the afternoon went on, many people came to speak with him, or be introduced. By the time the musicians arrived for the evening dancing, he had loosened his cravat and his posture was entirely relaxed as he chatted easily with farmers, merchants, clergymen and kelpmen. He seemed genuinely interested in everyone, and he and Alec even had an animated conversation about An Taigh Buidhe which caught Eilidh's ear. Eavesdropping yet again, she held her breath as Max asked where the Lidistrome Gatherings were held.

'Years ago, they'd have been in An Taigh Buidhe itself,' Alec offered with a shrug. 'There is a hall there which at one time was used regularly for Gatherings and parties—balls, even. We have nowhere like that now.'

'But why did I not know this before? So the house then was not just a residence for the Laird?'

'Not at all. It was the centre for our community, bringing us all together for winter nights and summer celebrations.'

'I see.' He thought for a moment. 'I think we must bring the house back to life, Alec.'

'I thought you might say so,' Alec murmured. 'The Lidistrome folk will be delighted.'

They were interrupted by little Mairead, who wanted Max to dance with her for the first dance. 'Oh, but I do not know your dances, Mairead.' He grinned at Eilidh. 'I wonder, could Monsieur Dupont travel here to teach me and Isabella the Highland dances?'

'Who is Monsieur Dupont?' asked Mairead, with a creditable French accent.

'He is a dancing master in London,' Eilidh offered. 'He helped me and Angus learn the London dances, and we practised with Isabella and Max.'

Mairead glanced towards the newlyweds. 'So Angus danced with Isabella, and you danced with Max?'

'That's it.'

The child considered this for a moment, thoughts flitting across her little face like scurrying clouds in the night sky. 'Very well. Eilidh, you should dance with Max, and I with Papa, for Mama-Lydia is too big to dance now.'

She would not listen to protests from either of them, protests which were, to be fair, half-hearted, and a few moments later, Eilidh found herself taking Max's hand for the dance. It was not particularly complicated, but he wore an adorable frown of concentration until he had repeated the figure often enough to begin to relax.

'See? You are a natural,' Eilidh told him, her tone half-teasing. 'Why, if you stayed you'd probably be a bard by Christmastide!'

He laughed at this, but the uncertainty in his eyes was clear to her.

I should not have said it.

Why was she trying to force the matter when she knew he needed time? Cursing her own impatience, she set out to ensure he enjoyed the dancing, which, to be fair, he seemed to—showing no signs of wanting to sit down. He danced every dance, sometimes with her, sometimes with other Benbecula ladies, young and old. And when the celebrations ended, he was included in the round of hearty and affectionate goodnights as though he had lived on the island all his days.

Progress indeed, she thought as she settled down to sleep. *A good day in all. Isabella is now my sister, and Max...well, who knows?*

Max lay in the darkness, his mind awhirl and his decision as elusive as ever. Today had surely been one of the most wonderful days he had ever experienced, and there had been many since leaving London. Seeing his darling sister marry Angus, Cooper walking her up the aisle, Eilidh attending her alongside Lydia—the English Lady of Ardmore… All of it had led to him feeling welcome, belonging, a part of it. Conversing with people from Lidistrome and further afield in this relaxed context had been good too he realised. Tendrils of connection were being created all the time—connections tying him ever more deeply to this beautiful place, these wonderful people. Connections tying him to Eilidh. Dancing with her had been exhilarating, and they had flirted unashamedly with eyes and smiles as they had danced their way around the set.

And yet his doubts remained. How could he ever make up for the neglect of generations of Burtenshaws? He might not be related to them by blood but he bore their name, had until very recently believed himself to be part of their family. He could not simply sidestep his way out of responsibility. Reality was not a dance, and the people here were not fools. His love for Eilidh was beyond question, and he was fairly certain she felt the same way. But speaking it aloud would not help, for he still did not know if it would be right for him to stay.

With determination, he steered his thoughts in another direction. A place to gather was as important in Lidistrome as it was in Broch Clachan—or in London, for that matter. An Taigh Buidhe had been asleep for decades. It was time to reawaken the house and fill it again with life, and people.

Tomorrow, he thought, *I shall meet with Alec and get things moving.*

Tuesday 4th June

What seemed like only a moment later, Eilidh woke abruptly to the sound of frantic knocking on her door.

'Come in!' she called groggily, pushing herself up to a sitting position and realising that soft dawn light was seeping into her chamber.

It was Mary, her maid. 'My Lady of Ardmore has need of you, Eilidh!'

Eilidh gasped, suddenly wide awake. 'The baby!'

'Aye. She's been griping all night and wants to go home as soon as she can.'

Eilidh was already climbing out of bed. 'Is there time? Should she not stay here?'

'Ach, there'll be plenty of time. First babies come slowly, most of the time.'

'Most—?' Eilidh clamped her jaw shut. 'I must speak to her. Here, help me get into this dress.'

A half-hour later, they were in the yard, ready to depart. Lydia was insisting that she was perfectly well, yet at times she wore a decidedly pained expression. Having made her comfortable inside the Ardmore carriage, Eilidh climbed up to sit beside her. Alasdair was already seated on her other side, but they had left Mairead behind, the child reportedly delighted she could stay a while longer in Broch Clachan.

'Max!' Alasdair's face lit up in a smile, and Eilidh twisted round to see the man she loved on horseback, looking roguishly handsome in the morning light.

'Thank you for doing this,' Alasdair continued. 'We shall follow you as quickly as we can, but the carriage will have to go steadily at some points. If you could ask the Ardmore staff to make all ready for my wife, I shall be eternally grateful.' He frowned. 'Are you certain you know the way?'

'Certain? Absolutely!' Max retorted. 'I have travelled these roads dozens of times since coming here, I think.'

This brought a thoughtfulness to Alasdair's expression. 'Dozens? Yes, I suppose that must be so. I am glad you are here, Max.'

'I appreciate you saying so,' Max returned quietly, and Lydia threw Eilidh a significant look.

Baby or no baby, the Lady of Ardmore still has her wits about her.

Tipping his hat to them, Max took off at a trot. Straining her ears, Eilidh heard the horse speed to a gallop once beyond the arch. It was good to know the Ardmore people would be ready, and that Max was the one to race ahead to tell them of their lady's impending confinement. Eilidh had given orders that the newlyweds in the Broch were not to be disturbed—there would be plenty of time for Angus and Isabella to discover that Lydia was on her way home to have the baby.

The driver took them at a steady pace, going slowly over the bumps and hollows and speeding his pace each time there was a good stretch of road. Alasdair held his wife's hand throughout, while Eilidh remained close to her friend, hoping and praying that the baby would not decide to come while they were travelling and with no midwife present. Thankfully, eventually the familiar sight of Ardmore Castle came into view and before long, they had arrived.

'And here you are,' clucked the older of the two midwives, stepping forward to help Lydia descend. 'Never worry, *a ghraidh*, for all will be well.' Lydia took a few steps then stopped, turning to lean slightly on the woman.

'Looks like she's progressing well,' the second midwife murmured to Eilidh.

'Aye,' Eilidh replied. 'She has gone into herself and barely spoke the past mile or so.'

'Good,' said the midwife with satisfaction. 'Now,

she will no doubt want you with her, but go you and get some breakfast before coming upstairs, you hear? There'll be time enough.'

Eilidh nodded, her eyes staying on Lydia as her friend disappeared into the house, the second midwife hurrying to catch up.

Max, who had been lingering to one side, now stepped forwards to greet Eilidh and Alasdair. 'I must say I am impressed by your people here, Alasdair. No sooner had I given them the news then the midwives were sent for, and someone to make the chamber ready, and another to offer me refreshments. But tell me, does the Benbecula doctor not concern himself with child-birth?'

'Lord, no, and the women would soon chase him if he tried!' Alasdair retorted. 'Childbirth is no illness, and what is more, it is women's business. The *bean glùine*—midwife—knows her work, and she will only call upon the doctor if she needs him. Now, come inside and we shall all have breakfast, for this is likely to be a very long day.'

'*Bean glùine,*' Max repeated carefully. 'Isn't *bean* the word for woman?'

'It is.' Eilidh beamed at him, naturally delighted by his show of interest in the Gaelic. 'Our word for midwife is literally "the woman of the knee"—perhaps because they kneel to attend to the woman giving birth. It also may be based on the phrase *bho ghlùin gu glùin*—from generation to generation. Literally, from knee to knee.'

'Like a child being dandled on the knee, then growing to hold another child in turn?'

'Exactly.' They eyed one another, and Eilidh wondered if he too had a sudden vision of them dandling their own child on their knees.

'Shall we go inside?' Alasdair asked, a hint of amusement in his voice, and they both made haste to agree.

A short while later, having taken her fill of creamy porridge, Eilidh rose to go to Lydia.

'I shall say goodbye now, Eilidh,' Max returned, 'for I mean to continue on to Lidistrome shortly. There is much to be done.'

'Of course.' Eilidh was conscious of the usual feeling of being torn. On the one hand, she was delighted by his taking his responsibilities so seriously. On the other, every goodbye was a wrench. 'I hope to see you again soon.'

'And I you.' He kissed her hand, leaving her heart thundering and her thoughts disordered. Before she was tempted into saying anything foolish, she turned and fled.

Max, nearing the last bend before Lidistrome, allowed the horse to drop into a walk. He always loved this part of the journey and today he was going to savour it.

There!

The incline fell away before him, the track sweeping its way down to the cluster of fishing cottages by the slipway. The sea was glistening, seabirds calling, and here and there small animals were scurrying through the bracken. The cottages themselves rested, nestling into the hill, solid and beautiful. They were as much a part of the land as the rocks and the heather.

Turning slightly, he fixed his gaze on the manor house standing proudly on the hill. From this distance, An Taigh Buidhe looked solid, peaceful and beautiful. Only when up close did the dilapidation become apparent. His heart leapt as he allowed himself to experience the joy of knowing he would revive the old place, re-awaken it, bring it back to life. The people needed it and maybe, just maybe, it might be a home again.

A home for him, for Eilidh, for any children they might be blessed with… The thought was tempting.

Bho ghlùin gu glùin. From generation to generation.

An old conversation with Cooper came back to him, one where he had recalled Mama talking about being reborn after being freed from Burtenshaw. Reborn. An Taigh Buidhe would be reborn and he, Max Wood— or possibly Max Cooper—would make it happen. He could stay a few weeks longer to help with the work.

It did not tie him to anything. Nor did it mean he had made any firm decision. No, of course not. He had good reasons to restore the house—reasons that were completely separate to decisions he must make about his own future, and Eilidh's. He would stay long enough to fix the house. For now, that was enough. It would have to be enough.

Chapter Sixteen

Tuesday 16th July

'That is the last of it.'

Max nodded to Alec with satisfaction. He and a team of Lidistrome men and women had just finished moving the furniture back into An Taigh Buidhe—the furniture that Anndra had been looking after for years. Once the roof and windows had been mended, Alec had confirmed the building was watertight and suggested transferring the furniture from the old barn into the house.

'Besides,' he had said, 'we have another shipment of wood due in the next few days and I have nowhere else to store it.'

The decision had been eminently sensible and logical, and yet Max's heart had warmed at the sight of tables and chairs, beds and nightstands being moved into the various rooms. Some of the sofas needed to be freshly upholstered and new mattresses, curtains, bed drapes and wall hangings were needed, but those details were cosmetic and could wait. Pushing away the notion that Eilidh should be involved in such decisions, Max concentrated on enjoying the sense of achievement currently coursing through him.

'The house looks and feels *alive* again, Alec,' he murmured, looking around the Gathering Hall. The place needed more work, of course. Some of the floor tiles were cracked, the paintings on the roof and in the panels had faded and the musicians' dais had rotted away, but Max could already see how beautiful the room was. Daylight streamed in through the line of windows down the whole western side of the room, although the terrace outside was in dire need of attention, Max recalled. But this was a house that a man could be proud of. And technically it was his. Therefore, for the moment, he was going to allow himself to feel proud.

'It does, aye.' Alec's eyes softened for a moment, then he was back to his usual brisk efficiency. 'Now that we have done the basics I want to lower the chandelier and check it, and set a couple of the men to building a new dais. I suggest we hold a Gathering here on Friday evening, if that suits you, sir?'

'So soon?' If the house was ready for a Gathering, then his work was done and he was free of any further obligations. The past month had been a dream for him, and he had loved almost every minute of it. Working in Lidistrome, learning more building skills—and plenty of Gaelic—from being around the people all day long, and falling into bed at night blessedly exhausted, seemed to suit him. He felt active, fulfilled, *useful*.

Generally, he slept in the cottage next to Anndra's, which served as Alec's office by day, but he made sure to stay in Broch Clachan at least twice a week. He also called at Ardmore on a regular basis. Lydia's baby—a boy—had been born that night, and the entire Ardmore community seemed to be besotted with him. Lydia, despite being an Englishwoman, was entirely comfortable living on Benbecula, it seemed. Temptation rose again to whisper within him, but he pushed it away with a stern reminder.

But Lydia is not one of the hated Burtenshaws.

Eilidh was always in his mind, in his heart. Yes, sometimes he would not think of her for minutes or even hours at a time, if he was absorbed in an important task with the Lidistrome people. But even then she was always present—an unseen witness to his attempts to assist them all.

As well as trying to make up for decades of neglect, he was conscious that it was *her* approval he sought, for she was to him the entire community in one person.

You are being fanciful, he told himself.

Yet every time he learned a new Gaelic word, or earned a kind word from one of the people, in his head he wanted Eilidh to know of it, to understand how hard he was working.

His evenings in the Broch were exquisite torture. Eilidh would be there, all beauty and sparkle and wit. He would talk with her and tease her and sometimes their eyes would meet or their hands would touch, and it would be enough to make him hold his breath briefly while trying to slow his racing heart. And every time he said goodbye to her, the racing thoughts would flood his mind.

Outsider. Sassenach. Burtenshaw.

He knew he was unworthy. He knew that part of him sought forgiveness from Eilidh, and it was because of that voice in his head, the one that had constantly told him by word and gesture that he was worthless. Lord Burtenshaw's voice.

The man he had believed to be his father. The man who had jeered at him and beaten him when he was an innocent, bewildered boy. That boy had come to believe bad things about himself, and Burtenshaw's voice in his mind drowned out everything else.

Lately, however, things had begun to change. Knowing Cooper, not Burtenshaw, was his father had come as a huge relief and it had also explained why Burtenshaw had treated him so badly. Isabella too.

Yet *knowing* it and *feeling* it were two different things.

I am making progress, though.

Now, he could picture himself answering the man, fighting back. Slowly, ever so slowly, he was loosening Burtenshaw's grip from around him. He was beginning to breathe, to lift his head and look about him, to feel a sense of control.

I have choices. I decide what I do.

'Aye, it needs to be soon.' Alec eyed him steadily and Max blinked, momentarily losing the thread of their conversation. 'The people have worked hard on this. They are itching to gather in An Taigh Buidhe, as their grandparents once did.'

'Of course, of course. No reason to delay, I suppose. Can you organise food and drink, Alec—and the musicians, of course?'

'You can certainly pay for the drink, which will be most welcome. In terms of the food, the women have already been making plans. Every house will contribute—'

'But I shall pay!'

Alec shook his head. 'Thank you, sir, but it is fitting to make this a shared table.'

'If it is a shared table, then I too can contribute. Perhaps something they do not normally eat. What can be bought from the mainland by Friday?'

'I shall go across to Skye tomorrow and see what I may purchase there. And sir, it would be your responsibility to hire the musicians. I can organise both. Do you wish to invite people from Broch Clachan and Ardmore, or keep it solely for Lidistrome?'

'Lidistrome only, I think—at least this first time.'

Alec nodded, an approving glint in his eye. 'It would be appropriate to invite the two Lairds and their Ladies, of course.'

'It would? And—'

'And the Laird's sister, yes.'

Max dropped his gaze, uncomfortable with Alec's knowing expression.

Lord, I want no gossip attached to Eilidh. If I leave, she must not be seen as having been jilted or abandoned.

If he left… In all honesty, with every day that passed, he found himself wishing more and more that he could stay. He just needed some sort of sign that would make it acceptable. As he was the owner of Lidistrome— a ridiculous notion, how could any man 'own' such a place?—they were his tenants and he their landlord. They would say whatever he wished them to say and he might never know what they truly thought of him.

Yes, they had been grateful for his funds, for the rent rebate and the help with repairs, but even now Mina Morrison remained cool with him, while some of the others actively avoided him. And could he blame them? Not one iota.

Having pushed away the time when he must decide, he saw now that he was fast approaching the crossroads. Lidistrome or London? Would he rather live out his days as a *ton* buck, or a Sassenach in the Hebrides? An outlander who might never truly be part of this place. Perhaps with a wife who would go through life feeling torn between loyalty to her husband and her people.

Would he really wish that upon Eilidh? It would be utterly selfish to do so.

So why was he hesitating? Walking through the house again, he noted the old and the new side by side. Burtenshaw neglect. His own repairs. Yet still the damage done was apparent. Perhaps it always would be. On and on it went, his mind veering from one option to the other, leaving him entirely bewildered.

Friday 19th July

Bidding a fond farewell to Lydia and her sweet baby, Eilidh made her way through Ardmore Castle and out to the courtyard outside.

'Ach, 'tis Eilidh Ruadh! How are you this fine day, miss?' It was the Ardmore housekeeper, who turned to walk with Eilidh as she headed for the stables.

'Mrs MacLeod! Lovely to see you. I am fine, thank you. And are you well?'

'I am, and delighted that the baby is doing so well. My lady is a champion feeder, and insists on having very little help with him.'

Eilidh smiled. 'And of course Mairead is delighted to be a big sister.'

Mrs MacLeod sighed. 'Aye, I am relieved all has ended well.' Unspoken between them was the memory of Hester, who had refused to look after her own child and had run away to the mainland months later, losing her life in a carriage accident on the way to Edinburgh. It was a timely reminder of the danger of bringing someone to live in the Islands who did not belong.

Mrs MacLeod was clearly thinking along the same lines. 'And how is the new Lady of Broch Clachan?'

'Isabella and Angus seem blissfully happy. I do think she will make every effort to settle here.'

'I am glad to hear it, for will is a good worker, as they say. Our choices are what make us.' The older woman paused, eyeing Eilidh keenly. 'And what of her brother? I hear he is making some amends over in Lidistrome.'

'He is.' Eilidh did not trust herself to say more. Mrs MacLeod was altogether too astute.

'And bending his back to it, not just opening his purse, I hear?'

'Aye. He has been staying in one of the empty cottages and working with the men.'

Mrs MacLeod nodded in satisfaction. 'Better a weary foot than a weary spirit. Are you going to the Lidistrome Gathering tonight?'

'I am. Alasdair will go, and Angus and Isabella. Lydia will bring the baby—his first outing.'

'Quite right too. New mothers and their babies should not part, for they are like one person.'

They had reached the stable, and Eilidh began saddling her pony.

'Eilidh…'

'Yes?'

'"*A' bheinn a 's àirde tha 's an tlr, 's ann oirre 's trice 'chi thu 'n ceo.*"' She recited the old proverb, adding an English version. '"The highest hill is like to be covered in clouds. It's a good man that knows not to hold himself too high."'

Eilidh nodded, her throat tight. 'Aye.' Her voice was husky.

They exchanged farewells, and Eilidh rode out. On impulse, at the crossing of the roads she went east towards Lidistrome, rather than westward to the Broch. It was only when she crowned the hill to An Taigh Buidhe that she realised there might be some awkwardness in her arriving unannounced.

What if Max does not want me here? What if he thinks I am pursuing him?

'Eilidh!' It was too late. He had just emerged from the back of the house and was crossing the yard towards her. 'What a delightful surprise!'

His smile was broad, his stance relaxed and open, and it struck Eilidh that today he had none of the London stiffness she associated with him. Suddenly she was glad she was wearing one of her most flattering dresses, a fine wool gown in cornflower blue. 'I hope you do not mind. I have been at Ardmore, and decided to come across to see how the work is going—and the preparations for the Gathering tonight.'

'Come and see!'

She jumped down and saw to her pony, then followed him inside An Taigh Buidhe.

They had entered via the kitchens, which were a hive of activity, the Lidistrome women busy baking and cooking. It looked as if there would be a veritable feast at tonight's Gathering. After exchanging greetings with the women, she turned to Max. 'My goodness— the ovens are working?'

'Aye, most of them. One or two will have to be replaced—and besides, there are better ovens available now.' He grinned. 'To think I know something of ovens—a subject I was entirely ignorant of just months ago! Ovens, and building, and weaving and farming... I even cut turf yesterday!'

She felt her own smile grow, delighted by his evident glee—and by his saying 'aye' instead of 'yes'.

Mrs MacLeod's words came back to her. *'Better a weary foot than a weary spirit.'*

'You seem…happy, Max.'

Instantly his smile faded, and she cursed herself inwardly for taking him out of the moment and into his own mind again.

'It has been a privilege. Now, come and see the Gathering Hall.'

In the end, he took her through the entire house, his pride evident at all the work completed so far. 'It is a long way from being habitable, of course. Just look at those damp-stained walls! But the roof is fixed, and I am assured it would be safe to redecorate if I choose to.'

And will you?

Thankfully, this time she had the sense not to give voice to the question bubbling within her. Yet she could not deny that hope was coursing through her. Never had she seen him so full of vigour, so enthusiastic, so animated. Having a purpose, doing good for others, working hard physically—all of it was changing Max. Did he even understand just how much he was changing?

The tour done, they made their way to the cottage Max had been using as his impromptu home. Averting her eyes from his bed, for she needed to keep her wits about her, Eilidh sat on one of the simple wooden chairs by the scrubbed table, questioning him on the work done throughout Lidistrome. He obliged, describing repairs to buildings, roads and hedges with the same animation as before.

'But this is astounding!' she declared. 'Max, you are a wonder!' He had given them some information during his visits to the Broch, but had, she now realised, played down the extent of his own involvement.

'Not at all,' he shot back. 'The *people* here are a wonder. I am simply fulfilling my responsibilities to them.'

Spoken like a true laird, she thought.

But before she even had time to consider saying it aloud, someone burst through the door and into the cottage.

Max felt as though he were in heaven, for Eilidh's response could not have been better. She had exclaimed and been delighted with every aspect of An Taigh Buidhe, and he now knew—if he had not before—that it was worth it. Every blister, every aching muscle. Every night he had fallen into bed exhausted.

There was no hint in her eyes or her voice of the woman who had spoken at the theatre of the softness of idleness, of selfishness, of self-indulgence. That night each word had stung—and it had stung because he had recognised himself in her words. Now he felt remade, reborn. He had chosen to embrace his Scottish and Hebridean ancestry and had rejected the life he had been reared to. Now could he possibly hope…?

Fate has given me responsibilities, and I am shouldering them as best I can.

A man and woman came through the door, both looking distressed, the man with a paper in his hand. Highly agitated, he was saying something in Gaelic, and Max had no idea what was wrong. Searching in his mind for their names, thankfully they came to him. Ronald MacLean. His wife was called Kenina. They lived in one of the fisher cottages near the slipway, and were among the Lidistrome people who still were cool towards him.

There was nothing cool about Ronald today. Max might not understand the words the man was saying but he knew how to read the man's expression, his voice, the language of his body. The man was furious. Furious and distressed, all at once. He glanced towards Kenina.

Fear. She was trying to calm her husband, fearful of something—perhaps of retribution from himself?

But why?

He had risen to his feet. 'Tell me what has happened,' he offered soberly.

'This!' Ronald declared in English, shaking the paper in front of Max's face. 'This has happened! They are slowly starving, and it is all the fault of you Burten-shaws!'

Max felt the blood drain from his face. 'Who? Who is starving? Tell me, so I may mend it!'

'Some things, Sassenach, cannot be mended!' Ronald almost spat the words at him. 'No, nor forgiven!'

'*Isht*, Ronald,' his wife hissed, taking his arm. She added something else—most likely a plea for him to leave the cottage.

'No!' Ronald declared. 'He shall hear of it. He must understand what he and his ilk have done to us! Done to Calum and Màiri.'

The names were unfamiliar as a pair. Might he mean Calum Bán Laing or his son, Calum Óg? Or perhaps he was referring to Calum Morrison, the weaver? Max could not recall any of them being paired with a Màiri. His mind was racing, as was his pulse.

'Wait, who are Calum and Màiri?'

'Calum is the son of Ronald and Kenina.' Eilidh spoke softly, a light frown creasing her forehead. 'He married an Ardmore girl called Màiri last year and they emigrated to Canada.' She turned to Ronald and Kenina. 'Is that a letter from Calum?'

Nodding, Ronald handed her the letter and she scanned it quickly. 'Oh, Ronald, Kenina! I am so sorry to hear this terrible news!' She turned to Max. 'Their money was stolen during the sea journey last year, but they never told anyone from home as they did not wish to cause worry. But they are not doing well. Work is hard to find where they are, and they have no money to travel to a better part of Canada. He writes to say farewell to his parents, and to ask them to let Màiri's family know. Unless there is some miracle, they do not expect to survive another winter. They are barely managing as it is.'

'And if Burtenshaw had done his duty by us, they would never have been forced to leave their home and go to Canada in the first place! Calum says he spent his last shilling sending this letter. I have no doubt he and Màiri did without food to pay the postage. They will not survive the winter!' Ronald raised an angry finger in Max's face. 'This is on you, Burtenshaw! Oh, you may pretend all you wish that you are not connected to that *monster*, but I *know*! I know you are his half-brother. Raised in wealth and ease while my boy starves. Landing here with your shiny boots and your gaudy yacht and thinking you can be forgiven. Well, I can tell you right now, you will never be forgiven! *Never!*'

Turning on his heel, he strode out. Kenina paused, squaring her shoulders. 'My husband is upset. But he has every right to be. You may punish us as you will. We have nothing more to lose.'

'Wait!' But she was gone, and ignored Max's plea.

He stood there in the stone cottage, stock-still as the world spun around him and all of his dreams crashed about his ears.

Chapter Seventeen

Vaguely, Max knew Eilidh was talking to him. He met her gaze and could see the distress in her expression. She would be trying to draw a veil over what had just happened, he knew, trying to console him, tell him it was not his fault.

But there could be no veiling it. No denying it. Calum and Màiri were *real*. They lived and breathed, and had suffered—were suffering even now, if they yet lived. Because of his family's selfish inattention. Abstractedly, he noted Eilidh's beauty, as if seeing her for the last time.

It cannot be.

He had been a fool even to hope that a life here might be possible.

'Worthless. Useless.' His father's voice.

'Idle. Selfish. Self-indulgent.' Eilidh's.

'Never be forgiven.' Ronald's.

This is who I am.

Eilidh seemed to have stopped talking and was simply looking at him, frustration and helplessness clearly writ on her features.

At least I know.

The other path, the one he had dreamed of for so

long, was vanishing before his eyes, leaving only the loneliness of London. Max found his voice, but even to his own ears it sounded strange. Tight, and faraway, and devoid of emotion. 'I must speak to Alec. Send them money for their passage home to Lidistrome. Ensure they have a home and decent work when they get here.' He looked about him. This place had felt like a home to him in a way that nowhere ever had before. 'They can have this cottage, perhaps.'

'Yes!' Eilidh laid a hand on his arm. 'That is exactly the right thing to do, Max, and it shows again that you are the right man, doing what is right.'

He looked at her blankly. Her words were so far from reality he could not even *begin* to challenge them. So he simply nodded, bowed and said, 'I must bid you good day, Eilidh.' The old cadence of London manners came to him, easy as breathing. He was a man of the *ton*, after all. Not a true Islander. Never that.

Striding across the yard, he made his way through the gardens to where Alec was helping rebuild the terrace.

I shall leave tomorrow, since I can bid farewell to everyone tonight. I will continue to send money to Alec for any future works, and ensure that the people have enough.

His heart was frozen, for fear he might feel it breaking. All around him, butterflies fluttered amid the beautiful flowers. He ignored them.

Eilidh stared out of the carriage window, ignoring Angus and Isabella's newlywed teasing, and tried to pretend all might yet be well. Max had done exactly as he ought on hearing the dreadful news about Calum and Màiri. Alasdair would no doubt also send funds, since Màiri was of Ardmore stock. The community would welcome them home, and they would never have to leave again.

Yet the feeling of dread within her could not be subdued. Max had taken Ronald's words hard.

Too hard.

Even now, she could recall with gut-clenching accuracy his pale, set face, stiff demeanour and clipped tones. Yet it was his eyes she remembered most. Those dark, beautiful eyes that had so recently gazed into hers with such warmth and animation. Earlier today, after hearing from Ronald, Max's eyes had been blank. Not cold, just…empty. As though Max had hidden himself away like a wounded animal.

It had been a shock, she had no doubt, and it would have felt like a blow—especially since Max had been working so hard to gain the trust of the Islanders.

What can be done? How can I make him see that he belongs here?

She had managed a word with Cooper earlier. Max's father was sitting alongside her in the carriage, deep in thought, but he had no immediate suggestions, beyond trying to reason with Max.

Reason with him? No, it is his heart we must reach. But how?

They had nearly reached Lidistrome, and soon the Gathering would start, and she was no nearer to knowing how to mend the situation. Earlier, when she had tried speaking to him, Max had looked through her almost as if he could not hear her. It had chilled her to the bone, and she shivered now just thinking of it.

Unusually, instead of driving round to the yard, the carriage pulled up outside the front door of An Taigh Buidhe, and as she stepped down, it occurred to Eilidh that she had never seen the house look more beautiful. Lanterns had been hung on either side of the front door and the windows glowed with warm candlelight. If she wanted to look closely, she would still see small cracks in the render and other signs of inattention. Instead she chose to notice freshly cleaned windows, a newly painted front door, branches of candles on the windowsills.

This house could be a home again. My home.

Inside were the same traces of care and attention, if you knew where to look. The black and white floor tiles had been scrubbed, the banisters on the wide staircase varnished. There was a scent of paint and polish and... and *love*. The house was awakening from a deep slumber, and it seemed to Eilidh that it wanted them there.

She caught her breath. At the foot of the stairs, where the host should stand, was Alec.

Where is Max?

They all greeted the steward warmly and he welcomed them to the Gathering, but no one was impolite enough to ask about the presence of the man who should have been there. Instead they made their way through to the busy Gathering Hall, which had been festooned with boughs and vases of wildflowers and where a hundred candles burned, supplementing the golden rays of sunset gently washing the room in warm light. The line of west-facing windows had been perfectly angled to catch the setting sun and Eilidh gave an inward nod to the unknown architect.

'What a beautiful ballroom!' declared Isabella, and Eilidh looked about the room anew.

Yes, in London this would be a ballroom.

The proportions, the dais, the long windows, glazed doors leading to the terrace and the hubbub of happy voices… Yet here it was rightly known as the Gathering Hall, with chairs laid out in rows for the formalities. Later, they would be cleared for the feast and the dancing.

There was no further time to talk, for people had already come forward to greet them. The next half-hour was lost in conversation, as Eilidh chatted with many people. All the while she looked for Max, without making it too obvious. He was nowhere to be seen.

Finally, Mina Morrison cornered her. 'I need you, Miss Eilidh. Will you come with me?' The expression in her eyes was one of determination, but her mouth was turned down and her brow furrowed.

'Yes, of course.'

Mina led the way through the kitchens, where dozens of people—women, girls and men—were making final preparations for the feast.

'Is he in yet?' asked one woman, rubbing the sweat from her brow with the corner of her apron.

'Not yet, no,' replied Mina grimly, picking up a cloth-wrapped parcel. 'But he will be.'

Eilidh swallowed, realising what Mina's mission must be. Sure enough, they exited to the yard and made their way across to Max's cottage, where the light from a single candle glowed through the small window. Dusk was rapidly falling, sunset a line of gold on the far horizon. Mina knocked sharply on the cottage door.

'Come in!'

Eilidh reached for the handle, but Mina forestalled her, handing her the package. 'He would not accept this earlier.'

Eilidh glanced down, abruptly realising what she held. Her eyes widened. 'You did this?'

'Aye. Me and all the weavers. He has earned it.'

Eilidh lifted her chin. 'I shall do my best.'

'Good lass!' Mina turned away and Eilidh squared her shoulders, praying for eloquence. The entire course of her future depended on the next few minutes. For a second, the enormity of it flooded through her, threatening to freeze her ability to think. Ruthlessly, she pushed away all thoughts of herself. This was for Max, and him only.

There was a murmur of voices outside the cottage door, though Max could not make out any words. It seemed to be taking an inordinate length of time for whoever it was to come in. He shrugged. It mattered little anyway. Continuing with his task of packing his clothes and personal possessions into the tea chest someone had found for him, he scanned the room. Really, it was surprising how many of his possessions had made their way to this cosy cottage during the past months. Carefully, he folded what had once been a pale-coloured jacket. Like all his work clothing, it had been carefully laundered by the Lidistrome women, but no laundering could remove the stain of his endeavours since joining in the work. His expensive clothing had been liberally marked with everything from soil to sawdust, and he regretted not a single moment of it.

There would be time enough for shining black boots and pale buckskins once he returned to England. By this stage, the Season was well finished and most *ton* families would be in their country retreats.

He would stay with Freddy for a few weeks, he supposed, and could check in on the work being coordinated by Great-Aunt Morton's lawyer to refurbish the Mayfair house. He had thought he might decide to let it out, not live in it. A good source of steady income, the lawyer had assured him. He could not imagine it would ever feel like a home to him.

I have no home.

His trunks, along with the rest of his possessions, had remained in Broch Clachan, but he could fetch those tomorrow, before he left. It felt strange to know that this would be his last night in Lidistrome, his last night on Benbecula. Tomorrow, and for many nights hence, he would sleep on the yacht.

His determination had, if anything, hardened over the past few hours, and his conviction that he did not belong here was absolute. How could he stay, wondering forever if there were others like Ronald, people who saw him for the fraud he was? Worrying every day what was being muttered about him in Gaelic. Always wondering, deep down, if he was truly wanted here. No, that was not a life any man should choose.

Alec, to be fair, had seemed genuine when he had expressed surprise and disappointment at Max's decision earlier. Max had asked him to maintain secrecy on the matter, yet only an hour later Mina had arrived with a parcel of hand-woven garments—a gift which Max had, naturally, declined. The last thing he deserved was gratitude from the Lidistrome people, who had been wronged by his family for generations.

My family. No matter how much he tried to deny it, he had been raised as a Burtenshaw in Burtenshaw House, and must share in the collective responsibility. The parcel had felt like a farewell gift with an air of *haste ye away* about it, not *haste ye back*.

The knowledge that he had alleviated some of the worst ills for the current generation helped a little. Ronald's letter had reminded him that he could do nothing about past wrongs. He could bring Calum and Màiri home, but he could not do anything to put right the hardship they had experienced since being forced to leave Benbecula. There had been no place for them here under Freddy's ownership, Inglis's management. No home, no work, no reliable income.

Ronald's anger—fuelled, Max knew, by concern for his beloved son and daughter-in-law—had been raw, intense and entirely justified, and Max could not stand against it. The best thing for everyone was for him to leave.

Everyone except himself.

Self-pity rose up within him and he turned away in disgust.

Even now, I am thinking of myself. Of my loss, my pain, when these people have endured decades of cruel neglect.

Thankfully, the door finally opened, offering him distraction from his thoughts, however temporary.

He stiffened. It was Eilidh, looking exquisite in the same dress she had worn at the Sandison ball.

Where I first kissed her.

Her hair was piled high upon her head, with one small auburn curl allowed to escape on each side. She wore no jewellery, save a simple necklace of green garnets, and as her eyes met his he knew himself to be in danger.

I cannot be alone with her!

He knew his resolve to be necessary, knew also that she was his weakness. How could he bear to leave her? Only by remembering that she would be far, far better off when he left.

'Max!' Her voice was soft, her expression concerned. He saw her gaze flick to his task, then back to search his face. 'How do you?'

'I am well, Eilidh,' he lied. 'And you?' The formulaic response rolled from his lips, honed by years spent in drawing rooms and ballrooms.

'I am not well at all.'

He blinked in shock. One did not say such things! People often jested that a person might be slowly expiring yet still reply that they were well.

'Indeed I am deeply distressed,' she continued, then paused.

He could not ask her why, for he did not wish to give her an opening. Instead, he simply stood there, like the fool he was.

'You will not ask me, but I shall tell you anyway.' Her expression softened. 'I am concerned about you. What happened earlier, with Ronald—'

'I do not wish to speak of it.' Retreating behind cold haughtiness, he ensured his expression was remote, his stance rigid.

'And I care not what you wish! On this, you must hear me!' She squared her shoulders. 'Ronald was angry, with justification. His anger was born of frustration, of worry, of concern for Calum and for Màiri. He was not directing it at you as an individual, but—'

'He was entirely correct in directing it at me. I am the *individual* who supposedly "owns" Lidistrome. I am a Burtenshaw. I am an English landlord. There is no getting away from it.' His tone was harsh, his words fuelled by self-loathing.

'This will be forgotten in a day, a week! You are bringing them home; *that* is all that matters. Over the course of a lifetime there will be many occasions when someone is angry with you. It does not mean—'

'Do not seek to diminish the significance of this, Eilidh. I know you mean well, but my mind is made up.' He took a breath. 'I mean to leave Benbecula and return to my true life in England.'

She gasped. 'You do not mean it! After everything you have done here? And what about…?'

Her voice tailed away. She was pale, he saw, and her evident distress pierced him like a knife. Still, she would be better without him.

'What about us, I think you mean?' She made no reply, just looked at him, her beautiful eyes shining with unshed tears. 'There is no us, Eilidh. It was always impossible. And what is more, we both know it. We knew it from the first.'

She swallowed. 'I no longer believe that. I have seen you change, become a better man. You could have a home here. You simply have to choose it. Choose me. Choose Lidistrome.'

'I shall never be good enough! Never!' The words erupted from the deepest part of his soul. 'Ronald's anger has simply shaken me out of my foolish complacency. He was right.'

She opened her mouth to argue with him, but he forestalled her.

'No, Eilidh. There is no point in you saying any more. My mind is fixed. I leave on the morrow.'

They stared at one another for what seemed like an eternity, then a fleeting expression passed across her face. 'Very well.' Her tone was low. 'I shall beg no man for his favour.'

Success had never felt so bitter. He had won the debate, and she would accept his decision. His mouth felt dry, his stomach sick.

She lifted her head. 'But if you are to leave, at least have the courtesy not to insult these good people on your last night here.'

'Insult them? How?' Now confusion was added to the mix of emotions swirling within him.

'You have failed to join them for the Gathering—the greatest insult you could give them.' Her face twisted. 'Highland hospitality has rules, Max, expectations. And they have worked alongside you these past months. The least you can do is *attempt* to suggest you do not think yourself better than them.' Her voice dripped with disdain, and every syllable pierced him like an arrow.

'But no! I do not believe myself to have any worth alongside them! That is why I cannot intrude on their Gathering.'

'You are mistaken.' She was ice-cold, her face pale, her tone harsh. 'If you wish to show them respect, you need to join them tonight.' She threw the parcel she was holding at his feet. 'And have the decency to wear the clothes Mina and the others made for you. You may leave tomorrow, and I may say good riddance, but tonight do not shame Cooper and Isabella with such a show of arrogance!'

'But I—'

It was too late. Whirling on the spot, she disappeared through the open door and was gone.

Eilidh hurried across the yard, shaking from head to toe. His self-loathing had caused him to break with her—to break with all of them—and even his love for her had not been strong enough to withstand it.

He is leaving tomorrow.

The realisation shuddered through her once again, and abruptly she swerved away from the kitchen door and away into the darkness. Making her way around the house, she paused between two candlelit windows, leaning against the cracked wall. Dimly, she heard the murmur of conversation through the open front door, voices occasionally raised in laughter.

Max should be among them, enjoying the Gathering. Yet he was quite ready to exclude himself, out of a mistaken sense of unworthiness.

She closed her eyes briefly, remembering the pain in his expression as she had flung at him accusations of discourtesy, of disrespect. At the time, it had been the only ruse she could think of to persuade him into the Gathering Hall, where at least there might be a chance of him seeing how well-regarded he truly was.

Of one thing she was certain: if he left tomorrow, she would never get him back. Tonight was the best chance she had of trying to open his eyes. Although she wished nothing more than to curl up into a ball in the darkness of the carriage until it was time to go back to the Broch, somehow she had to find the strength within to see this through.

Closing her eyes again and leaning against the wall of An Taigh Buidhe, she took a few deep breaths, almost sensing the house holding her up, strengthening her. Fanciful or not, her courage reasserted herself and she straightened.

If he does join the Gathering, I must be there.

With poise, elegance and a fiery dose of hope, she made her way back into the house.

Max sank to his knees on the flagstone floor, entirely unmanned by her scathing disdain. The harshness in her voice, in her expression, had cut him to the quick. As with Ronald, he knew her anger had come from pain, and yet it hurt. It hurt more than he could ever have imagined. Every breath now was an ordeal, every heartbeat agony.

Soon it will be over.

If he could survive it, by this time tomorrow he would be on the open seas with no one but his crew, and life for the people here would already be better.

Her words echoed in his heart.

A show of arrogance...have the decency...show them respect.

Slowly, slowly, he rose, reaching for Mina's parcel with hands that shook. One thing he understood as a Burtenshaw was duty. His father and brother had harped on about it for a lifetime. The notion that the cruel man he had called Papa was not his true father seemed unlikely now. He might have Cooper's blood, but he would always be the brother of Frederick, Lord Burtenshaw.

He closed the cottage door, then opened the parcel, stripping off his work clothes as he did so. A new linen shirt, bleached white by the northern Hebridean light. It felt soft against his skin, and abruptly he knew he would keep these clothes, would treasure them forever, even though he could not be certain of the sentiment behind them.

The jacket was next, soft wool in a moss green, expertly stitched. Caressing it briefly, he laid it on the scrubbed table, then reached for the tartan trews. His jaw dropped in shock, for what he held in his callused hands were not trews, but—

A kilt? I cannot wear a kilt!

The predominant hue was the same moss green, crossed with squares and thin lines of white, blue, black and red. Five colours. What did that mean? He could not recall. The intricacies of the pattern were a testament to the attentiveness with which the cloth had been woven. He knew enough now of the complexities of weaving to understand how much care had been taken to ensure the length of twill had been perfectly executed.

Having observed many of the Islanders donning their kilts over the past weeks and months, he knew the basics of what he needed to do. Laying the precious fabric on the floor, he pleated it carefully, threaded the finely-tooled leather belt beneath it, then lay down upon it, wrapping the kilt around himself and securing it tightly with the belt. Adding the belted sporran he found in the parcel, he drew the top layers of the plaid over his shoulder, front and back, securing them with a pin in what he hoped was a reasonable approximation of the Hebridean style. There were leather shoes to match, and he donned them over the new knitted stockings resting at the bottom of the parcel. Tightening the laces on the shirt, he reached for the jacket and found, to his astonishment, that, like the shoes, it was a perfect fit.

Well, of course it is!

The Lidistrome women, who had been cleaning the men's clothes and shoes throughout the building works, knew exactly his size and shape. They had no need for a tailor's measuring tape, for the experience of eye and brain were all the skill they needed.

Naturally, there was no mirror in the cottage, and he was not normally prone to fits of vanity. But never had he wished more to see his own reflection! Looking down, it was disconcerting to see an actual kilt, such as those he had been surrounded with these past months. It was also rather disconcerting to be…er…entirely naked beneath the kilt, and he reflected that a strategically placed sporran might have saved the blushes of many a young man.

He stepped towards the door, then hesitated. Was it really acceptable for him to attend the Gathering in a kilt, as if he were an actual Scot? But no, Eilidh had been most insistent.

Duty.

Very well. One last duty, then a farewell.

There was a knock on his door. He was not usually troubled by so many visitors in his little stone haven! Striding across, he opened it.

'Sir, there you are!' It was Alec. 'Nice kilt.' He grinned. 'Mina and the other ladies will be pleased that you wore it. As will the weaver men. Here, let me check it for you.'

Max stepped back into the centre of the room while Alec pulled and tugged the kilt into a slightly neater arrangement.

'Thank you, Alec. Is it really tolerable for me to appear in this, not being a Scot?'

'But you are half Scottish, remember? If I am right that is the Cooper tartan, with some white added. And yes, it will be seen as a compliment to the people here.' Alec fished in his sporran. 'But you will need this to finish it off. I found it in one of the old cupboards in An Taigh Buidhe.'

Max's eyes widened. It was a plaid brooch made of silver and jade, and the workmanship was exquisite. 'Oh, I cannot wear this!' he declared. 'It belongs to An Taigh Buidhe!'

'Which belongs to you!' Alec retorted, pinning it to Max's shoulder, and in that moment Max could not find the words to articulate just why he could not wear it.

I shall leave it behind me, he decided.

The clothes he would keep, one last memory of the place, but the jewelled brooch belonged to Lidistrome, and needed to remain here.

'Right!' Alec was suddenly businesslike. 'Are you ready?'

Ready for what?

Eilidh would be there, and somehow he would have to survive the coming hours with the ice of her disdain still piercing his heart.

Duty.

'Yes, I am ready.'

Alec led the way, taking him through the front door rather than the kitchens, which was novel. The hallway was deserted, but the hubbub from behind the closed double doors leading to the Gathering Hall was ominous. One last time, he would face them all, would withstand whatever they had to say to him. He could survive one night. Would Ronald and Kenina be there? No matter. It had to be endured.

Alec opened one of the doors slightly, then turned to face Max. 'Wait here, sir,' he said, 'for just one minute.'

Max frowned, but before he could question the steward, he was gone, and the doors closed in Max's face. He stood there alone, with an entire community on the other side of the freshly painted doors, and gave a sad smile. It was the perfect metaphor. He was the outsider. The Sassenach. The outlander. He was foolish to have thought he could ever be one of them.

He lifted his head as the noise within decreased, then ceased altogether, then suddenly both doors were flung open and Alec called from the dais, '*A chairdean! Friends! Please be upstanding to welcome Maximilian Wood Cooper of Lidistrome, the much-honoured Laird of Lidistrome!*'

For the second time that day, there was a roaring in Max's ears as he struggled to understand what was happening. Before him, row after row of Islanders rose to their feet, turning to look at him with glad smiles.

They are clapping, he thought dazedly. *Why?*

Some then began beckoning him to walk forward and, without really deciding anything, he did so, still struggling to take in this unexpected turn of events.

As he walked forward, they leaned towards him, reaching out to clap him on the back or pump his hand vigorously, and he found himself being kissed on the cheek by some of the older women, including Mina.

'Looks well on you, sir,' she declared, beaming.

'Thank you, Mina,' he managed. 'It is as fine a costume as I have ever worn.'

'Five colours for the Laird,' she replied, and he shook his head in bemusement.

'But you must have been working on this for weeks!' This was significant, but he had no time to work out why.

She could not hear him, for now Ronald stepped out from his row and stuck a hand out to Max. 'I am sorry for my harsh words earlier, *a thighearna*,' he declared. 'Will you take my hand?'

Max gaped, then took the proffered hand. 'I shall, and gladly,' he declared, 'but—'

Ronald was gone, his place taken by Calum Bán Laing, then another and another, until Max found himself at the front of the hall. In the front row were the Lairds of Ardmore and Broch Clachan, along with their close relatives. Even Lydia was there, her sleeping baby tied to her front with a soft shawl.

'Mealaibh ur naidheachd, a thighearna,' said Angus, a huge grin splitting his face. 'Congratulations, Laird!'

'But I cannot be their Laird! I have not the right!'

Why is no one listening to me?

In bewilderment, he looked from face to face. Angus. Isabella. Cooper. Alasdair. All smiling. All seemingly delighted for him.

I do not understand.

Finally, he allowed his gaze to rest on the woman he loved. The woman he had hurt dreadfully earlier.

'Max—' Eilidh's expression was serious '—you have been declared Laird not by blood, not by ownership, but by acclaim. The people of Lidistrome have chosen you for their Laird. Will you accept this honour?'

He stared at her as the world shifted beneath his feet and became changed forever.

'Will you accept it,' she continued, 'and all its duties and responsibilities? To care for the people and the land until your dying breath? To stay, and take this home that is being offered to you?'

A hundred thoughts flitted through his mind.

Duty. Responsibility.

It would be a burden at times, he knew. There would be no easy life, such as Freddy might enjoy. Here was work, and solitude, and remoteness.

But could he? Could he, really?

Home.

Here also was the home he had never thought to have, and possibly—

With a thousand thoughts flooding through his brain, he stepped on to the dais.

Eilidh released her breath, the slight dizziness in her head telling her she had been holding it a little too long. Max had stepped on to the dais and was speaking quietly to Alec.

What will he decide?

The entire course of her life would become clear in the coming moments.

Nodding, Alec stepped down from the dais, his expression neutral, and in the same moment, Max turned to face the crowd. The babble of conversation died down, leaving an expectant silence.

Please—Eilidh prayed—*please let him choose us, as we have chosen him.*

Beside her, Isabella reached for her hand and squeezed it briefly. Eilidh sent her a grateful glance, then turned her attention back to Max.

'*A chairdean*,' he began. 'Friends.' At this there were whoops from a few people, but he raised a hand to quiet them. 'I was born to Lady Burtenshaw in Burtenshaw House in Sussex, and until very recently believed myself to be the son of Lord Burtenshaw. My brother Frederick held the deeds to Lidistrome until I persuaded him to sell to me.

'My motives had nothing to do with the welfare of the people here, and in truth I had no notion of this place, or any of you. I must be truthful with you. My eyes were opened when I came here, and getting to know you all and work alongside you has been an immense privilege. So I must begin by offering my sincere apologies for every cruelty, every failing done in the name of Burtenshaw. I am most heartily sorry.'

The murmur of the crowd behind Eilidh was indecipherable, but she knew the people would be feeling a mix of pain at the memories, anger about the many injustices and gratitude for the apology.

'Since arriving in the Islands, I have come to understand something a friend tried to explain to me many months ago.' His eyes flicked briefly towards Eilidh. 'Everyone here works hard, including the Laird. *Especially* the Laird. This—' he gestured towards the crowd, his arm sweeping around the Gathering Hall '—is a duty, not a privilege. You are offering me no life of ease but one of responsibility. And if you are willing to have me—a half-English bastard—then...' he took a breath '...I gladly accept. I shall be your Laird, if you will have me.'

This was exactly what the Lidistrome crowd had been waiting for. As one, they rose to their feet, cheering their Laird. Eilidh too tried to rise, but her knees felt strangely soft and she sank back down again.

He is staying!

Around her, people began leaving their seats, wanting to move out of the rows of chairs to congratulate their new Laird, but he hushed them again.

'There is one more thing I wish to say. As well as my general comments to you all, and with a particular apology to Calum and Màiri MacLean, I must also give a personal apology—' he paused '—to Eilidh Ruadh MacDonald.'

Her heart thundering in her ears, Eilidh swallowed. She watched, unable to move a muscle, as he stepped off the dais and walked towards her. Mutely, she looked up at him.

'Eilidh.' Realising that she was unable to stand, he crouched down in front of her. A breathless hush filled the Hall as everyone present listened. 'Earlier, you asked me to choose, and I made the wrong choice. I could never have believed that the people here would accept me.' He grimaced. 'It will take some time before I fully believe it, I think. I have agreed to become the Laird of Lidistrome, and I mean to dedicate my life to this place and these people.' He held out a hand but she was incapable of responding.

He dropped his hand again. 'Even in London, I knew you were the Lady of my dreams. It is not just for your beauty that I admire you, but for your kindness, and your clear thinking and your courage.' Ruefully, he added, 'And for your ability to speak plainly of things I prefer not to hear. Eilidh, I know I have hurt you, and disappointed you, and frustrated you. I know I am not worthy of your regard. But, if you will have me, I should like nothing better than to be your husband.'

The wheels inside Eilidh's mind were turning frustratingly slowly.

'Why?' she managed, her voice croaky.

'Why? Because I love you, of course. I wanted to marry you in London, but I knew I could never ask you to leave your home. And now it seems I might have the chance to make my home here. This home. An Taigh Buidhe. Will you mend it with me and bring it to life again, and live with me here as my wife?' He shook his head and the look of desperation in his eyes almost undid her. 'I am quite prepared to beg, Eilidh. Will you at least consider my proposal?'

Eilidh heard the words emerge from her own lips. 'I have no need to consider anything.' He blanched and made as if to answer, but she lifted a hand to touch his face. 'I will marry you, Max.'

His eyes blazed and he claimed her mouth with his. Their kiss was brief, heady and full of promise, but the cheering all around them could not be ignored. Eilidh, her heart thundering, found that she was shaking from head to toe. Joy flooded through her, but her overwhelming feeling in this moment was one of relief. Somehow, the miracle had happened. He would be Laird of Lidistrome and she his Lady. Taking her hand, he pulled her to her feet and she went, smiling.

Epilogue

December 1812

Christmas was a special time in Benbecula. The planting done, the Islanders wintered together in cosy cottages and clachans, in warm stone-walled homes, with their animals safe in byres and stables and the people gathered together for long evenings of stories and songs, of reading in silence or playing cards and parlour games.

An Taigh Buidhe was no different. For almost seventy years the house had stood empty and cold, but this was the second Christmas when the house had been alive again. The Laird and Lady of Lidistrome had moved into the newly-refurbished house a year ago, just after their Christmas wedding.

The staff quarters at the rear were also occupied, with Calum and Màiri MacLean leading the team of staff who ensured the Laird and Lady, along with Alec, their steward, had all they needed. All three led busy lives, organising supplies and repairs and meeting the ongoing needs of Lidistrome and its people. Max had become adept in his role as leader and arbiter of small disputes between neighbours, and his Gaelic was improving by the week.

Lidistrome maintained its close relations with both Broch Clachan and Ardmore, and the Lairds and Ladies visited each other with frequency, even in winter, dashing to each other's homes between the winter storms. Cooper spent his time between Isabella's home and Max's and had visited Islay in the late summer, tracing cousins and an elderly uncle he had not seen for over thirty years. Lydia's baby was now a sturdy toddler, while Angus and Isabella's daughter was already sitting unaided and waving farewell when prompted. Angus had pronounced her a genius and his wife a marvel.

Eilidh lay in the bed she shared with her husband, her hand creeping to rest on her still-flat stomach and her heart slowly returning to its normal pattern following their delightful exertions of the past hour.

'That was wonderful, Max,' she murmured, 'as always.'

He kissed her, staying on his side and gently stroking her back. His hand swept to her shoulder, then down to her stomach, where he covered her hand with his own. 'When are you going to tell me?'

Her eyes widened. 'You know? But how?'

He grinned. 'I can count, my love. And I have noticed that you have been particularly tired these past weeks.'

'Oh, Max!' She shuffled on to her side to face him. 'I cannot know for certain yet, but I believe…that is, I hope—'

'Me too.' They kissed, and he lifted his hand to trace her face. 'I am surely the luckiest man on earth, even without this possibility. Never could I have imagined a life so fulfilling, so wonderful. And you, my love, are at the heart of it.'

'Then a second year of winter storms has not tempted you to prefer the glitter of the London Season?'

He shuddered. 'A thousand times no! It was never for me. I would rather a hundred storms than one more day of house calls and soirées.'

'But we do house calls here too!' Her eyes danced. 'Why, today I called on Mina Morrison *and* Mrs MacKinnon!'

He matched her tone. 'And I visited half a dozen farmers to discuss our plans for the spring. My conversations were purposeful, and meaningful, and...*real*,' he declared. 'And every evening, I come back to you, and to the knowledge we may sleep in one another's arms for another night.' Half rising, he bent his head and pressed a gentle kiss on her stomach. 'And now this.' Propping himself up on his elbow, he gazed into her eyes. 'I love you, Eilidh Ruadh.'

'And I love you.'

They kissed again, then he raised his head to add, in a firm tone, 'And the best choice I ever made was to become Laird of Lidistrome.'

* * * * *

If you enjoyed this story,
make sure to read the other books in
Catherine Tinley's Lairds of the Isles:

A Laird for the Governess
A Laird in London

And why not check out her other great books?

Captivating the Cynical Earl
A Waltz with the Outspoken Governess
"A Midnight Mistletoe Kiss"
in Christmas Cinderellas
Rags-to-Riches Wife

WOOING HIS CONVENIENT WIFE (Regency)
The Patterdale Siblings • by Annie Burrows

Jasper's out of options when feisty stranger Penelope offers him a lifeline—marriage. It's a practical match...until an inconvenient desire to share the marriage bed changes everything!

AWAKENING HIS SHY DUCHESS (Regency)
The Irresistible Dukes • by Christine Merrill

Evan is stunned when Madeline takes a tumble fleeing a ball...and accidentally falls into him! Now the situation forces them somewhere the duke didn't want to be—the altar!

THE GOVERNESS AND THE BROODING DUKE (Regency)
by Millie Adams

Employed to tame the Duke of Westmere's disobedient children, Mary should avoid entanglement with their widower father. If only she didn't crave the forbidden intimacy of their moments alone...

HER GRACE'S DARING PROPOSAL (Regency)
by Joanna Johnson

Widowed duchess Isabelle's wealth has made her the target of fortune hunters. A convenient marriage to mercenary Joseph will protect her but could also put her heart in danger...

THE EARL'S EGYPTIAN HEIRESS (Victorian)
by Heba Helmy

Ranya's mission is clear: restore her family's honor by retrieving the deed to their business from the Earl of Warrington. Until she finds herself enthralled by the new earl, Owen...

A KNIGHT FOR THE RUNAWAY NUN (Medieval)
Convent Brides • by Carol Townend

Having left the convent before taking her Holy Orders, Lady Bernadette is horrified when her father wants her wed! The only solution—marrying childhood friend Sir Hugo.